THE HOSPITAL

Alastair Wilkins

First Published in Great Britain in 2022

Copyright © 2022 Alastair Wilkins

A CIP catalogue record for this book is available from the British Library

ISBN 978-1-7396748-0-9 (paperback)

ISBN 978-1-7396748-1-6 (ebook)

Cover Design by Creative Covers

Typesetting by Book Polishers

To my family

1.

IT SEEMED THAT the corridor stretched on for miles, drawing the eye to an indiscernible vanishing point, along glistening well-scrubbed synthetic floors, past defunct automatons which lined up along the yellow-stained walls and which invariably bore the sign CONDEMNED. At intervals of six or seven paces, side passages leading to wards or offices would appear and, dangling from the ceiling, sets of signs indicating the destinations to be reached gave information to the weary corridor-walker – information that appeared archaic and was, in all likelihood, inaccurate.

The corridor was the pride of the hospital. Sources now unknown had made the (probably apocryphal) claim that it was the longest corridor in Europe. The lack of evidence to the contrary and the absence of any significant penalty should this prove not to be the case meant that the hospital authorities did all they could to perpetuate the claim. It did sound impressive, they reasoned, and being in possession of such a record, indeed such an accolade – which had little to do with the reputation of medical care there but was solely a feature of architectural design – was not to be scoffed at.

At night, the poor illumination of the corridor lent it an eeriness; an unwelcoming air that many felt to be at odds with the purpose of the infirmary – although others felt that this feature discouraged people from loitering in the facility. Myths were disseminated about the sort of clients who skulked in the side tunnels late at night, ready to pounce and commit some desperate atrocity. Even the porters, that band of resilient floor stompers, often refused to walk alone at night. They treated the hallowed ground with a healthy respect and an almost magical solemnity. But in the daylight, it became a different environment altogether. Wheeled beds dodged the elderly; walking frames collided with X-ray machines; doctors stopped to consult colleagues; pushchairs carried their screaming loads onward. The corridor was the heart of the hospital, the epicentre of a sprawling establishment into which flowed the dying and the cured, transporting each to their next destination in the process of infirmity. And it seemed symbolic that at one end was the maternity suite and at the far end the mortuary. From cradle to grave. A stroll, a push, or a run from one end of the corridor to the other: a journey through life.

Somewhere near the middle, on a side road off the sickness highway, like some marooned Ark, could be found the offices of the management. Plush, resplendent, and devoid of any reference to the suffering that surrounded them, the rooms at their hub could be entered only by a locked door and a series of secret codes. In this isolation worked the executives and their minions who decided the fate of budgets and changing priorities with one eye on the paymaster and the other on the clock.

John Such, newly elevated sub-chief executive, sat in one such office: large, open-plan and uninspiring in its decor. His brow was furrowed, and his coffee was cold. In his hand he brandished a sheet of paper festooned with the latest figures, facts and fallacies relating to the hospital, keeping it arm's length, ready at any moment to bury it under a pile of similar documents lest he should be discovered in possession of such information; those who found him might pin the blame on him and inflict some arbitrary punishment. He wasn't in the mood for explaining himself, having recently developed intractable migraines and a lethargy for life. He picked up another sheet of paper from his in-tray. This more sparsely populated document related to recent instances of 'never' events: occurrences within the hospital that should never, *not ever*, happen (but commonly did). 'Never' events included giving the wrong drug to the right patient; or giving the right drug to the wrong patient; or giving the wrong drug to the wrong patient; or not giving the drug at all. The fact that 'never' events occurred regularly did not deter the evangelists from espousing the use of this nomenclature. Attempts were made to change the name to 'almost never events' or 'shouldn't happen events', but it was felt that this would be contrary to the ethos of the hospital and would concede to the inevitability of imperfection. The official failure of these attempts did not, however, stop several other informal names for these events arising.

A colleague who had been doing the rounds of the office appeared in front of John Such's desk holding an identical sheet of paper in one hand and a cup of coffee in the other.

'Have you looked at these?' he asked, thrusting forward the paper.

John Such glanced at the sheet, then at the one in his own hand. He nodded and made a non-committal noise which indicated his lack of desire for a conversation. The man walked off, spilling coffee on the patterned carpet as he went.

The sub-chief executive put down the paper and looked up into the soulless open-plan office. In the periphery of his vision, he noticed a familiar blurring sensation. Closing his eyes, he confirmed the presence of black and white lines zigzagging in an imperfect arc, heralding the onset of another migraine. These had become daily events. His doctor had told him that this visual phenomenon was called a 'fortification spectrum' and was so named because it resembled the outline of the battlements in a stylised Mediterranean hilltop fort. Or maybe he had misremembered this. How he longed to be in a warm Mediterranean hilltop village now, even with a migraine, rather that this office of numbers, strategy, and the overwhelming sense of knocking a square peg into a round hole. He rested back in his chair, closed his eyes, and began tracking the movement of a zigzag arc of light to the outskirts of his peripheral vision.

2.

DR BARNABY SMITHERS had reached that stage in his career where he was feeling things starting to slip away. Having been appointed as a hospital consultant two years earlier, his enthusiasm and desire to please had gone and the dreary prospect of thirty more years doing the same job was beginning to take hold. As a younger trainee doctor, he had assumed that becoming a consultant was all that he would need from a career perspective and that on reaching this pinnacle his life would be complete. But looking out from the top was not as he had expected. Every day seemed rather misty, and the view was not so great. It was as though he had climbed the highest mountain only to discover a fast-food takeaway at the summit. There were so many consultants these days that it didn't carry as much status as in years gone by. The perks of the job had all but gone. He often thought back to when he had started his training – a time when such privileges as a consultant's dining room and a named parking space in the hospital car park had existed. Now he had to slum it with the rest of them.

His wife had encouraged him to take up hobbies; she had presented to him a series of possibilities ranging from golf to carpentry. But generally, the job drained him, and he disliked the prospect of enforced sociability. Family life took up much of his off-duty time, and when evening came he was always ready to drink wine and fall asleep in front of the television. In addition, he had to take work home with him. The various hospital committees he had been cajoled into joining generated

a large amount of paperwork which he could not complete the allotted daytime hours.

After his appointment as a consultant, he had been ask on an almost daily basis to take on some management role other. The natural course of events was that the least popul ones were the first to be put before newcomers; the consultan who had been in post for a few more years than Dr Smithe wanted to offload the duties that had previously been offloade onto them. He found it hard to refuse and, in the early days least, had wanted to immerse himself in his job. Membershi of the patient safety committee would be – he had though when accepting the position – a fairly straightforward (an not very time-consuming) role: six meetings a year and a fev emails every now and then. After six months, however, due t various government inspections, the committee had taken o newfound importance and had become rather onerous. The chiel executive of the hospital herself had started to take an almosl obsessive interest, attending all the meetings and insisting on being copied in to all the correspondence. He had thought this behaviour slightly paranoid and reckoned she would have been better off concentrating on the dire financial situation into which the hospital was spiralling. Nonetheless, she had persisted, and he now frequently received emails from her (generally sent at 2am) asking about such and such an incident of patient safety transgression. Nothing got past her.

The next patient safety committee meeting was the following day, and Dr Smithers had a stack of papers to get through. It was 8pm by the time he got home, and he was on his second glass of wine before he started reading them. He knew from past experience that the meeting would be unlikely to get beyond the third item on the agenda, so he took out the documents relating to the first two items, figuring that he could bluff his way through the third or make some excuse to leave at that point if necessary.

The first document concerned the recent failed fire drill. As far as he could make out, the main reason the staff could

not evacuate the patients from the simulated fire was the poor design of the hospital wards. There was simply no way that non-ambulant patients could reach the designated exit points given the architectural layout of the ward and hospital passageways. This had been discussed on all the previous committee meetings he had attended, and the response was always to repeat the drill in the vain hope that it would succeed next time. Save for knocking down the whole hospital and rebuilding it, it was hard to imagine any other solution. He sighed and put it to one side. At least this one wouldn't take up much more of his time, given the inevitable repetition of previous discussions that would take place.

He took a large gulp of wine. The alcohol was having its soporific effect and he yawned loudly. The second agenda point related to issues of 'informed consent'. This was guaranteed to send him to sleep, not only this evening but in the actual meeting. The hospital governing body had employed an ethicist to steer through the difficult ramifications of the issue. When he had first heard about this, he had thought it was a good idea. However, there was no getting away from the fact that ethicists liked to balance the issues on either side of the argument to such an extent that no decision could ever be made. This appeared to be the ethicist's badge of honour: exactly matching up the pros and cons of an ethical dilemma to achieve some form of perfect counterpoint. It didn't help that the ethicist the hospital had employed was so dull and ponderous that the discussions took an age, meaning that most people simply switched off – especially as they were not really true discussions but more monologues delivered in a slow monotone, rounded off by indecision. During the last committee meeting, Dr Smithers had felt himself drifting off to sleep but had become curiously fixated on the slow-moving lips of the ethicist as he delivered his dreary soliloquy. The lips appeared disembodied from the face and indeed the whole body, rather like Beckett's *Not I*, which Dr Smithers had seen performed the previous year. The lips rambled on and on, circumnavigating the sea of moral honour and turpitude with no apparent final

destination. Beckett's words had been more engaging and had made more sense than the ethicist's, which was saying something.

He cast the documents aside, content that he would be able to hold his own in the committee meeting. He checked his phone for emails. Amongst the many (mostly regarding bed occupancy numbers), he noticed one from the chair of the patient safety committee which informed him that the ethicist had broken his arm and would not be attending the meeting. This was bad news, as it meant that Item 3 might be pushed up the agenda. With a further gulp of wine, he returned to his papers and located the relevant documents. However, before he had got beyond the first few lines of the page outlining a new traffic light system for drug errors, he had dozed off to sleep.

He woke an hour later with a jerk, confused and with wine stains on his trousers.

3.

IN AN ATTEMPT to look stately and authoritative, the hospital's chief executive had commissioned a style consultant. As part of her make-over, she had taken to wearing high-necked collars and dark suits which, irrespective of whether they had made her look more impressive, were so tight and uncomfortable that by midday she had a strong desire to change into baggy clothes. Nevertheless, she was willing to endure the discomfort in furtherance of her mission to achieve a greater sense of confidence and authority. She had been chief executive for just over six months, during which time she had come to the realisation that exerting any sort of influence would be highly challenging – hence the need to strengthen her persona from all angles. People around her simply didn't listen, or if they did listen, they didn't take much notice of her words. She had a vision for how she would like things done and worked hard to instil her values in those around her, but a general apathy for change combined with the rigid structures which had been in force for decades worked against her. Perhaps a more snappily dressed version of herself would hold sway to a greater extent.

Her style consultant had suggested all manner of changes to her wardrobe, many of which were impractical and not suited to the hospital environment. Indeed, the chief executive had wondered whether the consultant had any concept of the work performed in the healthcare sector, since many of her recommendations seemed best suited to the catwalk. The consultant even seemed to harbour a disdain for people working in the healthcare sector, making no secret of her disregard for the 'illness industry', as she called it. She refused to have meetings in the hospital and spent a good portion of their style sessions trying to persuade the chief executive that she would be better employed in some other sector of business.

Undeterred, the chief executive took on board her recommendations and went along with her fashion suggestions. Initially she experienced some glimmers of newfound confidence. At the very least, those around her seemed to pay her more attention, even if it was mostly out of curiosity as to what outfit she would turn up to work in the next day. In her work clothes, she imagined herself as an army general in resplendent uniform, geeing up the troops for one final push in a battle which could not be won. The title of chief executive, like a row of metaphorical medals, showed who was in charge and inspired others to go the extra mile in pursuit of the goals of the hospital. The foot soldiers needed guiding and only respected unwavering authority. Any crack in the veneer – any loss of impenetrability – would be noticed and the drive towards the ultimate goals of the campaign would falter. At least, that was how she tried to think. She wore the façade of authority in a manner she felt was appropriate to her status, but it wasn't easy. The splendour of her external appearance betrayed an inner uncertainty, a weariness and a feeling of indifference which had been poking at her enthusiasm for some time. She often considered admitting that she didn't know which direction she was heading in, which plan to take, which challenge to prioritise. Yet, there was nothing to be gained by admitting this, and the outward portrayal of implacable confidence which she had learned over the years remained.

In her private life, the situation was very different. She felt no need to display a perfect home life. Her work and her career progress had consumed so much, and this had inevitably led to the destruction of her marriage. When the first rumbles of marital discontent had appeared several years earlier, she had reasoned that she had a simple choice: save the relationship or save her career. The volatility of her husband meant that the safer option – and the one she could control more effectively – was the salvation of her career. The marriage went into freefall, and neither party showed much in the way of resistance. Half-hearted attempts to open the parachute were made, but each of them landed in different fields, battered and broken, only able to be patched up into more dilapidated versions of their former selves. Her husband had left the country and embarked on a voyage around the world to discover himself. He had returned several months later and bought a large house several streets away. She would catch a glimpse of him from time to time, but they no longer talked, and she never had found out what he had discovered about himself.

Single life had driven her to ever-higher career responsibilities. However, as promotions and greater authority were thrust on her, she had become increasingly uncertain as to whether this really was the destination she had desired. Although undoubtedly her younger self would have looked on at her current self and concluded that she had succeeded beyond all expectations, she now experienced a sort of malaise bordering on resentment. Yet she felt powerless to change. What if she were to give it all up and start a new career? She would return to the bottom of the pile, and that seemed so much more unbearable than the recurring unhappiness over her current predicament.

She had employed a life coach who had made her draw up a matrix of values and score the potential life choices she could make against those things she thought really mattered to her. Time and time again, leaving her job came up with the highest scores. And yet she knew she would never have the heart or courage to make that change. The lack of a life partner was a big factor, as she was dependent solely on her own salary, but a smaller salary and a simpler life – one without the exotic holidays, the gym and the spa breaks – would be the solution. This was the modern executive's problem; the dilemma of those who have thirsted for power and then achieved it. Most people in her position (she thought) wouldn't see it as a problem, and none would show their doubts in public. Membership of this exclusive club made rules against that sort of insurrection.

4.

THE HEADQUARTERS OF the local health authority were situated within a grand house built in the prosperous years of the seventeenth century. During the First World War, the lord of the manor had allowed the construction of twelve huts in his vast acreage which served as wards for the injured returning from the Western Front. Ever since that time, no attempt had been made to reclaim the land for the estate and, after the fifteenth earl died childless, the land was taken into trust and handed to the health authority.

The main hospital was constructed a mile away on the site of the old smelting mill, but the estate and the manor house were retained as the headquarters of the health authority in all its fading grandeur. The land on which the early hospital huts had been built was sold off piece by piece, such that the grand old house and its associated tennis courts were rather incongruously surrounded with modern three-bedroomed detached executive houses with their postage stamp gardens. The old dining room of the house was now the boardroom and was used for many of the meetings the chief executive needed to attend. The mile distance from the hospital could be seen as either a blessing or a hindrance. Some separation from the chaos of the hospital was, on occasion, a godsend.

The boardroom was high-ceilinged, with stucco plaster designs around the main chandelier light fitting and along the covings and cornices. The windows were high and without curtains or blinds, but despite their size the room always seemed rather dark.

A solid white door with chipped paint was the only way into the room, since the French windows which led out to the small lawn had been made unopenable. The remains of a serving hatch, through which the food had been delivered during the erstwhile banquets, had been boarded over and made into a noticeboard. In the centre of the room, several large tables had been placed together to make a roughly rectangular shape. It was of such a size that when refreshments were placed somewhere near the middle, they became impossible for everyone present to reach at once, which meant either some of those attending the meeting went thirsty or there were moments of awkward shuffling of cups and coffee pots. Twelve Regency-style chairs surrounded the table, their reupholstered splendour rather at odds with the grubby-looking collection of veneered plywood tabletops in the middle.

The chief executive, having arrived early for the meeting, sat alone in the chair nearest the large sash window, which let in most light. She had walked from her home to the headquarters, so would need to walk the mile to the hospital after the meeting. It was a fine day, so this prospect pleased her. She would decline the offers that were likely to be made to drive her that short distance after the meeting since the prospect of time in a car, however short, with someone trying to bend her ear about some clinical issue – or, more likely, trying to ingratiate themself with her to increase a vague prospect of promotion – was something she couldn't bear at the moment. And anyway, she had discovered a new route, slightly longer than it needed to be, which took her down to the river and along its bank and which avoided the busy main roads. It was thinking time, if anybody asked.

Through the window, she could hear the gentle rumble of traffic interrupted at intervals by the shrill staccato of a blackbird's warning call. Piled on the table in front of her were copies of the agenda for the meeting and other necessary paperwork. She had spent the previous evening scrutinising their content and was not overly enthusiastic about the forthcoming hour of discussions.

The door opened with a baritone creek and Eric, the splendidly titled director of transformation, appeared. No sooner had he acknowledged the presence of the chief executive than he dropped the sheaf of papers he was carrying. He fell to his knees to pick them up, but this seemed to trigger the influx of the rest of the meeting attendees, who had to side-step him as he tried to gather up the papers in some sort of order.

The chairman of the board took his place at the head of the table. As he sat down, a young woman in a smart suit who had been trailing him placed three distinct piles of paper in front of him and poured out a glass of water. The chairman took out his reading glasses, wiped them with a cloth from his jacket pocket, and briefly surveyed the top sheet from each of the piles. He turned to the young woman, who had been waiting attentively, and smiled. This was the cue for her to leave and she trotted off, dodging Eric, who was still scrabbling around on the floor near the door.

The chairman took a sip of water, cleared his throat and intoned, 'Welcome, all. Are we ready to begin?' He peered over the top of his reading glasses at Eric, who had retrieved his papers and was headed for the only empty seat.

'Eric, are you alright?' the chairman enquired, more out of annoyance than out of concern.

'Yes. Sorry,' said Eric taking his seat and trying not to look too flustered.

'OK, well let's start. You've all read the minutes from last time? Any issues?' He was expecting no answer. 'Good. Well, let's crack on. We're starting with a financial update. Elise, would you like to take us through this?'

He turned to Elise, the chief accountant, who sat to his left. She was a small woman with angular spectacles and black hair swept back into a short ponytail. Her strong Glaswegian accent had not softened in the six years she had lived in England.

'Thanks, Pras. Table 1 in Appendix 3 of the documents you were sent shows the year-to-date figures for the hospital's financial position.' There was a shuffling of papers while everyone turned to the relevant page. The chief executive had already placed this page uppermost on her pile. The numbers at the bottom of each column were exclusively in red ink, which said it all, really.

'It's fiscally important – going into the depths of winter with the projected rise by twenty percent in expenditure during this time – that we resolve the issue of excess costs,' continued Elise.

The chief executive reflected on the fact that this could have been any meeting for the past five years. The numbers changed but the messages remained the same: cut costs, generate more income. Only now, things looked worse than ever. There was no prospect of the usual bailouts, and the possibility of closing parts – or even, as unthinkable as it might sound, the whole – of the hospital was being entertained at higher levels. The previous week, the chief executive had received a delegation of besuited dignitaries from the Department of Health, who had delivered, albeit in a smiling (and what they stressed was a supportive) way, an ultimatum that costs had to come down from the current unsustainable levels. The usual excuses concerning the higher-than-average age of the population and the large areas of social deprivation to the north of the city were heard, but not accepted.

'Can I cut in there, Elise?' asked the chief executive, who had not really been listening as the accountant went through the individual figures.

Elise looked up, disgruntled to have been cut off mid-flow. She glanced at the chairman, who nodded at the chief executive.

The chief executive gave a brief smile. 'From the figures you have calculated – and bearing in mind the added pressures for the next few months – just how much exactly do we need to cut costs in order to balance these awful figures?'

Elise took off her glasses, shuffled through her papers and pulled out a sheet of dense type. 'If you look on page seven of the same appendix, it indicates that if we take into account our historical debt, the costs relating to the refurbishment of the maternity unit and the seasonal variation of admissions to the hospital, then a reduction in costs of at least ten percent is required to get anywhere near breaking even in the next quarter.' She paused and put her glasses back on, avoiding the gaze of the chief executive.

'Is that clear?' the chairman asked the chief executive, who was trying to think up a way of making it apparent that she had indeed read that part of the appendix.

'Yes, exactly,' she said, standing up and leaning forward. 'I just want everyone to be sure of the challenge we face. It is crucially important that we all understand this is a watershed moment for our hospital, and the DoH visit last week was a warning from on high that we cannot simply carry on as we are. We are talking about closures, job losses, redistribution of clinical services. Anything could happen.' She paused for dramatic effect.

Eric sneezed to break the silence. 'Excuse me,' he said, digging in his pocket for a tissue.

'Ten percent. No less,' repeated the chief executive.

Eric, not having found a tissue, picked up a pen instead and wrote '10%' in large figures at the top of his agenda.

'So, next board meeting,' continued the chief executive, 'I need everyone to bring a concrete plan as to how to save at least ten percent in each of your respective departments. No excuses for the complexity of your department's work or the patient caseload. Everyone, and I mean everyone,' again she paused for effect and looked at each of the faces around the table, 'needs to think of a feasible way of doing this. Think radically, think big. If we fail in this endeavour, then who knows what carnage will be unleashed on us.'

She remained standing for a few moments to let her words sink in before sitting down and folding her arms.

All sat in silence, unsure of what to say. Eric looked down at his papers and underlined what he had written on his agenda, twice.

5.

THE CONCEPT OF a good death has occupied the thinking of philosophers and ethicists since debates began. Given that death is inevitable, most would accept an end without protracted pain. Ethicists, advising those who take charge over the dying, have defined a good death as one that is free from avoidable distress and suffering and is in line with the patient's wishes. Some have even gone so far as to use the term *successful dying*. Yet dying seems such an improbable goal and the parameters of success and failure are so hard to define that this concept sits uneasily. The commonest written epitaph – *he died peacefully* – implies that the optimal way to depart the earth is via a death with no resistance. But medical science is built on the principle that resistance to death is necessary; that treatments make people better and oppose the process of dying. Indeed, another epitaph runs: *he lost his fight with the illness*. So, which is it to be: capitulation to the inescapability of death, or a full-blown battle? When does the dying man know he is beaten and wave the white flag? When does the doctor turn from recommending all-out assault to surrender? What is the point at which death is preferable to an imperfect life?

Going by the ethicist's definition, Muriel Frank's death was not a good one. Even though her heart was still beating, there was little doubt on the part of her and those around her that she was in the last phases of her death. Six months after an operation to remove a twisted section of bowel, she was still in hospital enduring the full force of medical intervention. She had been back to theatre on umpteen occasions to revise colostomies, to drain abscesses, to remove further bowel tissue and, most recently, to remove the lower part of her leg after a blood clot had led to gangrene. She remained septic, and the bugs were doing their best to achieve what medical science was trying, but failing, to avoid. Her abdomen remained open, packed with dressings soaked in antiseptics. The risk of closing up her abdominal wall was that further abscesses would form, so she lay like a dissected cadaver on her bed, not moving but being moved every six hours to prevent pressure sores. On her remaining leg she wore an inflatable compression device which blew up intermittently to prevent further clots forming, and she had twice daily injections of medicines into her bruised and scarred skin to do the same. A plastic tube leading directly into her stomach came out of her nose and was forever becoming dislodged, so that she had to endure the ritual of having the semi-rigid tube rammed down her nose, across her gag reflex and ever downwards. The latest prospect she was facing was the insertion of a long line into a major vein into her neck, since the veins in her limbs, through which she was receiving antibiotics and all manner of other drugs, had packed up after multiple stabbings on a daily basis and were no longer viable.

Her surgeon, Mr James Barabas, who had performed all her operations bar two, had seen her devotedly four or five times per week, even coming in at weekends when he was not on duty. The initial procedure to remove a section of infarcted bowel had seemed relatively straightforward, and the first hours of the post-operative period had been as they should. Before leaving the hospital on the evening of surgery, he had called into the intensive care unit to see how she was recovering. He had been given no cause for alarm. The next morning, however, during the ward round, he had been directed to her bed as a matter of priority. He had learned that she had been back in the operating theatre for much of the night having a blood vessel which had been damaged in the first operation repaired, but only after it had bled most of her blood volume into the cavern of her abdomen. From that moment, medical complications spiralled. From that moment, her death began.

Mr Barabas approached the high-dependency side room gingerly, half-wondering what further problems he would be faced with behind its door. His patient had been stepped down from the intensive care unit three weeks earlier and was now on a general surgical ward. This did not mean that she had recovered, but reflected the unwillingness of the intensive care doctors to keep her there any longer. She still required the same amount of exhaustive treatment, so the nurses had to manage as best they could. The senior sister and the junior ward doctor joined Mr Barabas as he took a big breath and entered the room.

Inside, he was greeted with the usual scene: bed sheets, machines, tubes and monitoring equipment. A nurse wearing a plastic apron, bright purple gloves and a face visor was draining the catheter bag, lifting the tubing to encourage flow into the jug. She looked up as the surgeon and his entourage entered.

Mr Barabas paused at the door and himself donned the obligatory apron, gloves and mask. The barrier between him and the patient being complete, he approached the bed.

'Hello, Muriel,' he said, his voice muffled behind the surgical mask.

The patient shifted her gaze, slowly and deliberately, and sighed audibly.

'How are you today?' he asked, holding her gaze. He asked the question but knew he was unlikely to get an answer. He was not sure he really wanted one anyway.

Muriel raised her eyebrows and looked away. She had not said much for weeks now, and the surgeon did not push her to talk. She had been assessed by a psychiatrist when the nursing staff had suspected a depressive illness as the cause for her lack of social interaction. Of course, this was not unexpected, given all she had been through, so they knew the answer before she had been assessed by the mental health team. The psychiatrist had used terms such as apathy and abulia, secondary to a reactive depression. Anti-depressants were prescribed but did little good. More drugs, more papering over the cracks.

The surgeon turned his attention to the machines that recorded her blood pressure and vital signs, which were then recorded on the charts at the end of the bed. 'These look fine,' he declared, reassuring himself on these numerical figures. 'How about fluid balance?' he asked the nurse, who had now finished emptying the catheter bag.

'Positive one litre,' she snapped back, 'so we're fluid-restricting'. The game was to balance the books of fluid – too much fluid retained meant less fluid was given; too little fluid peed out meant it had to be given into the veins. At least that was easy to control.

'Very good,' declared the surgeon, pulling at the fingers of one of his plastic gloves. Looking back at Muriel, he smiled and laid his gloved hand on her arm. Then he left the room, removing his protective clothes and throwing them in the bin by the side of the door.

This was a fairly standard interaction, and it had been like this for months. It was stalemate. They were balancing the figures of fluid and blood pressure, but she wasn't getting any better and everyone involved in her care knew that she wouldn't get better. The ward sister had given up asking about the way forward, the plan to break the impasse, as she knew there wasn't one. Just keep going.

They had to keep going. He, the surgeon who had nicked the blood vessel and caused the catastrophic bleed, had to keep going. He needed to put right what had occurred (undetected at the time) on that inauspicious day during a routine operation. He had spoken to Muriel's relatives on multiple occasions, reassuring them that he would do all he could to get her through the stormy post-operative course, as he had put it. He had fallen short of admitting the blame for the complications and they, having an all-too-common reverence for the magical powers of surgeons, did not think to apportion blame. However, he knew that this whole catalogue of problems – in fact, this disaster – was due to the inadvertent slip of his scalpel. He was not a bad surgeon, he knew that, and all surgeons make mistakes, but this was the first major catastrophe of his career, and he didn't really know how to deal with it. He just knew that he had to do all he could to keep her alive in the desperate hope that she would recover somehow and walk out of the hospital. After a few weeks, everyone providing her continued care, himself included, knew that this would not happen. But what could they do? They would carry on, despite the pain and anguish, despite being as far from giving Muriel a *successful death* as could be imagined. To stop treatment was unconscionable.

6.

THE DIRECTOR OF transformation was concerned. He had been appointed to the role just over a year earlier and, on honest reflection, could not claim to have transformed anything. If he were to truly fulfil his duties as the director of transformation, he should be well into a programme of transforming the operating procedures of the hospital, redefining the way the hospital ran. Others in his position may have made a more nuanced interpretation of his title, but he had always been a concrete thinker and saw the lack of transformation as a sign of failure. He was the kind of person who would draw up lists: *things to be transformed, things I have transformed* and such like.

During his childhood, his parents had fretted over his inability to comprehend beyond the literal meaning of words and phrases. They had taken him to see a child psychiatrist, who had asked him what he understood by terms such as 'raining cats and dogs', and what the meaning was of 'people who live in glass houses shouldn't throw stones'. This had baffled him at the time, and it was only years later that he discovered he had been diagnosed as being on the autistic spectrum. On learning of this diagnosis (as an adult), he had become profoundly affected by the need to engage with the full spectrum of the disorder. To his mind, having been diagnosed with an autism spectrum disorder by an expert in the field meant that his lifestyle and behaviour should reflect a fulfilment of the diagnosis. His life became more ordered and disciplined, perhaps out of relief over no longer having to suppress his thoughts – or maybe through a newfound sense of destiny.

Working in the regimented setting of hospital administration seemed to suit him. His early jobs, which involved balancing the books and moving numbers on spreadsheets, seemed made for him. It was only later, as he began to be rewarded for his unfailing accuracy and attention to detail and was promoted to more managerial and supervisory jobs, that he started to struggle. He couldn't understand why the people he was managing didn't see things in the same way that he saw them. He had been surprised, therefore, about his promotion to director of transformation. The senior executive team had sent him on courses in abstract thinking and surrounded him with a team of meticulous attention-to-detail types. For a while, as he found his feet, all had seemed fine, but soon his growing sense of anxiety became apparent. In truth, the senior team had made an error by side-lining him into a role with the remit to accomplish what was essentially an unachievable goal.

There was a knock on the door and a young man in a pinstripe suit came in.

'Eric, can I have a word?' he said, holding up a sheet of paper with one hand and clinging on to the door with the other.

The director of transformation stood up abruptly, took off his glasses, and indicated that the young man should sit down. He glanced furtively at his diary, which lay open at the desk, and then at the clock. There was nothing in his diary for this time. Impromptu callings such as this made him anxious. Nonetheless, he sat down behind the desk and tried not to appear flustered.

'Yes, hello ... What is it?'

The young man, Tony Pilkington, who worked in accounts, loosened the collar on his shirt and placed the sheet of paper he was carrying on the desk.

'Well, I've been looking at the data on length of stay and patient tariffs. I've looked at specialty costs in order to identify high spenders. The surgeons seem to have cut back on their expensive new toys ...' he looked up to see if this would raise a smile in Eric. No such response.

'So not much luck there.' He paused, seemingly for dramatic effect.

'But if you look on a yearly *per patient* basis – i.e. how much individual patients cost to have their treatment per year – then it is really striking. About one percent of the patients take over twenty-five percent of the total budget for the hospital. In fact, in the medicine department there are about five or six patients who take up just under ten percent of the whole budget.'

The two men stared into each other's eyes for the briefest of moments before Eric looked down at the pile of papers on his desk. He noticed that the top few papers were out of alignment with the rest of the stack, so he corrected the asymmetry.

'I think we already knew that there are certain patients who have very expensive treatment pathways,' Eric replied, shifting the pile of papers a few millimetres to the left.

Tony appeared a little deflated.

'But the figures suggest a larger issue than we had suspected, don't they?' Tony replied, not letting the lack of expression on the director of transformation's face put him off.

'Yes, I agree … but what is the practical implication of knowing these numbers?'

Tony sat back and ran his hand though his thick black hair.

'I don't know,' he conceded.

For a few moments, the two men sat in silence, avoiding eye contact, each trying to think of something to say.

Eventually, Tony broke the silence. 'Listen, Eric. On Friday at the board meeting, we have to come up with some ground-breaking new idea to cut our spending by at least ten percent. We have squeezed every last penny out of the places that can be squeezed. There's just no more to give. What are we meant to tell them on Friday?'

Eric glanced at the diary again. The hospital board meeting was indeed on Friday at eleven o'clock, and each member of the team had to propose a novel mechanism for saving money. They had been asked to 'think radically'. That and other nonsensical jargon that Eric so abhorred had been spouted in an attempt to generate fresh thought in the stale environment of senior management. Yet, Friday was fast approaching, and he had not come up with anything remotely resembling a plan. He sighed, stood up and looked out of the window.

'So, what you are saying is ...' he began, considering his words carefully, '... that if we didn't treat five or six patients in each department then we could save ten percent of the budget?'

Tony looked down at his shoes, then up at the window. 'Well, I'm not sure I'm saying that ... but, yes, I guess so,' he said rather cryptically.

'Preposterous,' said Eric. And with that, Tony left the office.

7.

It was a common sight: an individual or a small group crying outside the door to a ward, on the benches outside the hospital, or in the cafeteria. Perhaps a young girl, unable to comprehend her predicament, head buried deep in the bosom of her mother, or a young man with reddened, deep-set eyes; perhaps an elderly man who had lost his companion of many decades, frozen in disbelief, tears running down his cheeks. This was the place of such terrible revelations. The unwritten code dictated that the outpouring of grief was to be respected as a private act. No one would approach the distressed. The corridor, the side rooms, the open spaces, despite the ever-present hustle of human traffic, became the most private of places. A metaphorical screen was erected around the grief-stricken which none would breach. To violate the sanctity of anguish with a question – *are you alright?* – or a reassurance – *it'll be fine in the end* – was not something to be considered. Distress was ever-present as an unwelcome yet inescapable aura.

In the offices of the registrar, all births and deaths were recorded: a blue form for new arrivals to the world and a yellow form to record the departed. Appointments to register one or the other were made according to their occurrence, and the registrar had developed the skill of flipping between joyful congratulations and solemn condolences with alacrity. She had been told that around four out of five people in the region died in hospital and that, in this ageing population, the deaths far outnumbered the births. Although many of the appointments to register a death were not difficult experiences – often by the time the relatives had reached the point of filling out the formal register of death, their emotions had been spent – she naturally preferred the registration of new life. She was interested in the latest trend in first names and in the evening would report back to her family the latest weird name with which a child had been burdened and which would, one day, be recorded on the yellow form, when a future registrar would raise an eyebrow and report back to his or her own family on the ludicrousness of parents so many years earlier. A name in and a name out.

On this morning, the registrar was signing the paperwork to validate the entry into this world of twins; girls born by caesarean section in the maternity unit two days earlier. The mother was wheeled down to the offices along with two midwives, each carrying a new arrival, both infants sleeping in their many layers of blankets. The details were taken and the forms were signed with little fanfare. Usually, multiple births were heralded with more flourish, but the mother was clearly still recovering from the operation and didn't seem in the mood for small talk. She declined to give the name of the father of the children. That was her prerogative, and no reason was needed. The registrar wondered whether the mother was going to raise the two babies alone, but it wasn't her business to know such things.

After the signing, the monosyllabic mother and her entourage received the necessary paperwork. The wheels on the wheelchair made an annoying squeak as they left. The registrar watched as they departed. There was no place for sentimentality and even less for judgementalism, yet she was concerned, on this occasion more than others, about the fate of the three family members. Did the mother have post-natal depression? Even the midwives had appeared rather cold and uninterested.

The process was over more quickly than most encounters. There was often small talk appropriate to the particular situation: a few words about how calm the baby seemed, or condolences and a hand on the wrist. But this birth seemed more like a death to the registrar; in fact, she had experienced more upbeat death registrations. Only the day before, a woman had registered the deaths of both her parents, who had passed away within hours of each other. The woman, newly orphaned, saw their simultaneous deaths as a reason to be thankful. The fact that their forty-six-year marriage had ended abruptly and that neither parent had been left behind seemed to comfort her. There would be no grief in the remaining spouse, no loneliness. The registrar wondered if the lives of the twins whom she had just registered would progress with such symmetry.

8.

A SENSE OF foreboding and a morbid fascination with the ideas discussed meant that Eric could not stop thinking about the conversation he had had with Tony. It was only two days until the board meeting at which he was required to present his radical new idea for reducing costs by ten percent. He glanced at the whiteboard opposite his desk and the multiple scribblings in red and blue ink. Red represented previously tried (and failed) schemes for cost reduction; blue was for new ideas. There was a noticeable lack of blue. The majority of red words were synonyms for 'cost reduction' which, if he thought about it, didn't really provide solutions – just reinforced the difficulty of the question. One of the more radical blue ideas was to close the maternity unit, but he knew that the outcry which would ensue when it was proposed that pregnant women would have to travel thirty miles or more for assistance with giving birth – that most sacred of all the medical services on offer – would doom the idea to failure before it was even half-baked. Pregnant women and new-born babies were not to be messed with.

The previous chief executive had organised almost monthly newspaper stories, proclaiming the first birth of the year, the first quadruplets in the county since who knew when, the two hundredth IVF baby, and so on. Maternity was high-profile, kudos for the hospital. But if it had been up to Eric, he'd have closed it in an instant. He couldn't stand the place. Every time he had to enter the maternity unit (as part of the senior management walkabouts) his heart sank, and he would become nauseous.

The thought of what was going on behind the curtains – the unmuffled screams, the blood and unspeakable body emissions – filled him with such horror that he would see it as his number one priority to get out of the maternity unit walkabout. In fact, the chief executive was quite happy for Eric not to join the maternity tour, since she felt his presence would most likely lead to heightened anxiety in an already fraught atmosphere. Nonetheless, Eric lost sleep over the matter and felt compelled to devise more and more complex methods of evasion.

His eye was drawn to a star diagram in the top left-hand corner of the whiteboard. On each point of the star was an acronym. The list of groups of letters which stood for some important concept in the world of healthcare was endless. Not a meeting went by without him having to spend time trying to work out what was meant by FFT or BHOM or other such mysteries. One point of the star had a downward arrow followed by the letters LOS. Length of stay – this was one of the more common acronyms used and repeated endlessly. LOS had been underlined several times and was connected via thin lines to several other letters: DL (discharge lounge), HAH (hospital at home) and TMED (time-monitored early discharge). He had no idea what the latter really meant but had never had the interest or the energy to ask for an explanation. Length of stay reduction – reducing the amount of time patients spent in hospital beds – was a key priority for saving money, but the sick usually remained sick wherever they found themselves, and the whole process was like shuffling the deckchairs on a sinking ship.

Eric picked up the blue marker pen from his desk and approached the whiteboard. For several minutes, he stood studying the words before him, as though he were a wartime cryptographer trying to break an enemy code, but this was a conundrum with no solution and the words didn't join up to form any clever pattern. He tapped the blue pen against his forehead and took a step closer to the board. Without really thinking, he took the lid off the pen and wrote the words: *KILLING OF*

FIVE in the bottom left-hand corner of the whiteboard.

He stepped back and was about to rub out the words when his gaze was diverted to a fox which was standing outside his window. It looked as though it had just emerged from a gap in the hedge. It stood still, gazing straight at Eric. Its coat was rather ragged, and its paws were caked in mud. The black tip of its tail was threadbare and greying. It had a hungry look about it which was undoubtedly the reason for the boldness of its stance. It stood for about a minute, impassive, while the soft rain dripped around it, before disappearing back behind the hedge from where it had come.

Eric kept looking, imagining and maybe hoping it would reappear. Large puddles had formed in the patchwork lawn outside his office. An untidy blackbird landed by one puddle and took a drink, while the rain, which had become harder, bounced off its wings. It hopped around splashing in the expanding pool before flying off, heavier, more iridescent.

The alarm went off on Eric's phone. It was time for another meeting. He left the office, slamming the door behind him.

9.

THE HOSPITAL LAY at the base of a shallow-bottomed valley flanked by rolling hills. The easterly slope was the steeper, zig-zagged haphazardly with dry stone walls forming a patchwork of brown, yellow and green. Flocks of sheep occupied alternate fields, their diminutive figures clinging to the land in its perilous attitude. On the western side of the valley, hedges and stone walls formed altogether more geometric designs. Some of the fields were laid out to crops and others were used as meadowland to nourish the occasional cow. Expansive trees grew in the corners of these fields, acting as shelter for the beasts from the inevitable rain. Across several fields, well-worn paths meandered, oblique lines descending from way-marker to way-marker. After sunset, a gloom descended on the valley. Then, the hills appeared draped in dark tarpaulin glistening with the sheen of ever-present drizzle. In winter months, little light seeped into the valley floor even in the daytime, and the residents of the narrow streets would settle in for the prospect of darkness for weeks on end. The hospital, lying at the lowest point of the valley floor, was thus bound in a disheartening form of half-light for the majority of the winter.

It was speculated by many that this darkness contributed to the general increase in depressive illnesses, the sufferers of which flooded through the doors of the psychiatry department. Investments in ultraviolet lamps and an increase in the lighting bills were put into the budgetary calculations, but it was impossible to provide a true antidote to the gloaming. Most of the workers accepted this hardship during the winter months, the prospect of the valley's beauty in summer months being their incentive to carry on. Indeed, on a summer's evening, many of the hospital's staff would don walking boots and ramble over the fields, climbing to the best vantage point where the town and the hospital could be assessed and put in its place.

Far to the north of the valley floor, following the gentle course of the river, lay the Black Witch Hills, so named because of the witchcraft that was reputed to have occurred in caverns at the base of the hills. In the late sixteenth century, seven local women had been tried, found guilty and hanged. The caverns retained a sense of menace, of evil deeds. Local industry had perpetuated the memory of those witchcraft trials, reflected in the shops and tourist trails of the region. Indeed, a macabre enchantment with the lunacy of the past was evident in much of the county. When planning the new hospital in the late 1950s, the architects had wanted to incorporate aspects of local history into the design of the buildings. The hospital was to be built on the site of the old workhouse, which, as an aside, struck fear into many of the older inhabitants of the town, such that many refused to attend appointments at the new hospital and would only be admitted under duress. The workhouse had been linked to a smelting mill, and two colossal chimneys had dominated the town for a century. So, the architects had designed the main hospital corridor to run in a line connecting the former locations of the chimneys, resulting in the corridor being referred to locally as 'the chimney'. It wasn't until work had started on the construction of the new build that residents pointed out that the toxic fumes produced day in, day out by the burning of noxious chemicals had done much to harm the health of the locals for generations. The planners and health authority officials had responded by releasing statements claiming that it was time to replace the destructive nature of the chimneys with a healing atmosphere inside the new facility. But the memory of the old workhouse, the years of unclean air and the general superstitious nature of the population meant that the new hospital was viewed with an air of apprehension and mistrust for its first few years.

Fifty years later, no one remembered the workhouse or the chimneys. Now the calls were for a new hospital. The corridor was dated, and the open-plan wards were no longer acceptable to those who felt the sick should be afforded more of a hotel experience. Debates about mixed-sex wards raged, but ultimately there was no money to replace the hospital with a brand-new building. The government had put a hold on the disastrous money-borrowing schemes which had funded other healthcare buildings. The realisation that the vast sums of money borrowed could never be repaid had dawned on the health authorities, and the prospect of huge and interminable interest repayments meant that leaking roofs and crumbling brickwork had to be tolerated.

Several years earlier, a previous chief financial officer had been convicted of embezzlement of hospital funds. He had received a five-year jail sentence for syphoning off large amounts of money to a fake company that had purported to supply surgical devices. This deception had gone unnoticed for at least two years, and the perpetrator had become increasingly bold in the amounts of money claimed. The exact figure was unclear due to the complex accountancy arrangements which had been introduced to hide the misdemeanour, but probably ran into millions. The court had ordered the money to be paid back, but it had long been spent, and the hospital only received a fraction of what had been taken. The chief executive at the time had been sacked, and although he was himself cleared of any wrongdoing in court, there was a likelihood that he had been in on the scheme all along.

Even though the hospital had effectively been robbed of this money, the Department of Health expected it to be able to reclaim the missing money, which increased the financial fragility of an organisation in an already perilous situation. The stolen money was, rather euphemistically, called the historic debt, although it was not clear to whom the hospital was indebted other than the profligate lifestyle of their corrupt former employee.

Money was at the heart of everything they did. The great dream of free healthcare for all irrespective of individual circumstances was tempered by ever-rising costs. The managers who had an altruistic calling to work in this sector realised very quickly that their jobs were not to assist in alleviating suffering but to squeeze every last penny from the process of illness. On the face of it, their spreadsheets concerning numbers of deaths from sepsis, numbers of failed hip replacements, numbers of maternal deaths were a litany of human suffering. But these phrases became the macabre mantra which translated to targets and which, in turn, translated to money generation. Of course, no one (other than those who were driven to distraction and resigned within weeks) really thought deeply about the suffering which lay behind the spreadsheet columns of the various forms of death. This was the currency of the hospital, and the one by which it would survive or crumble.

10.

ON THE DAY the local newspapers carried incriminating photographs of a group of foxes going through the bins on the hospital site, the chief executive had seen several of the beasts strolling across the car park as she pulled into her parking space. As soon as she saw the newspapers – she had been briefed by the press officer the moment she appeared in her office – she was determined to do something about the animals; a resolution which was undoubtedly strengthened by the morning's encounter. She was naturally inclined to live and let live, having had a keen interest in the natural world as a child and a series of beloved childhood pets. But the damage that *rampant vermin* (as the papers called them) within the hospital grounds would do to public confidence made their presence problematic. Previous public health outcries had done significant harm to the hospital's reputation, most notably the discovery of *Legionella* (the bug that causes Legionnaires' disease) in hospital water supplies shortly after it had been built.

The fox issue, as it turned out, was much more controversial than previous pest-related problems. Many people wanted to protect foxes, whereas no one spoke out in favour of bacteria or rats or even mice. It drove passionate debate. The chief executive was in two minds about her best course of action and felt it best to delegate the issue to her deputy. Although clearly important to the image of the hospital, she reasoned that she had more pressing issues to deal with, and time taken away from the financial problems was not in the best interests of the institution.

She happened to bump into her deputy, John Such, later that morning as she was walking along the corridor. She had been asked to officiate in the opening of an art display in the maternity unit and was returning to the management offices. The officiation had gone well. The newspapers had been there in force. She made no secret of the fact that she wanted to promote certain departments more than others. Babies were good for public relations. The art display had been put together by local artists who were celebrating the thirtieth anniversary of the first test tube baby born in the unit. After the ceremony, in which the chief executive said the usual few paragraphs about how bringing artists and the hospital together bonded the local community, she had chatted to a few of the artists before taking the long walk back down the corridor. She spotted John Such talking to a surly-looking nurse, his shoulder leaning against the wall. He looked deep in thought.

As the chief executive approached, the nurse stopped talking and glanced at the advancing figure. Immediately recognising her, she smiled and then walked off. The chief executive often had this effect on people. At least it made it easier to get the attention of those to whom she needed to speak.

John Such straightened, standing to attention.

'How are you, John?' she enquired.

'Yes – fine, thanks,' he replied.

'Have you seen the papers today?'

'Which ones?' he stuttered.

'The foxes. The story about the foxes in *The Herald*. Foxes all over the hospital, apparently.' She paused, realising that he had no idea what she was talking about.

'Oh yes,' he lied. 'I'll get onto it.'

The chief executive gave him a look which indicated that she knew of his bluff.

'John,' she continued, staring directly into his eyes, 'I want you to sort this out. With all the other problems we are facing, I simply haven't time for this.'

She raised her eyebrows while John Such nodded vigorously. 'Yes, of course,' he replied.

'OK. Speak later.' With that, she marched off. The click of her heels against the hard floor echoed faintly down the corridor.

John Such headed off in the opposite direction, towards the hospital shop, where he would be able to get a copy of *The Herald* and assess the damage.

Later that day, he added *fox trouble* to the list of problems that was forever growing.

11.

AAMAAL HOSSEIN, WHO cleaned the offices and administrative areas of the hospital late at night, had a lot on her mind. Her husband had recently been diagnosed with lung cancer and could no longer work due to the harsh side-effects of chemotherapy. She had five children who were still at home and endless unpaid bills. She worked in the hospital at night and at her local supermarket during the day, leaving little time for sleep or looking after her children. Her eldest daughter took most of the responsibility for ensuring the younger ones had clothes for school and adequate nutrition. The younger children had adapted to the new family hierarchies, wanting little and doing their best to support the new family routines with largely absent parents.

Her husband's prognosis was dire, and she was facing the prospect of life as a single mother, probable homelessness, and, even worse, having her children taken from her due to excessive debts which had accrued over the years. As if life had not been bad enough before the cancer diagnosis, the decline of her husband from breadwinner to burden was a final kick in the stomach, flooring the whole family. They were ready for the knockout count. Other close family members had either died or returned to Pakistan, so she was increasingly alone in trying to make a living and a life for her dependents.

Cleaning on Saturday nights was less onerous than on other nights, since the offices were not used as much at weekends. The usual mess in the kitchen area was generally absent, although the paper recycling bins were often much fuller. Perhaps the office workers were keener to get rid of documents at weekends. But other than the degree of messiness of the offices, little changed from night to night. The same desks had debris spread around. The same bins were overfilled. The same carpets needed stains removing. Aamaal had a routine of clearing the mess first from the kitchen and then from the large office. She followed this by washing the tiled floors and hoovering the carpets. She then tackled the individual offices, ending up with the chief executive's office, which was the largest of all the individual rooms and often the one that needed the most attention. The chief executive had a habit of making piles of documents on the floor around her desk, which made cleaning rather difficult. Coupled with the presence of countless ring binders full of paper which were stacked on tables and windowsills, it was often hard for Aamaal to know where to start. Minimalism and order were not the chief executive's way of working.

This was in contrast to the normal state of the director of transformation's office, which was pristine and ordered. However, on entering his office this Saturday evening, Aamaal was immediately struck by its untidiness. Not that it was any more untidy than other offices – but the usual fastidious attention to order made by its occupant was not apparent. An empty coffee cup lay on the floor, papers were strewn across the desk and several document folders were positioned on the top of a bookcase rather than in their allotted storage space. Furthermore, the chair which was normally neatly placed beneath the desk was positioned by the side of the door under the air conditioning unit, giving an appearance that someone had been standing on it to inspect the unit. She wondered whether someone had been hurriedly trying to find something.

She picked up the chair to replace it, but while she was carrying it the short distance back to its rightful place, a pain in her abdomen – which had been troubling her episodically for several weeks – recurred, causing her to put the chair down and sit on it while the pain resolved. She had not yet managed to see her doctor but imagined it was something to do with her gall bladder, which had troubled her for years. Indeed, her mother and all her sisters had had their gall bladders removed at an early age. Aamaal had resisted having the same operation, not because she was afraid or didn't trust the doctors, but simply because she'd had no time for it.

The waves of colic persisted for longer than during past episodes, and she started to sweat. She would have to do something about it. She was in a hospital, surrounded by surgeons and experts, but there was no way she could ask for advice from any of them. She was one of the invisible nocturnal underlings to whom no one paid much attention.

After several minutes, the spasms of pain resolved. She felt nauseous and her heart was racing, so she remained seated for a little while more. She had, by chance, placed the chair opposite the whiteboard and now started to read the collection of words written in red and blue. As English was not her first language, some words she recognised and some she didn't. Some words seemed to be a random assortment of letters and were unlike any English words she had ever read. There were many red words and letters, but fewer blue ones. The blue words were mostly written on the left-hand side of the board and were connected together by a series of arrows. Some had been crossed out and some circled for emphasis. Of those that were neither crossed out nor circled, one word stood out: KILLING. She knew well enough its meaning, yet it seemed so out of place in the institution in which she worked that she was puzzled by its presence. Why would someone write KILLING on the whiteboard of an office in a hospital? Next to this most ominous of words were OF FIVE, which added to the menace. Clearly five people had been selected for the act. This wasn't just a concept but a specific action to be carried out. Or maybe it had already been carried out.

The words frightened her, and she felt she needed to leave the office as soon as possible. But if the room remained uncleaned and the bins unemptied, then she would be at risk of losing her job. Where would that leave her and her family? The occupant of the office had previously left a note for her when the windowsill had been (in his opinion) greasy and not properly wiped down. She was in no doubt that if she left things as they were, she would get into no end of trouble. So, she resolved to put the words out of her mind and get on with her job.

Before too long, the office was looking as it should. The chair was repositioned under the desk and the windowsill was sparklingly clean. She opened the door and was about to turn the light off when she looked back once again at the whiteboard. Again, she read *KILLING OF FIVE*, but this time, rather than feeling scared, she wondered whether the words might be an opportunity. She had heard of people selling stories to the newspapers, and scandals concerning the hospital were often in *The Herald*. She would read the headlines in the canteen at the end of her shift. They reported dirty sheets, patients left unwashed, bad food, leaking roofs. Surely this was worth something to the papers. A whole new level of scandal. The hospital was actually killing its patients.

She grabbed her phone from her pocket and took a photograph of the whiteboard before switching off the lights, closing the door quietly and leaving.

12.

John Such had taken the day off to go birdwatching. It was bright and warm, reportedly the warmest stretch in winter months for a decade. The reeds of the marshland swayed in synchrony with the gentle, awakening breeze. Cold rivers flowed vigorously. Spring flowers had shown themselves, boldly, heralding an early start to the year. Birds fluttered, waddled, cooed in the bright sun. A large flock of wigeon made their way through a meadow, foraging whatever they could from the hard earth. Three cranes, majestic and so different to their squat wildfowl colleagues, stood motionless on the distant shoreline. All this was far away from the grind and complexity of the hospital, the demands, the spreadsheets and the targets.

The three cranes flew off across the estuary, disturbed by an unseen predator. Seeing them reminded John Such of an ex-colleague who had given up his life as an accountant to become a conservationist. His specific project had been the reintroduction of the Eurasian crane to England. He recalled the enthusiasm of his colleague's explanation of this calling. He had been disturbed by the knowledge that cranes had once been common in England but had been wiped out through hunting and loss of habitat, and had thought it important to restore the natural order. Similarly, he had talked with passion about the reintroduction of beavers to the waterways of Southern England and, perhaps alarmingly to many, backed a move to see wolves roam freely in the Highlands of Scotland, as they had centuries earlier.

Above him, a buzzard floated into vision, gliding on a forceful air current. He wondered what had become of his ex-accountant colleague, whom he had not seen for some years. Had the escape from the office routine been worth it? At least he had helped to restore the cranes to the local area, which was something, and was undoubtedly more life-affirming than balancing the books of a provincial hospital. Maybe there were cranes nesting back in Cranesborough, the old village that had been named after the bird in medieval times, but which had not been host to them for centuries. That very fact: the lack of cranes in a village named after the bird had been the most important influence on his colleague. 'What's become of us if Cranesborough no longer has cranes?' he had repeatedly asked those around him. Most dismissed this a being rather fanciful and even fanatical, but maybe he had a point. At least he had a passion and was courageous enough to take a stand. What was he, John Such, so passionate about? Would he change the world or take on a worthy cause?

He continued to walk through the watery landscape. Beneath him, the ground had become marshy, and his feet sank a little with every step. The path headed towards a ploughed field, which he crossed before entering a small copse. Tree branches were strewn on the ground, the result of the previous night's storm. At one point along the path, a tree had fallen and blocked the way completely. He struggled to climb over and got his coat snagged on one of the branches. He sat down on a nearby log to inspect the damage. At that moment, he heard a faint rustle and, looking up, saw a deer doing its best to hide in the undergrowth. The animal was looking directly at him. Alert, ready to run at any moment, the beast maintained its position. This was its land, its home. It was accustomed to intruders, yet was powerless to defend its territory. One more move from the intruder and it would have no choice but to run. John Such remained seated and still. It was a roe deer, he thought, maybe a younger animal. It had the beginnings of antlers between its two large ears. Its back was faintly mottled, and it had the recognisable skittishness of all deer. After another moment of this uneasy standoff, it ran deeper into the trees.

Seeing this made John Such think about the fox problem. Who was the intruder? The fox in the hospital grounds? Himself in the woodland? The cranes which were now repopulating the estuary? Should he preside over the extermination of the foxes, just as those before him had got rid of the cranes?

He rebuked himself for thinking about work when he was meant to be getting away from it all. *Think of the trees and the birds and the sky*, he told himself. He got up and walked further in the direction of the retreating deer.

13.

WARD 17 RAN with the efficiency of a colossal beast, only moving when necessary, consuming vast resources and trampling all in its path. The beds were arranged around a central nurse's station, in a spiral fashion, rather like Matisse's snail. A huge TV screen recorded the comings and goings, the daily sojourn of each individual into their disease state.

In Bed 4, an old man was the latest arrival. Mr Alyoshin, although a newcomer to the ward, had long since been overcome by his deep affliction. His move from home to hospital had made little impact; the change of scenery was just from one wall to another. His emotions were dulled and drab; his thoughts, chequered by the experience of regret, were replayed minute by minute and consisted predominantly of his lack of foresight, his previous inertia for living. The ephemeral man begins dying from the moment he knows he is beaten. At home, he had repented daily, staring at his bare cupboard and empty plate and chastising himself for his lack of forethought. Not a day went by when he did not think he should have made provisions for this day. Not a day went by when he didn't come to the conclusion that this suffering could have been dulled by companionship – even if it were one minute before the invading tumour had been diagnosed. Just one minute is all it takes. But now he was a condemned man, newly arrived in his sterile prison cell, knowing this day would be among his last. This was the fate of this ephemeral man, living out the rest of his time in company and alone.

Mr Alyoshin sighed deeply, his head slumped forward, his

fingers jerking, his gaze fixed and lowered. A nurse, rushing and unobservant, appeared beside his bed and switched on the television.

'I thought you'd like to watch something,' she said, not waiting for or indeed expecting an answer.

Mr Alyoshin shifted his gaze to the screen. At home, he had diligently watched the 24-hour news channels, which told him about the war on terror, about the stock exchange and about why children were developing mental health problems in ever greater numbers – a crisis which would unfold in the coming decades to bring society to its knees. He had been fascinated by the complexity of his damaged society, but at the same time had no inkling of why he needed to know all this information, why he needed it presented in a bite-sized format. He watched constantly, nonetheless.

The nurse, who was a fleeting presence, reappeared by his bedside.

'This is no good,' she said, referring to the TV programme. Holding the TV remote in her left hand and a catheter bag in her right, she flicked through the channels.

'Nothing on …' she mused before putting down the remote control. The TV programme which played after she had finished her browsing concerned the life of a twenty-five-stone child who had become a chess grandmaster at the age of fourteen but had died of obesity one week after being crowned national champion. Mr Alyoshin watched, distracted from his unholy thoughts. At least the obese boy had enjoyed that one week of glory.

Mr Alyoshin had come from a long line of maestro violinists. His great-grandfather had been in the court of the Tsar in imperial Russia, achieving great riches and fame before the revolutionaries and idealists deemed that music was superfluous to the greater cause. Subsequent generations had continued the musical tradition in disparate lands or by stealth. The musical instinct could not be suppressed, no matter how often their instruments were considered counter to the ideals of a new philosophy and reduced to mere firewood. Mr Alyoshin's father had wandered Europe before settling in Vienna, where he had eked out a living as a bar room fiddler. His wages barely paid the bills and the family lived in poverty.

However, his son's talent was such that he was accepted on a full scholarship into the finest music school and tutored by the leading musicians of the erstwhile Austro-Hungarian Empire. At the age of eleven, Mr Alyoshin was giving recitals in the palaces of the land. He was spoken of as the next great violinist of Europe. But shortly after his twelfth birthday, he was struck down with polio, which caused his left hand to become weak, and he was no longer able to press down the strings on the fingerboard. Thus, his prospects and career were ended, almost overnight, in this cruel way. His father was devastated, since he had tolerated his soul-destroying job only because he had vicariously used his son's success as a way of surviving. He took to drink and died a few years later. Mr Alyoshin's mother, having failed to reconcile the terrible fates of her son's hand and her husband's melancholy, was admitted to a psychiatric institute and never seen again by her family. The children – Mr Alyoshin, his sister and his younger brother – were taken in by the city's institutions and put up for rehousing to whomever might have them. At the time, Mr Alyoshin was nearly fifteen and plotting an independent life, but war in Europe and his disability meant that he was put on a train which ended up at a coastal town near to the English Channel. He took a boat to England, and there he had stayed ever since.

He had eked out an existence as a music teacher in a large boys' school and, latterly, as a private tutor to middle-class children whose parents wanted some extra skill for their young ones which would ease their passage to university. Music was all he knew, yet the regret of his lost career, felt every day, was all-consuming. He struggled to comprehend the gifted child who was indifferent to his talent given that there was no physical impediment to him becoming a virtuoso musician. He resented the mediocrity of the musicians who were playing only because it was expected of them. He abhorred the parents who were interested solely in certificates, and he was intolerant of the rigidity of the syllabuses which encouraged the pupils to be just good enough to play an uninspiring composition nobody wanted to hear. Perhaps more damningly, he rejected his teacher colleagues, who had no interest in culture and had never heard of Rachmaninov. He had been married briefly in his late twenties, had a daughter whom he rarely saw, and drifted into his own obscurity.

Slowly grinding to a halt, he had retired at sixty with just enough pension and had lived alone for ten years before his final illness showed itself: at first a pain in the chest and then coughing up blood. He had not sought medical attention for this, both out of terror of the possible diagnosis and also out of resignation to his fate, but he had been forced to confront it when he collapsed in his local shop as a result of a massive lung haemorrhage. He had been taken to the hospital, where the diagnosis of lung cancer was confirmed. A prognosis of a few months was given. He had gone home to die, with handfuls of pills to be taken daily, one of which caused the salts in his blood to become massively deranged (as his general practitioner had put it). Hence the current admission. The general practitioner had said that he was confused as a result of the salt issue, but he had long since lost the ability to differentiate reality from the unreal. He was too weak to resist the ambulance teams and so had ended up in Ward 17. He knew for sure that it was where he would die.

14.

Foxes belong to the biological family of mammals called Canidae – dog-like creatures which live on every continent apart from Antarctica. In popular folklore, they are portrayed as sly, clever and quick-witted. They have large ears, giving them an excellent sense of hearing, and a pointed snout for seeking out prey. The red fox (more of a dirty orange) is the commonest type on these shores. Other members of the Canidae family include wolves, jackals and racoon dogs …

So began the talk that John Such was preparing for the next day's meeting of the fox committee. He had collected the majority of the information from several (possibly unreliable) internet sources, trawling the vast array of information and deciding to include anything vaguely plausible. He had been asked not to express any strong pro- or anti-fox feelings and to produce a dispassionate introduction to the subject. He was not sure he really had any strong feelings about the animals anyway.

The fox committee had been assembled in a rather hurried manner as a response to the increasing number of stories appearing in *The Herald*. The stories were becoming more outlandish, and the chief executive had made it clear that the issue needed resolving. The problem was that strong pro- and anti-fox lobbies had materialised as soon as the stories emerged. It wasn't just a matter of getting rid of the foxes. This would enrage the animal rights campaigners. But at the same time, *The Herald* had the bit between its teeth and was pushing the issue, so it couldn't be ignored. John had little doubt that should the foxes be exterminated, the newspaper would turn from outrage over the risk to human health to indignation over the abuse of wild animals.

… a group of foxes is sometimes referred to as a skulk, a leash or an earth …

That will get the chief executive going, he thought. The thought of one of the blighters is enough to send her into a cold sweat, but a whole skulk … or a diabolical leash? These names seemed to underpin the importance of the fox in olden times, when words and languages were being developed. There were so many words relating to the variety of fox life – vixens, kits, tods, reynards, vulpine. Presumably, in former times the creatures needed describing in great detail. At least his reports in the coming months could avoid repetition.

… foxes are omnivores and commonly live in urban settlements, foraging for discarded food …

In his internet searches he had found a video of a fox bouncing on an outside trampoline. Tentative at first, the sly old thing had worked out the object's purpose and had seemed to enjoy several minutes of jumping. Should he include this in his presentation? It would be amusing, but was it too light-hearted? Would it suggest he wasn't taking the issue seriously enough? He decided against it but viewed it one more time for good measure before turning off his computer and making some tea.

During John Such's childhood, his father, who had lived all his life on a farm, had told him stories about nature and the lives of animals. Bedtime was filled with mystical tales – such as those explaining why the auroch had disappeared from England and why owls hunt at night – mixed with harsh realities of lambing and winters holed up in deep snowdrifts. His father had been particularly enraptured by the fox. He spoke of his uneasy relationship with the beast; on the one hand, he had always been on the lookout to prevent the animal from committing the carnage of farmyard raids, but on the other, he had a deep respect for the adaptability of a creature which had grasped its opportunity in human methods of farming. He had told one especially odd bedtime story, half-nonsense, half-cautionary, about a fox who wanted to become king of the forest. This particular fictional fox decided to take on the might of the wolf and, by guile and promises of glory, enlisted a whole host of woodland animals as allies. The wolf, having heard of this subterfuge in the offing, had also gone about building an army of like-minded creatures to square up against the new pretender. A fierce and bloody battle ensued, and all were killed, save the fox, who now ruled the woodland. However, having no other animals to rule, his victory was hollow, and he learned that treachery of this sort never pays.

John Such's father had told other similar stories, the meaning of which were sometimes hard to fathom, but this fox story was the one that had stuck in John's mind ever since. Maybe he should recount it at the next meeting of the fox committee. Or would it imply that he thought the fox would always win? Or that defeat of the fox would be a pyrrhic victory? He was rambling and his thoughts were becoming irrational, so he went to bed.

15.

A COBWEB, CONSTRUCTED in the right-angle of the car park sign, glistened in the morning light. Heavy dew and the bright sunshine combined to turn that which was constructed to be invisible into a work of beauty. The chief executive, just arrived at the hospital, stopped to admire its splendour. Several of the threads were disrupted or missing but its imperfection only added to her feelings of wonder at the creation. The sun was low in the sky. Looking beyond the cobweb towards the hospital buildings, she had to shield her eyes to avoid its full glare. The wintry light made faint silhouettes of the low-built structures.

She continued to shield her eyes as she walked on. She could just about make out a collection of people carrying a banner at the front door of the hospital, but she couldn't read what it said. It was most likely something to do with the dissatisfaction of the Public Services Union because of the recent pay freeze the government had announced for all healthcare workers. As she approached, however, the group dispersed, and she was unable to ascertain the reason for their gathering. Someone would tell her later, no doubt.

The day was scheduled to be meeting followed by meeting. The patient safety committee was first up, followed by the senior management review of cost pressures. The main hospital board was the next day, by which time they would have to have made at least a half-baked plan for the ten percent savings. She was relying on her colleagues to have some radical ideas, as she had none.

She arrived at the front door and stepped inside the hospital.

A warm front of air greeted her, contrasting with the coolness of outside. The corridor was quiet; the occasional nurse or doctor scurried by, but it was too early for relatives. She preferred these calm hours in the hospital. On the odd occasions that she worked at weekends or overnight, she enjoyed walking around, the peaceful nature of the surroundings more conducive to the proper function of the institution, the regaining of health. She avoided the corridor around lunchtime, when it became a highway of chairs, beds and people, some running, some blocking the way with their walking frames and attendant physiotherapists. In the summer months, many would take the alternative routes which led outside, but in winter the warmth of the enclosed walls attracted those who refused to brave the cold and it became even more rammed full. The hospital board had tried to introduce a one-way system, like that seen on underground railway escalators, but it was unobserved and merely caused confrontation and further congestion as the rule-enforcers clashed with the rule-breakers. Everyone had somewhere to go on that chaotic highway.

After walking halfway to her destination, she noticed that a new art collection was being displayed on the corridor walls. The hospital had encouraged local artists to show their works in an attempt to add colour and interest to the surroundings. Reports in medical literature had indicated that a pleasant environment – art, music and the like – might be helpful in speeding up recovery from illness. The new art collection was a series of lino prints of wild animals – badgers, rabbits, and squirrels, amongst others. She paused. A large print of two boxing hares caught her eye. Both animals had the intense expression of battle, front legs reaching forward, hind legs off the ground. The artist had captured the passion of the conflict. Next to it was displayed a smaller print of a seal in blue ink. The animal was perched on a rock, head upright, looking as though it were about to topple over at any moment.

'At least there are no foxes,' came a voice from behind her. She turned to see John Such, smiling at his interjection.

The chief executive smiled. 'Morning, John. These are rather good, aren't they?' she said pointing at the display of monochrome prints.

He nodded, scrutinising the boxing hares, which was the most striking of all the prints. He regretted bringing up the subject of foxes. She was bound to start interrogating him about his plans on the subject.

'We need to talk later,' she declared. He knew what was coming. 'About tomorrow's board meeting,' she continued before he had a chance to formulate the anticipated answer about the fox problem.

'Yes – sure,' he replied, relieved, not only at the subject but also the word *later*. He would have time to think about his response, forewarned. Whereas a solution to the fox issue was expected, there was no genuine expectation of an answer to the ten percent question. Nevertheless, he would need to come up with an idea; something that sounded different to previous suggestions, something which was perceived as innovative, or at least vaguely plausible.

The chief executive was about to resume her journey down the corridor when she stopped, looked John Such in the eye and said, rather quietly, 'Have you noticed anything odd about Eric recently?'

John Such was not sure what she meant by this or what type of answer she was expecting. 'No. What do you mean?' he asked.

'He seems distracted, rather on edge.'

'Maybe,' replied John Such, not really sure what she was driving at. 'He's got a lot on his plate at the moment.'

'Haven't we all!' said the chief executive, studying the print of the hare once more before continuing her walk to her office.

16.

THE BODY LAY behind the curtains, hidden from the rest of the ward. Beside it, a solitary nurse was making the necessary checks and gathering up belongings. The ward sister had called the doctor to certify the death, but he had been busy attending to the living and had told her he could not attend for a while. The dead could wait.

On such occasions, the ward became a quieter place. Conversations became hushed. Death pervaded the atmosphere with the reminder to all, not least those in hospital beds, who were nearer than most, that their turn would come too. Nurses stopped their chat. Cleaners wiped down the walls with more intensity than usual, as if to ensure they had wiped away the stain of dying. Porters were alerted that they would need to send out the special trolley, the one draped in blue canvas, which they would push a little more slowly, as though it were a hearse.

The curtain rustled and the nurse emerged holding a bag of clothes, upon which was written *For Incineration*. She drew the curtains together but unintentionally left a small gap so that, from a certain angle, it was possible to see the dead man, his pointed nose and open mouth visible, his body cloaked beneath a pristine white sheet. None looked through, however, having no desire to see the remains of a life. Those working on the ward had seen death on many occasions, and the patients had no wish to be reminded of it.

When the doctor arrived, the ward sister handed him a pile of notes pertaining to the deceased and took him behind the curtains. Being new to the job, he had not seen many dead people; not newly dead, at least. His first few months in medical school had been spent in dissection rooms, learning anatomy from cadavers. It was alarming to him that after a few weeks, a body was no longer regarded as a former person; it was seen more like a collection of bones, sinews and muscles. The lack of reverence given by his colleagues, who knew nothing of death, was, looking back, unsettling. It was the way to learn the structure of the tissues of the human body, and that was all it meant to those fresh-faced youths, most of whom could not imagine the end of a life. After anatomy had been learned, their training was with the living, and the dead were of no more interest to them.

He looked at the body before him, then glanced at the notes.

'What was he in for?' he asked the ward sister.

'He had metastatic lung cancer,' she replied. 'He came in with confusion and deranged electrolytes'.

The doctor nodded and looked back at the man. He had a waxiness of skin which was commonplace in the newly deceased. His mouth was open, revealing an edentulous mouth, and a few untidy whiskers sprouted on his chin. His eyes were closed, or, more likely, had been closed as part of the ritual of laying out. The doctor's role was now to confirm death: no heartbeat, no breath sounds, no response to painful stimuli. That would do it. A few minutes to determine that a long life had ended. He put his stethoscope on the man's chest, listening for thirty seconds or so. He took the man's left hand and pressed down hard on the nail bed of his middle finger to ensure there was no flinching. It seemed ridiculous to be doing this to a corpse.

He nodded to the sister, and they left his bedside, drawing the curtains once again. The doctor scrubbed his hands, then sat at the work bench, opening the tome which contained his clinical notes. He started to write: *no heart sounds, no breath sounds, no response to painful stimuli; declared dead at …* He glanced at the ward clock. He had to be somewhere in ten minutes. *Declared dead at 12.10pm RIP* he continued to write before putting down his pen. He riffled through the notes. Since he would be required to sign the death certificate, he needed to acquaint himself with the cause of death. He ascertained that the man had had terminal cancer and that low levels of sodium in the blood had caused his admission with confusion. He looked at an electrocardiogram, which had been performed the previous morning. The heart rate was perilously low; only around thirty beats per minute – barely enough to sustain blood flow to the organs. The man had had complete heart block; the chambers of the heart were out of sync, so blood pumped in a chaotic fashion. Under normal circumstances, this would be treated with a pacemaker, but perhaps they had decided not to go down that treatment path, given his poor prognosis with the cancer. That was a reasonable call, but they might have considered giving a drug to speed the heart rate, which might have made him feel better – at least in the short term. He looked at the drug card. In fact, rather than having been given a drug to increase his heart rate, the man had been given one which would slow it down even further. That morning, he had had a large dose of a beta-blocker, a drug used to treat fast heart rates.

He showed the drug card to the ward sister, who was now sitting next to him.

'He was given a beta-blocker this morning,' he said, pointing at the offending drug name.

The ward sister looked at the drug card and scrutinised the writing that detailed the timings of drug administration.

'Yes, looks like it,' she replied, not sure of its relevance.

The doctor picked up the electrocardiogram and showed it to her, as though it were an exhibit in a court case. 'He had complete heart block and severe bradycardia. The drug would have caused his heart rate to drop further.'

The ward sister looked from drug card to electrocardiogram and back again. Her expression became more concerned. As soon as the connection had been made, they both knew that the act of administering the drug had, in all probability, killed their patient. They looked at each other.

'What are we going to do about this?'

17.

THE RISE OF the various groups in support of or vehemently against the presence of foxes was worrying the sub-chief executive. It was not only deeply troubling, but baffling: he couldn't understand why so many people would take up arms over the matter. At the time of the initial outcry, spawned by the scaremongering newspaper article, he had suspected that, given time, the problem would go away: either the foxes would move on, or people would become less bothered by their presence. The storm of protest and letters to the press could only be described as an overreaction, to put it mildly. It seemed that people held strong views and had the time to express them. Thus, the scene that greeted him that morning – at least eight protesters standing outside the hospital gates holding *SAVE THE FOX* signs – filled him with incredulity. How this had escalated from a scurrilous story in the local newspaper to picketing was beyond his understanding. He was so taken aback by their presence that he stopped next to them as he was making his way into the hospital, as though the shock had paralysed him into a state of confused inertia. One of the protesters approached him, placard in one hand, leaflets in the other. John Such's brain was still trying to make sense of what he was seeing. The protester, clad in a heavy duffle coat and wearing a bright orange beanie hat, thrust the leaflet at him, giving him little option but to take it.

'Save the fox, mate!' said the hatted man.

John Such nodded and walked on, saying nothing.

Once he had arrived at his office and after having made

himself a large coffee, he inspected the leaflet. He had thought to throw it straight into the bin but reasoned that he needed to have some idea what he was up against. The hospital board had not decided one way or the other about the fate of the animals. They had certainly not hired a firm of pest controllers to exterminate the foxes, as seemed to be implied by the protests. Not yet, at least. The leaflet was printed in red (maybe the blood of the fox?) with a picture of a large-eyed fox cub. The emotive language was juvenile and amateurish, he thought. It was signed off at the bottom FOX DEFENCE LEAGUE. He sniggered. This is a league, is it? A few disgruntled types banding together for the sake of protesting, and it was now a league?

A colleague, dressed in a smart blue suit, entered the office. Equally flabbergasted at the delegation which had greeted him at the hospital gates, he held up the same offending fox leaflet.

'Have you seen this?' he asked.

John Such held up his own copy.

'Crazy lunatics!' exclaimed the other man, making a gesture of screwing up the leaflet and throwing it in the bin. 'Mass hysteria!' he continued. 'As soon as there is a whiff of something, they all crawl out of the woodwork.'

John Such smiled and nodded. He wasn't in the mood for a protracted discussion about the level of perceived insanity of the protesters. He sat down and switched on his computer. The daily trawl through emails would shortly begin. He glanced back at the leaflet, which he had placed beside his coffee cup. *Meeting 17th February 7pm: Brewers Arms* was written by hand at the top of the sheet. Maybe he should go. Infiltrate the group to discover its tactics? He was being sucked into their world of madness. Of course, he wouldn't go.

He opened the browser on his computer to read his emails. On the homepage was the headline: 'GOLD STAR FOR THE HEALTH SERVICE'. This referred to the local initiative to honour those working in the health service by displaying a gold star in windows of homes and workplaces. Local businesses had signed up to this, and those with a gold star would also give a discount to healthcare workers every Monday. Children would be making them in schools and placing the stars on their classroom windows to show their appreciation. The health authority was right behind this and had commissioned a local artist to make a large artistic interpretation of a gold star. This was going to be made of wire and papier mâché and would be sited halfway down the corridor near the management offices. The cost was undisclosed but was likely to mirror the size of the thing, which was vast. He had seen the design and thought it ridiculous. To him, its resemblance to a star was hard to see. The official unveiling of the *Star of Thanks*, as it was called, was in a week's time, and local dignitaries would attend the ceremony. He wondered if there would still be fox protests outside the hospital by then. Maybe there would be some protesting against the *Star of Thanks*.

He opened his emails. The majority were from finance: approvals for various costs, loans, interest payments. There were several from the chief executive, sent at some ungodly hour and marked with a red flag. She used this priority signal with a frequency that befitted her status. He knew what their content would be. The chief executive had become obsessed with the ten percent saving mission. There had been similar calls in the past, but this time the zeal of action was heightened to new levels. Whereas before, similar calls had been considered in a slightly half-hearted way, the push to achieve this goal had taken on warlike dimensions. Indeed, the chief executive had signed off many of her emails (which she had clearly copied and pasted from one email to the next) with: 'failure to reach our ten percent savings target will have dire consequences'. It felt like a threat. John Such, reading between the lines, had surmised that her own job would be in jeopardy should this not be achieved.

His phone rang.

'Morning, John,' said the voice. 'I've got the chief exec on the line for you.' Before he had a chance to answer, he was put on hold. Hastily, he attempted to open his emails to give the impression that he was starting to address some of the problems she had presented to him.

'John, how are you this morning?' said the chief executive, her tone rapid and urgent. 'These wretched people outside the gates – how are we going to get rid of them? I've got the Quality Commission coming today and the minister's office tomorrow. It will look terrible having that bunch of hippies outside as they drive in.' She paused, and it sounded as though she were taking a sip of her coffee.

'Yes, I've just seen them,' replied John Such.

'Well, we need to get rid of them, and quickly.' By *we* she meant him, of course. He couldn't see how he was meant to achieve this. Peaceful protest was not illegal. They were not technically on hospital grounds, so security or the police would not be able to remove them.

'It's not something I've had to deal with before,' he replied, making it clear that he was asking for suggestions.

'Well, I'm sure you'll think of something.' She paused again for a further drink before continuing, 'Oh, and have you read my emails? We need to meet later to thrash out some ideas about the cost savings.'

'Yes, that's fine. I'll be there,' he said, wanting to get her off the line so he could get on with solving the unsolvable.

'OK. Catch you later.' And with that she was gone.

Cost pressures versus fox saviours. Which was to be first? He had such bizarre choices.

18.

WHEN BARNABY SMITHERS had first heard the term patient safety committee, he had thought it odd. Why did such a thing exist? Why did patients need to be kept safe in a hospital, of all places? People came to hospitals to be cared for, to be made better. They would expect to be in an environment conducive to wellbeing and away from the hazards of the outside world. But the more experience he had of working in healthcare institutions, the more he realised that hospitals were one of the most unsafe places to be for the ill and the infirm. So many things could and would go wrong in an institution whose existence was predicated on changing the natural order, on fighting against disease by any means possible. The simple act of giving a drug was fraught with all manner of dangers. The idiosyncrasies of metabolism and the peculiarities of the immune response meant that pharmacology was beset with risk. Even if one in a thousand had a drug reaction, so many drugs were given that such a thing was commonplace. Yet, that was the least of concerns. A drug reaction was random, unpredictable, nobody's fault. Drug errors were the main problem. The complex nomenclature which had arisen in chemistry laboratories coupled with the huge variety of dosing schedules caused no end of problems: wrong drug, wrong dose, wrong frequency. Such issues consumed much of the agenda of the patient safety committee.

With Item 1 on the agenda taking very little time, and with the item on informed consent postponed due to the ethicist's accident, discussions turned to the development of a new system for reducing drug errors. Dr Smithers had read a little about this over breakfast and had got the gist of what was proposed. It was based on the concept of a traffic light, with red intended to mean the person giving the drug should stop and check the drug card to ensure the correct drug was being given to the correct patient at the correct dose; amber indicating that the drugs themselves should be inspected to make sure they were correct and in date; and green signalling that they should proceed – but only when the drug was with the patient and a further check had been done. This procedure was followed already, but apparently someone had decided that if the process were made analogous to driving a car, it would reduce the number of drug errors. *People are more likely to jump a light than give the wrong drug*, he thought halfway through the dry and ponderous presentation on the subject.

'The traffic light gives a bold and memorable aide memoire to the busy nurse,' concluded the speaker in a louder voice, perhaps having noticed that Dr Smithers had dozed off. He woke with a jolt and was momentarily unsure of his surroundings. He glanced up at the screen, saw a traffic light and recalled the subject of the meeting.

'Any questions?'

An older man in theatre blues, wearing half-moon glasses, raised his hand and asked, 'Is there any evidence that this works? From other hospitals or other countries, maybe?'

The speaker started to press some keys on her laptop before replying. 'If you remember the slide I showed at the start of the presentation,' she looked up and shone a light on the screen, 'this is the evidence from Scotland, where this has been in place for some time.' She looked back at the man who had asked the question. Her displeasure that he had clearly not been listening (coupled with her awareness of Dr Smithers' sleep) was apparent in the curtness of her response.

Dr Smithers looked out of the window. It was gloomy outside. It would be a few months yet before summer would fill the valley with light for the majority of the day. For now, darkness and damp were the principal elements of the environment. In the winter months there was not enough natural light through the windows and so the hospital neon strip lights were on almost permanently. Their artificial nature gave the impression of a subterranean bunker to much of the hospital. In the quiet of the night, their electric hum was faintly audible, giving an oppressive feeling to the many who stomped its lonely corridors.

The discussion had turned to matters of training. Dr Smithers was feeling sleepy again. He had not slept well the night before and had been woken by one of his children in the early hours. His phone rang. Apologetically, he stood up and rushed to the door before answering it in hushed tones.

'Dr Smithers?' asked the voice at the end of the line.

'Yes?' he replied, now outside the meeting room.

'Can you talk?'

'I'm just in the patient safety meeting,' he replied, although it was not clear why he needed to justify his location to the person on the phone.

'It's Imi, your registrar. I need to speak to you about one of your patients.' He sounded rather vexed. He had been on Dr Smithers' team for over four months and rarely rang, so this was likely to be important.

'Yes, go ahead,' he replied.

'It's about the Russian man who died today.'

Dr Smithers had not been aware of anyone dying, although he did recall seeing a man with a Russian-sounding name on the ward round the previous day.

'Mr Alyoshin,' continued the registrar, 'the man with end stage lung cancer and hyponatraemia.'

'Yes, I remember. I didn't know he had died. That was very quick.' Death was not uncommon on the wards, and the man in question had had an end-of-life plan in place.

'Do you remember that he had complete heart block?' asked Imi.

'Yes, we decided not to give him a temporary pacing wire

given his prognosis but to ask for a cardiology opinion later today,' replied Dr Smithers, unsure of where the conversation was going. Heart failure was one route out of the misery of the man's cancer, so if his heart had stopped, then so be it.

Imi was quiet and seemed to be hesitating, before spitting out, 'It's just that he was given a beta-blocker this morning.'

'Oh f—' He stopped himself swearing in front of his junior and continued in less vulgar terms. 'This is bad news.'

19.

CIRCULARS FROM THE Department of Health had arrived, warning of a possible pandemic. In the email alerts, reports of a mysterious new illness originating in Manila and now spreading rapidly in East Asia, were brought to the attention of the planning committees of hospitals the length and breadth of the country. The disease was heralded by a peculiar rash, which invariably led on to breathing difficulties. The illness, presumed viral, caused people to stop breathing for a period of two weeks. Untreated people died within five days of the skin lesions appearing. The rash resembled a red crescent stretching below the collar bones, leading the illness to be called the crescent moon disease. Scientists were rather baffled by its origin, and the lack of parallels with other diseases was leading to generalised panic and the re-emergence of the usual doomsayers.

Curiously, if patients were identified and placed on life support – if full ventilatory support of the lungs was instituted – they almost universally survived without any other form of therapy.

This near-universal survival following treatment was what vexed the health planners the most. A disease in which death was common was easier to plan for. The excuse that someone was unlikely to survive a period of time on the intensive care unit (as a reason for discontinuing treatment) did not hold water for this disease. The turning off a ventilator when hope seemed lost was no longer an option. In places where the disease had taken hold, intensive care units filled up with people 'biding their time' on a ventilator until they got better. This was a resource nightmare. Planning frenzies and stockpiling of ventilators were in full swing in certain parts. Manufacturers of washing machines and tumble dryers were given governmental edicts to turn their hands to the manufacture of intensive care unit ventilation machines. One inventor had put in a patent application for a respiratory support device which could be used at home by hooking it up to a household vacuum cleaner. There was no end of possibilities.

John Such surveyed the memo from the Department of Health. 'What's the point in a disease that doesn't kill people?' he thought, grumpily. This news would signal a new round of planning, a brand-new chain of command. It had not yet reached these shores, but all indications were that it soon would, since maintaining free will and the ability to travel outweighed any public health concern (at least until controlling the pandemic had become completely impossible).

He rubbed his eyes and dropped his head. He knew it would not be long before he was summoned before the chief executive and yet another project was dumped on his desk. He checked his phone. There were messages, fifteen of them, unread in a group message 'chat'. He had no desire to chat to half these people. He hesitated before reading them, knowing that once he did, everyone in the group would know he had seen the messages and would expect some sort of reply. Some things were better not read, or, at least, it was better that other people knew they were unread. Ignorance – albeit temporary – delayed the urgency, put off the moment. Some things go away. Ideas change. The ability to contact a whole cohort of people, meaning that large numbers contemporaneously knew your thoughts, was undoubtedly overrated.

He was mulling over the prospect of opening the messages when the phone rang. Another momentary dilemma over whether to answer the phone presented itself to him. But there was no hiding place. If he didn't answer, the chief exec would be pounding on his door within minutes.

He picked up the receiver after three rings. 'Hello, John Such,' he said.

'John. Crescent moon ...' said the familiar, curt tones of the chief executive. He was unsure if this represented a question or a statement.

20.

DR MATT BUTCHER, newly qualified doctor, had worked on Ward 19 for a few weeks. He had decided long ago that his future lay in surgery, and he was committed to the prospect of spending the next fifteen years training to achieve his goal. He knew the career was the toughest: mammoth shifts, endless theatre sessions, operations going wrong; but, emboldened by the naivety of youth, he had figured that it would be fine. Life at the bottom of the surgical career ladder was about five percent operating, ninety-five percent being a dogsbody, but he bided his time, hanging around after his shift with the hope of donning the surgical garb and wielding the scalpel.

For now, though, most of his time was spent seeing patients before their operations and, more challengingly, after their operations. The ward round of people in various stages of recovery often took all day. His job was to order and check a variety of tests which would determine the process of recovery: how well a patient's kidneys were working; their blood count; whether they had developed blood clots or patches on their chest X-ray which would indicate lung collapse. There was a never-ending throughput of patients, each staying somewhere between a day and several months. He understood that once a patient had been operated on, most surgeons lost interest. It was his job to keep the post-operative demons at bay. Most were straightforward; bodies had a remarkable way of healing themselves after the horrors a surgeon could inflict. Other patients were more challenging, and some were a catalogue of complications: the surgical manifestation of sod's law.

He had first come into contact with Muriel Frank on a night shift; one of his first, just a couple of weeks earlier. The nurses had asked him to replace a cannula – a small tube delivering life-preserving fluids and drugs – into Muriel's vein. This was a standard activity for a doctor of his rank, and he had performed it hundreds of times during his training and in his early days on the job. He had assembled the materials he needed – tourniquet, cotton wool, tape, sharps bin – and entered the patient's room.

The nurses had given him no warning of the difficulties others had encountered in performing this task on Muriel. He had introduced himself to the patient, but on receiving no reply had assumed that she was barely conscious, and so continued with the task in hand. He had put the tourniquet in its usual position, tightening it until the veins bulged. But none did. The area at the front of the elbow joint, from where blood was normally forthcoming, was bruised and oedematous. He tried to feel for the vein beneath the skin, but again, nothing was apparent. He took the tourniquet off and tried the other side, but the procedure met with the same lack of success as before. He went to try Muriel's feet, but found that one leg had been amputated below the knee and the other leg was mottled and cold, so he aborted the attempt. There were no options left, so he returned to the first limb he had tried, which, by now, was looking like the best option. Again, he set up the position of the arm, applied the tourniquet and waited for blood to pool in the veins. Still nothing. He needed to make an attempt, however, so he plunged the needle into where he expected to find a vein. The patient flinched and drew away her arm. He grabbed the arm, too roughly in retrospect, and snapped 'Keep still!'. He tried again, waiting for the flush of blood to appear and signal success. But none appeared in the tiny chamber behind the needle. So, again he tried, by which time the patient was becoming agitated and Dr Butcher was losing his temper. For several minutes, he attempted to perform something unachievable, sweat dripping down his forehead, his anger rising. It wasn't until a nurse came in and suggested they call for senior help that he stopped, storming out of the room, thinking only of his inadequacy.

He had retreated to the hospital canteen, giving no explanation for his rapid departure to the nurses on the ward. There, he drank coffee by himself and wallowed in his thoughts of failure. Maybe he should give up on his surgical career now. He was clearly not cut out for it.

Back on the ward, small droplets of blood appeared on the arm of Muriel Frank. The nurse wiped them away and applied a bandage.

Muriel Frank looked at the kindly nurse. 'Angry man,' she said in a voice that was barely audible.

21.

'John, can I catch you for a few minutes?' Eric asked, spotting the sub-chief executive walking towards him in the corridor.

John Such looked at his watch and stopped. 'Yes, of course – what is it?'

In truth, this was not a random meeting, since Eric had been tracking the movements of the sub-chief executive all morning, trying to fashion an impromptu discussion. It was just under an hour until the board meeting, and he knew that both of them would need to leave for the headquarters of the local health authority shortly. He hesitated before asking, 'What is the chief executive really expecting from us today?'

John Such laughed, then patted Eric on the back. 'Eric, it will be fine.'

'But have you had any ideas? We're struggling to come up with anything.' He felt like a school child asking a fellow pupil for the answers to the test or help with his homework.

'You'll be fine,' repeated John Such. He smiled and then started to walk away, but stopped and turned to Eric. 'Oh, would you like a lift to the HQ?'

Eric accepted, reasoning that this would give him some time to quiz his colleague on financial strategies.

'Meet me by the entrance in twenty minutes,' said John Such as he walked away. 'And not too close to those bloomin' protesters!'

Eric headed back to his office to pick up his papers and read over the notes he had prepared for the board meeting. He arrived at the agreed meeting place five minutes early. The band of protesters outside the hospital had mostly dispersed, and now only two people stood behind a sign which the rain was slowly destroying. He could just make out the slogan *SAVE THE FOX*, although the card on which it had been written was now sodden and crumpled. He checked his papers once more to ensure he had picked up the correct documents, then rehearsed in his head what he was going to say when asked about his ideas for saving ten percent of costs. They were neither radical, nor realistic.

At the agreed meeting time John Such appeared, and they drove the short distance to the old house which served as the headquarters of the local health authority. Despite his plans to quiz the sub-chief executive on the possible outcomes of the meeting, Eric was so anxious that the journey passed in near silence.

Most of the meeting attendees were already sitting around the table when Eric and John Such entered the board room. A round of pleasantries were dispensed with before the chairman brought the meeting to order. Since the meeting was almost exclusively to discuss the financial crisis, he invited the chief executive to introduce the issues at hand.

'Thanks, Mr Chairman,' she started, rather formally. 'The situation is …' And thus she expounded that which had been expounded on multiple previous occasions. Everyone present had heard the words before, not only by the current speaker but by countless others before her.

After the introduction, the attendees took it in turns to deliver a novel strategy or, at least, attempt to fashion something new from tired and previously discarded propositions. Eric sat in nervous anticipation. He was due to give his ideas after everyone else had spoken, allowing him time to listen to others and judge the validity of his own cost-cutting proposals. He heard about introducing intermediate discharge teams to reduce the length of stay of the chronically ill, charging (those who were able to pay) a bed occupancy tax, closing down the money-draining emergency short stay unit and moving the services twenty miles down the road, and so on. Although they were all presented with great conviction, the presenters knew that their suggestions were flawed: they were either impractical or they just shifted the financial problems to another struggling organisation within the health authority. But they had done what had been asked of them, more or less.

Eric looked down at his own notes and shuffled his papers, making them line up neatly. When his turn came, he read calmly from his prepared speech. His idea focused on charging patients for food, linen and toiletries during their stay. After admission to the hospital, a patient would be given a bill for the cost of such things as laundering of sheets and towels, plus the cost of all the meals. This had been carefully costed and on average, twelve percent of the cost of an admission was for so-called *hotel costs*. The idea was similar to the bed occupancy tax proposal which was gaining some support in higher management circles of the health authority. The big problem was that such a charge or tax would never be acceptable to the public, thus making it impossible to get it passed through government legislation. Any government which passed a motion to legalise such a tax would be out on its ear at the next election.

After all the proposals had been heard, the chair suggested a tea break to give people a chance to stretch their legs and consider the proposals. They would reconvene in ten minutes to discuss the ideas. The chief executive went over to the table at the side of the room, on which sat an array of teas, coffee pots, milk and biscuits. No one followed, and there was a distinct absence of conversation, given the overwhelming lack of a breakthrough. They were still no nearer finding anything resembling a solution. After the allotted time, cups were returned to the side table and the committee members trudged back to their seats.

A sinking feeling infiltrated the collective mood of the meeting, and after an hour of going round the houses on the proposals, they were no clearer on the strategy to be presented to the Department of Health team. Potentially a combination of generating income from the least unpalatable bed tax elements plus an early discharge plan? It was unlikely that this would reduce the net budget expenditure by ten percent; it would be two percent if they were lucky, and more likely, given the extra infrastructure required to implement these changes, they would end up losing more than they gained.

It was time to wrap up the meeting. The chairman tended to allow people to ramble when it was clear they had exhausted the possibilities, so the chief executive, wishing to draw proceedings to a close, asked, 'Do we have any other ideas? Be as radical as you like!'

For some reason, her gaze rested on Eric as she said these words. It was unplanned and in no way indicated an expectation that he would say something. Yet Eric felt that he was being specifically asked for his further input. With a sense of moderate panic, he picked up the sheet of paper which was topmost on his pile and, with the discussion he had had with Tony entering his thoughts at that precise moment, spluttered out, 'We've looked at the breakdown of our expenditure per patient and it is interesting that ...'

He wasn't sure he should be saying what he had started to say, but carried on, all eyes on him. He felt unreal, that it was not really him talking, as he repeated the figures concerning the five most expensive patients taking up ten percent of the costs. His mouth was dry and his collar tight.

'I don't think there is a practical implication to any of this,' he concluded, 'it's just something we noticed.'

John Such, lightening the mood, but also attempting to stop Eric digging himself into a hole, smirked and said, 'So, we could bump off our most expensive patients!'

No one else seemed to find this funny, and John Such raised a hand in apology.

The secretary to the board, who had been sitting quietly in the corner of the room, taking the meeting's minutes, looked up with a surprised expression on her face, and then continued to type away at her computer keyboard.

22.

A SCRAPPY-LOOKING AREA just behind the management offices which had been designated a wildlife reserve was, despite its unkempt nature, a common place for hospital workers to spend their lunch breaks. Several well-worn benches were placed at intervals beside a pond, and a few picnic tables, which had seen better days, were usually occupied by midday. Families of ducks had made the pond their home, and the yearly cycles of eggs, ducklings and fully grown adults were keenly observed by workers hungry for respite from the chaos and suffering a stone's throw away. In the small copse behind the pond, felled tree trunks had been arranged in a circle around a charred mound of stones, although the lighting of fires was strictly prohibited.

On one of the tree trunks sat Dr Matt Butcher. He had taken fifteen minutes to escape from the ward, asking a colleague to take his pager while he made an important phone call (so he had claimed). He needed some time to himself. The copse was barely twenty trees, but the covering of branches was dense, and the variety of wildlife was surprising. In spring, bluebells and primroses grew in irregular patches and wild garlic flourished, giving the area a distinctive, pungent smell, powerful yet sweet.

Matt took his book out of his bag. He thought that if he read for ten minutes, it would relax him. He was reading *Dead Souls* by the Russian writer Nikolai Gogol. He looked at the cover and then the last page to check how many pages were left. He had only read about a hundred, and there were several hundred to go. It was not a relaxing read, and the light was not good where he sat, so he put it back in his bag. He was finding it hard to follow the plot of the book and had needed to refer to various online synopses. The main character, Chichikov, travels around the Russian countryside buying up the ownership of serfs who have recently died. Newly deceased serfs still counted in taxation calculations for landowners, hence their wish to be rid of them. The reason for Chichikov wanting to buy them was (at least not at the point to which Matt had read) not that clear. The book was steeped in old Russian law and the social mores of the time, and many of the concepts were hard to understand for a modern reader. Yet the concept of the book – the trade in dead souls – fascinated him, and he had a newfound yet deep passion for Russian literature. He vowed to carry on at a time when he would be more receptive to its words. He had read that Gogol had burned the final part of *Dead Souls* and, indeed, the published text finished mid-sentence. It seemed that Gogol had sought to rationalise the incongruity of a close friend's death and had turned to a spiritual healer. With the healer's help, Gogol had become convinced that *Dead Souls* was the work of the devil, hence the burning of the manuscript. Subsequent to that, he had refused food and had died after enduring some form of psychosis, while mystics and quacks had tried to effect a healing, most likely through leeches and incantations.

A woodpecker flew onto a nearby tree. It turned its head to the side, listening for danger and, in a flash, flew off, its red underbelly disappearing into the trees. It was nearly time for Matt to return to the ward. He checked his phone for messages and saw that his consultant wanted to meet at two o'clock. That would mean seeing Muriel Frank again. The thought depressed him. He knew that he would be asked to perform some procedure on her: probably taking blood or inserting a new cannula. He would rather stay in the woods all afternoon to avoid the futility of what was about to happen.

He took his book out again and flicked through the pages, delaying the moment he had to leave. What would Gogol have done? Probably, he would have gone mad trying to understand his duties; to understand why he had to prolong such a life. He had read that another great of Russian literature, Chekhov, himself a qualified physician, had at the end of his life opted for champagne rather than any further medical intervention. He had known that his time had come. If only that option were available in the crumbling walls of Ward 19.

23.

AN EMAIL REQUIRING attendance at a rapidly convened patient safety committee had appeared in Dr Barnaby Smithers' inbox, suffixed with a red exclamation mark. He knew exactly what the meeting would be about, since he had alerted the patient safety officer to the drug prescription which had, in all likelihood, contributed to the premature death of his patient on Ward 17. Although errors of this kind were not infrequent, the hospital was keen to adopt a zero-tolerance policy for such misadventures. This would be the second time in as many weeks that they would meet to discuss drug errors. It was unsustainable to keep meeting at the drop of a hat, and they had decided that from next month there would be a monthly gathering dedicated solely to the discussion of such incidents. *More meetings*, he thought, closing his laptop and picking up a medical journal perched on a pile of miscellaneous professional debris. Opening a page at random, he read the first few lines, which were about a trial of a novel therapy for brain tumours involving inserting small sections of genetic material directly into the brain to block the replication of the cancerous cells. The trial had prolonged survival, but all the participants had died in the end.

He put the journal down and decided to get himself a coffee from the café which was situated a short way off the corridor. He picked up his ID badge – *Dr Barnaby Smithers, Consultant Geriatrician* – unravelling the thin strip of fabric before placing it around his neck, like a medal. He was one of the few remaining consultants to use the title *geriatrician*. The idea of treating people based on their age was old-fashioned to many: why would you treat someone differently because they were eighty rather than eighteen? This moral code was all well and good for issues of etiquette or societal rights, but age was an unignorable factor in recovery from illness, and the acceptability of risk was dependent on what might lie ahead. Age did affect how people were treated in hospital, and having specialists who were experienced in treating patients at one end of life's spectrum always seemed to him to be a good thing. He had chosen geriatrics for that very reason: he could balance up the risks to a life lived against the prospects of a life yet to be lived. Yet, the term continued to cause offence to some, with many thinking it to be pejorative, discriminatory. He remembered one man suffering great indignation at receiving a letter requiring him to see a geriatrician. He was not to be referred to as geriatric, he told the doctor when they met, before he had sat down. He even went so far as writing a formal complaint over the use of the word. Dr Smithers continued to use the term with impunity. He doubted paediatricians had the same problem.

He picked up his laptop and walked to the coffee shop, ordering a large black coffee and resisting the cakes. The café was mostly empty, so he picked a seat near the window, sipped his coffee and switched on his laptop. He would need to consider what to do about the drug error. The procedure was standard, albeit lengthy, with numerous forms to fill out. He would meet the relatives of the deceased (*Were there any?* he wondered) and ask the doctor who wrote the beta-blocker prescription to reflect on his practice. *Reflective practice* and *culture of no blame* were the latest buzz words in education; no one made mistakes anymore – they were actions which could be reflected on to learn how to do things better in the future. It had been different during his training. Such an event would have been dealt with by humiliation, in front of the whole team, like a sharp rap on the knuckles. Who knew which was better? For sure, though, he would forever remember his most calamitous of errors, and they were never repeated.

He texted his secretary, asking her to find out whether the deceased man had any relatives, before opening the incident form on his laptop which would report the drug error, the tortuous truth of the blunder. He hadn't got much beyond filling out his own details – qualifications, medical council number, et cetera – when he received the text reply from his secretary. It read: *Yes, daughter rang office today asking to speak to you. Would you like me to set up phone call?*

He didn't reply. He would see her in person later and ask her to set up the meeting. He resumed the filling out of the incident form.

24.

An organisation which is so adapted to chaos, which is so acclimatised to achieving only a minority of its goals, yet which is adept in its resiliency, trundles on. It is not until an event occurs that is alarmingly catastrophic that it confronts the fragility of its being.

Thus, one morning, after a night of the worst storms in a decade, an event of the greatest magnitude upset the fabric of the hospital to such an extent that all its workers felt that a destructive endgame had been initiated. An air of distress emerged overnight in the management teams and a state of insecurity permeated the lower ranks, reducing morale to an all-time low. A large oak tree had fallen and damaged the roof in the southern section of the corridor. A temporary diversion was put in place and the maintenance team had erected signs and warning barriers to prevent injury from the hazard. Daylight was visible through the damaged roof, and debris from the storm was strewn over the corridor's floor. A haulage company had been called to bring their largest crane in order to remove the old oak tree's trunk, which lay precariously against the corridor wall. Spectators came to marvel at the sight; the force of nature inflicting its worst. The cost of repairs would run to tens of thousands.

But the fallen tree was the least of the chief executive's worries. That morning, the local newspaper had run an article titled: 'KILLING OF FIVE: THE UNCARING FACE OF HOSPITALS'. Beneath the headline was a picture of Eric's whiteboard and the damning three words. The article asked why such a thing would be written down in full view of everyone. Furthermore, a transcript of the recent board meeting, in which ideas relating to saving money and 'withdrawing treatment for an economic reason' (as the paper had put it) had been obtained by the press using freedom of information powers – although the lack of any approach to the hospital for such information made it clear that the meeting minutes has been leaked to the newspaper. The conclusion the article drew from these pieces of evidence was that the hospital was actively engaged in shortening the lives of its patients. It was not even euthanasia, the article continued, since there was no consent; no discussion with the patients that their deaths might be sped along.

As ever in these reports, the conclusions went way beyond what was reasonable. The press had no desire to regulate its allegations. Dull stories which were balanced and modest in their content did not sell newspapers. Hyperbole, which lay just below the libel threshold, was the order of the day as they sought to attract readers.

The chief executive put her head in her hands as she sat behind her desk. In her office the sub-chief executive, the director of transformation and the press officer were nervously awaiting her proclamations. Eric had not uttered a word since reading the article, his face ashen and unmoving.

'I just don't know ...' the chief executive started before breaking off. She had been woken at six o'clock that morning with news of the tree fall. That alone was enough to send her into a panic about the cost of repairs, and she had just got out of the shower – in which she had formulated plans to convene a committee to determine the best way of repairing the damage to the corridor – when the phone rang again. This time it was the press officer who, having been tipped off by her contacts in the media, told her, in a staccato voice, about the revelations that were to be released to a general audience. To be rang twice before the sun had risen from behind the hills was clearly not going to be a cause for celebration.

She looked up from the desk, avoiding Eric's gaze. Having written the offending words on the whiteboard, his fate as the chief architect of this debacle was, to his own mind, not in doubt. He stood upright, but trembled visibly, gazing down at his feet.

John Such broke the unpleasant silence. 'How did this get out?' he asked rhetorically, then added, 'Who took that photograph?'

After that, there was silence for several more minutes, followed by a faint rap on the door.

The chief executive stood up and walked to the door. She put her hand on the door handle, but before opening it, she turned back. 'We'll talk later,' she said as a cue for the three of them to leave the office. They obediently stood up and started filing out, past the chief executive's secretary, who stood at the door holding a cup of coffee.

The chief executive ushered her in and took the hot drink. The secretary, Jan Marling, who had worked in the hospital for thirty years, awaited instructions. She had seen much over her time, notably the embezzlement scandal which had swamped the hospital and had led to the unceremonious sacking of her former boss. Somehow, she knew the current problem was even bigger than that. In her opinion (which no one ever solicited, despite her experience), the days of the current chief executive were numbered.

'This is bad, Jan,' said the chief executive after a few more moments. She was gazing out of the window, eyes fixed on the distant trees. Jan said nothing, as was her way. The chief executive turned, sat down and beckoned the secretary to do the same.

'I just don't know ...' she began, just as she had done minutes before. Ignorance was all she had to offer at this point. She looked at Jan, seeking inspiration.

'Jim Spier's team have been on the line, asking for an urgent meeting,' Jan said apologetically. Jim Spier was head of the local health authority. He was an unpleasant man who appeared to have a grudge against the hospital management and was always happy to point out their shortcomings. 'I've put him off until this afternoon,' Jan continued.

'Thanks. That's all I need: a mauling from Jim.'

'And we've had lots of calls from *The Herald,* and a few have started to come through from the national press.' Jan paused. 'I've directed them to Sue and the press office team.'

'Let the floodgates open …' the chief executive declared ominously.

25.

THE HILL FORT of Old Graseby was situated three miles from the hospital, on the southern boundary of the county. Bordered on one side by the Carthen Ridge, it offered stunning views across the valley: rolling hills and, depending on the weather, the distant, menacing peaks of the western range. On a good day the whole extent of the county could be seen, slopes and plains in the patched landscape. The earthworks of the fort, consisting of a semi-circular ditch and a steep rampart dating from the Iron Age, were constructed to fend off the influx of invading barbarians or their like. Legend states that the Romans, ever resourceful and not afraid to recycle the works of a former age, refortified the encampment and located a garrison of soldiers there as a strategic site from where legions could be dispatched to repel the threats of the Picts. The Roman road connecting the two most important trading points of the north of England ran a short distance away, passing below the ridge and stretching to the southern valley, the most green and fertile in the region. Small villages dating from those times continued to prosper after the Roman road was converted to the major north-south thoroughfare, bringing its trade and passing pilgrims as it had done for centuries.

The fort itself was a peaceful place. From the grassed banks, little could be heard other than a gentle rumble of traffic and the irregular song of birds which came in and out of hearing, buffeted by the wind. Occasionally a kestrel or a buzzard would fly overhead, pause and hover in the sky, surveying the ground below whilst fighting against the forces which would blow it away. Higher still in the sky, red kites, newly returned to the area after relentless persecution had led to their elimination a hundred years ago, would ride the wind currents fanning and tilting their tail feathers to direct their passage on their aerodynamic path.

Eric visited the place regularly to sit and look out across the bountiful land. He had known it since childhood, growing up a mile down the road in a small village also known for its Roman connections. He walked to the seclusion of the hill fort often, in all weathers, sometimes taking sandwiches. Previously he had visited with his old dog, which had plodded slowly and refused to climb on the ramparts. He had wondered if the dog sensed the ghosts of the past, since it would tread cautiously at certain parts, stopping and sniffing and refusing to be led on. In its younger days, the dog would jump up as if asking for reassurance when they reached the ridge overlooking the valley, and would often disappear in a frenzy of activity through a gap in the hedge, returning minutes later with as much excitement as it had entered. Maybe it was just that the rabbits were more interesting in those parts. He had read of similar stories concerning animals that acted strangely in ancient burial sites, reputedly detecting ancient souls who acted as guardians of the sacred land – so perhaps there was something in the idea that his pet had discerned an unusual presence in the fort.

His dog had long since died, and now Eric faced his problems alone. He had been sent home after the meeting with the chief executive, during which he had said nothing. But the walls of his house echoed the cries of his predicament, and he felt the need to get out. He had no one to whom he could offload his burden of torment, as he lived alone and never socialised. His solitude was rarely unwanted, but today was an exception, so he drove to the hill fort, forgetting his coat. Along the short, tree-lined track up to the fort he met several walkers, whose dogs came up to sniff his feet and wag their tails. He avoided eye contact with the walkers and ignored their dogs.

On reaching the wide-open expanse at the top of the track, he headed for the far corner and a wooden bench which looked out over the edge of the ridge. There he sat, alone and undisturbed. He had left his mobile phone at home on purpose.

The wind was strong where he sat, being exposed to the up-currents which were a result of the turbulence created by the ridges and which allowed for the birds to hang effortlessly above him. Within minutes he began to feel the cold, yet he felt the need to be there rather than anywhere else he could think of. He pulled the sleeves of his jumper down over his hands, then folded his arms round himself and stamped his feet to restore some of the circulation.

He had not been up to the fort for several months, the recent pressures of work having reduced his leisure time. When he did visit, he would often sit on this bench and think. Now, there was only one thought in his mind, and it was the image of the words he had written on the whiteboard – words that now accompanied a headline on the front of a newspaper. He had reached the conclusion, almost as soon as he had learned of the impending scandal, that he would have to resign. There was no way out of this mess. The words were no longer written down in their original form: he had wiped the whiteboard the morning after he had written them – yet although no one had explicitly asked him, he was certain that everyone knew he was the culprit. Indeed, the limited talk that he had heard was not of who had written the words, but of who had leaked the picture to the press. His guilt was, to his mind, already established. The chief executive had not spoken to him specifically, only in the company of others, and her rage was such that she appeared unable to address him and his foolishness. After the meeting, John Such had taken him aside and told him to go home. Maybe he didn't need to resign, as it was highly likely he would be told to leave.

The cold was becoming intolerable, and he was about to move on when the sun appeared from behind a cloud and the wind died down, making him not altogether warm, but at least not as unbearably cold.

His thoughts raged. He felt a throbbing rising from his neck arteries and a tightness around his temples. His breathing was irregular; he held his breath for no purpose and then exhaled forcefully through pursed lips. In his chest, his heart pounded, sending pulses of pressure to his cold extremities.

For some time, he had been visiting a counsellor as part of his treatment for anxiety. The counsellor espoused the virtues of mindfulness and was attempting to train Eric to perform certain techniques at times when his anxious thoughts took over his whole mind. The counsellor had explained that it was a method of using the body's natural physiology to calm the mind. *Focus on the breathing and not your thoughts*, she had repeated.

Eric breathed the cold air in through his nostrils, expanding the lower recesses of his lungs. He tried to focus on the air moving through his respiratory passages. He breathed out slowly through his mouth, pursing his lips slightly. When his lungs were empty, he repeated the process. But he had only managed three cycles before the images of *KILLING OF FIVE* flashed back into his thinking. He clutched his head.

The sun went back behind the clouds and the wind picked up.

26.

LATER THAT DAY, the chief executive summoned John Such to her office. She looked pale and wore a pair of thick-rimmed glasses which he had not seen her wear before. They made her look less approachable, more like she was about to chastise him for some frivolity or for not performing a chore. She took them off shortly after he entered the room. Her eyes were tired.

She beckoned him to sit down and closed the lid of her laptop. The newspaper carrying the damaging story was on her desk, neatly folded. He waited for her to speak, sensing her anger was inhibiting her ability to express her thoughts in a fluent way.

When she finally spoke, the subject was not the one he had expected.

'I've just about had enough of those fox protesters,' she started in a quiet voice, looking beyond John Such to the painting on the opposite wall.

'Yes …' he replied, feeling uncertain. It was only the second day that the protesters had been outside the hospital, but he could see that they presented an image problem. Not, however, as big as the one that looked out from the pages of *The Herald*.

The chief executive shifted her gaze to look at John Such. He could see she was expecting a more thorough analysis of the problem and a solution.

'Look, haven't we got a much bigger issue?' he said curtly, eyeing the newspaper that sat on the desk.

The chief executive picked up the paper and looked at the front page. Her eyes scanned from top to bottom and from left to right in jerky saccades, not appearing to focus on any aspect for more than a fleeting moment. As she did so, she chewed on her bottom lip, showing the imperfection of her upper incisors.

'I'm not sure there is much we can do about that,' she concluded, placing the newspaper down and picking up her glasses, which she relocated on her nose. 'We'll just have to let it run its course. It will go away after a while.'

John Such was taken aback. He had not expected this. Indeed, her words were utterly incongruous with her agitated state. He reasoned that she was trying to reassure herself rather than present a plausible strategy. The story was not going to go away.

'Well, I guess so,' he offered in reassurance. He agreed on one thing; like her, he wasn't clear on what could be done about the newspaper headlines. The hospital would, of course, issue the press with statements rebutting the nature of the allegations and assuring the public of the hospital's commitment to excellence in healthcare. Perhaps, after the initial furore, the uproar would die down, but this was clearly a major crisis they were facing. The most worrying aspect, however, was that sources from within the hospital had sent the picture to the press, and had also sent the minutes of the board meeting. This was hugely concerning and made the hospital vulnerable to further leaks and allegations.

'How is Eric?' the chief executive asked. There was something about the way she spoke his name that revealed her ambivalence to his welfare.

'He's in a bad way. He was unable to speak, poor fellow, so I sent him home.'

'Why the hell did he write that?' she interjected, her anger showing more and more as they talked. 'It's inconceivable,' she added, before returning to chewing her bottom lip again. It was a tic he had never seen her display before.

'I don't think we should pin the blame on him,' John Such said, feeling the need to defend the director of transformation. 'He's usually so meticulous and considered in what he writes on his whiteboard – or anywhere, come to that. It's very unlike him to write this sort of thing.'

'But he did …' interrupted the chief executive.

'Yes, well, who knows why he wrote it? But the fact is that he wrote it in a private office, that should … that was his own space.' He was getting flustered. The chief executive's raging threat was rubbing off on him. 'We should be asking who decided it was a good thing to send the picture to the papers.'

The chief executive stopped chewing her lip and breathed out deeply.

'Yes, you're right,' she said in a calmer voice. 'It's not Eric's fault. It was stupid of him, but he clearly didn't mean all this to happen.'

She looked at her diary, which was open on the desk next to her. 'Can you tell him to see me tomorrow at ten? Make it clear to him that I am not holding him responsible.' She looked at John Such and smiled. 'We need to support Eric through this,' she said, although neither of them believed that this was the real sentiment behind her words.

27.

DISTRACTING HIMSELF FROM greater matters, John Such opened the folder on his laptop computer labelled *Foxes*. The fox committee had yet to meet, having been postponed on a few occasions when more pressing issues needed to be considered. He had not been able to impress on other members of the committee (nor himself, if he were being honest) the importance of addressing this awkward dilemma, which could cause significant harm to the reputation of the hospital. So, the timetable for deciding the fate of the foxes drifted further, overtaken by changing events and prescient threats.

As yet, his presentation on foxes had not seen the light of day. He thought it rather ridiculous anyway and more like a natural history talk than a public health presentation. He would have time to change it, if need be. The other document in the folder labelled *Foxes* was titled *Fox Strategy*, but it was blank, save for the title. He opened it and considered jotting a few notes but didn't really know where to start. His policy of putting things off until the last minute, until just before they were required, was generally effective given the shifting nature of priorities and the regular emergence of new crises which demanded immediate attention.

The protesters were out in greater numbers that day. The day before, their first official picket of the hospital, they had appeared a disorganised rabble, but they had become more orderly; their banners seemed more professional, their attire more coordinated. Whilst walking past that morning, he had noticed that they had with them an oil drum filled with charcoal or a similar flammable material. It was unlit, but presumably was there to provide heat for them when the temperature dipped. *They must be in it for the long haul*, he thought. It had reminded him of footage of the miner's strike that he had watched on the six o'clock news as a child.

He opened the web browser on his computer and called up the website of *The Herald*. He skipped the articles concerning the main news story, looking for reports of the fox demonstrations, but found none. He had some time before the next assault on the hospital began to be played out in the local rag.

After visiting the kitchen area just off the main office to make himself some coffee, he returned to the *Fox Strategy* document and contemplated its future content. He started by writing two headings: *Elimination* and *Management*. He would write down under each heading a list of reasons to adopt that particular policy. By 'management', he meant finding some way of allowing the foxes to live on the hospital grounds without incurring the indignation of the press and some parts of the public. This was the more complex plan, and it was unclear to him how it could be achieved, even if it were deemed to be the right course of action. They couldn't simply ignore the animals. That would risk further expansion in their numbers and invoke more accusations of a vermin problem. But what to do with them? Create a wildlife sanctuary where they would live and ensure they would not come within a few metres of the hospital? A vulpine restraining order?

He walked over to the window of the open-plan office, from where he could see the protesters at the front gate, some way off in the distance. There were fewer of them than when he had arrived first thing. He suspected some had sloped off to the pub for a lunchtime drink or two. Perhaps he should ask them what they thought the hospital should do with the foxes. He considered this and decided it wasn't a bad idea to engage them in dialogue. The chief executive would not approve, though. He knew that for sure. She took a combative approach to these sorts of problems and any attempt at discussing the problem with the crowd outside would be seen as conceding advantage, as giving in. He started to trudge back to his desk and noticed that a leaflet identical to the one he had been handed yesterday had been pinned to the bulletin board next to the window. Taking hold of the paper, he gave it a sharp tug, detaching it from the clip that was holding it in place. He reread the leaflet and the message written in freehand at the top: *Meeting 17th February 7pm: Brewers Arms*. He looked out of the window again, then back at the paper in his hand, and decided he would go to the Brewers Arms the next week, just to see what it was all about.

28.

DR SMITHERS ARRIVED at the ward office in good time. It had been reserved for his meeting with Mr Alyoshin's daughter; the meeting in which he would have to explain the prescription of the drug which had hastened her father's death. His duty was to provide complete honesty, but his instincts were to downplay the error in the interests of the greater good. The hospital being sued was the last thing that was needed, and expensive litigation costs and pay-outs would cause further damage to a cash-strapped system. Mr Alyoshin had been going to die before too long anyway; some might say that this occurrence had prevented weeks of further suffering. At least, that was one argument which many might veer towards, although only when looking for an excuse. But it was, he told himself, inexcusable.

Serena Alyoshin arrived a few minutes after Dr Smithers and was ushered into the room by the ward sister. Offers of tea were declined. She shook the hands of the doctors and sat down in one of the hard-backed chairs positioned around the table. Her black hair streamed down across her shoulders, glinting as it caught the sun. She wore a heavy raincoat and carried a large umbrella of the type seen on golf courses. Her face was rather pale and she had dark, deep-set eyes. Her expression was sullen.

'First of all,' began Dr Smithers, 'I'd like to say how sorry I am for your loss.' He paused, expecting an acknowledgement, but getting none, continued. 'Your father was a very ill man. As you know, he had terminal cancer and was admitted to the hospital a few days ago. He was very frail, and he was placed on an end-of-life pathway when he arrived.'

Serena Alyoshin remained impassive, but it was clear to Dr Smithers that she was listening intently. He continued. 'In the end, his heart was very weak, and he passed away.' He disliked the use of euphemisms for death but found he couldn't help using them in these situations. It seemed to be what was expected. The bluntness of the word death was repellent to many.

Serena Alyoshin took a tissue out from her handbag and pressed it gently to her nose. Her lack of interaction was making Dr Smithers nervous. The bereaved often helped him out. They realised the difficulty of his job and would say things like *you did all you could* or *I'm sure he was comfortable at the end*, even though they had no idea whether these things were true. The consoled needed themselves to console. But when it came to Mr Alyoshin's daughter, Dr Smithers had no idea what she was thinking.

'Do you have any questions?' he asked, trying to get her to say something.

Serena Alyoshin dabbed her nose again and then shook her head. Finally, she broke her silence. 'I hardly saw him. He was a strange old man.' She paused, clearly unsure about whether she should speak of a dead man, her father, in this way. 'He had no time for me. No time for anyone.'

Her bluntness was not uncommon in this scenario. Members of feuding families died, and death did not usually heal the rifts, despite the common misconception that it would. But Serena Alyoshin seemed colder than many. There didn't seem to be an ounce of sadness for her deceased father. Dr Smithers wondered why she had bothered to come, as she was clearly not interested in her father – neither in life, nor in death.

He paused and considered what to tell her next; whether he should tell her of the drug error. Maybe this was his get-out clause. Nothing would change if he didn't disclose this information. The daughter, it seemed, wouldn't have cared if he had been run over by a bus or shot in the head during an altercation.

He was about to find a way of terminating the discussion

when she asked, 'Doctor, why did you bring me here?' The question was blunt, to the point. Of course, he hadn't asked her to attend a meeting just to offer his condolences. He pulled his chair closer towards the table and placed his elbows on the table, hands clenched.

'All deaths ...' he started, but then corrected himself. 'Every case where a person is admitted to hospital and dies within twenty-four hours needs to be reported to the coroner,' he said rather clumsily. 'In your father's case, there was also a complication.' He felt his palms become sweaty, his pulse quicken. Serena Alyoshin raised her eyebrows a fraction, widening her eyes.

'There was a possible com...complication,' he stammered.

'What do you mean?'

'We're not sure the extent to which ... exactly what happened.'

'Doctor, what are you talking about?' She was now speaking more aggressively.

'Mr Alyoshin was given a drug just before he died.' His obfuscation was making the situation much worse. If he had just told her in bland, authoritative, matter-of-fact way then she probably would not have been interested. Initially indifferent to her father's death, now she was becoming suspicious.

'What drug?' she asked.

'Your father had a very slow heartbeat, and he was given a drug which may have further slowed down his heart,' he said quietly, choosing his words carefully. 'We're not sure what effect it might have had on him.'

Serena Alyoshin was silent for a few moments, contemplating her next move.

'So you killed him, is that what you're saying?'

Dr Smithers shook his head and raised his left hand, but before he had a chance to say anything further, Mr Alyoshin's daughter stood up, grabbed her umbrella and stormed out of the room.

29.

As if the newspaper problems and the fox infestation were not enough, the incidence of crescent moon disease was rising globally and the hospitals in the south of the country had started to see their first cases. The illness continued to baffle scientists and public health doctors alike. The disease was poorly defined and, together with its alarming rate of spread, this was causing widespread consternation in the healthcare community. A new faculty within the Department of Health was hastily set up. It sat within the Department of Communicable Diseases, which had already received a sizeable budget. Experts who advised during seasonal influenza outbreaks had been gathered to thrash out a policy for coping with the potential spread of the disease. Forecasts were dire and there was talk of intensive care units being swamped.

The chief executive read the latest memorandum from the Department of Health. Each health authority had been tasked with developing a plan for the epidemic in the likely event of its widespread manifestation within the next few months. The need for ventilatory support for patients with the disease, in the form of intensive care beds and ventilators, was a huge challenge, since most hospitals already ran their intensive care units at full capacity. The challenge was how to find extra resources and physical space for the influx of patients without impacting on the current services. This point had been emphasised in no uncertain terms: there could be no reduction in the normal activity of the hospitals. The targets that the Department of Health had recently set needed to be abided by. There would be no excuse for increasing waiting times or cancelling operations. It was like planning a meal for six people – a meagre one, at that – and then being told that sixteen people were turning up and they all expected a portion of the size originally planned, despite the amount of raw ingredients remaining the same.

The chief executive was used to this kind of problem. If such a disease took hold, there would be cancellations of operations and waiting times would rise – there was no question about that. Money and resources were finite; diseases were infinite and ever-changing. She recalled the days of planning for a mysterious neurological disease which was linked to eating infected pork. Projections for widespread contagion came to nothing, and multiple documents detailing contingency plans were unused but still kept in files on her hard drive, like an apocalyptic manual. Nothing changed in healthcare planning except the (often extravagant) names of the illnesses. They would use many of the files from the hard drive as templates for the new round of pandemic planning. In addition, she had decided to ask Eric to lead on the plans. He was good at that sort of thing, planning to the finest detail, envisioning the full range of possibilities. And, of course, it might take his mind off the newspaper leak and reduce his sense of guilt over what had happened. Putting him in charge of this – which, she would emphasise, was one of the greatest challenges for the coming year – would tell him that she had confidence in his abilities and that she did not hold the whiteboard words against him. She would run it by John Such and then tell Eric when they met the next day.

After skim-reading her latest emails, she got up to stretch her legs, walking the length of the corridor – an executive perambulation, so to speak. She commonly walked the floors for no reason other than to increase her presence and profile. Often, she would meet someone she needed to talk to and, just as often, there would be unsolicited approaches from someone who needed to vent frustration or bring an incident to her attention.

Most of the people trudging the corridor, however, either did not recognise her, or, if they did, had no desire to engage with her and so walked past, eyes low. Even though there were uncomfortable moments – gripes and groans, requests for mediation, invitations to experience the hardships certain members of the workforce were enduring – she enjoyed her morning walks.

On this day, she had only walked a few paces when she was accosted by the head nurse, who was dressed in casual clothes, rather than her matron's uniform. Because of this, the chief executive didn't recognise her at first.

'Chief exec!' the head nurse called from the other side of the corridor before dodging the few souls who stood between them. The chief executive stopped and smiled. 'Jennifer,' she said. 'How are you?'

The head nurse had been working in the hospital for at least three decades and knew nearly everything that was worth knowing. She carried a half-full coffee cup in one hand and a blue cardboard folder in the other.

'I'm at a training day today,' she explained, even though the chief executive was not looking for an explanation of why she was dressed casually.

'Oh good. Hope it's useful,' replied the chief executive.

'Yes. Child protection.' She raised her eyebrows. 'Pretty depressing stuff.'

The chief executive nodded, thinking it was the end of their conversation and expecting to continue her walk. Jennifer leant in closer and in a quieter voice said, 'Did you hear about Graham Perry?' She looked at the chief executive, waiting for her recognition of the name, and, seeing none, added, 'The old chief exec. A few before you.'

The current chief executive did indeed know all about Graham Perry. He had been in charge during the embezzlement crisis which had resulted in the hospital acquiring huge debts. These were still being paid off and would be until the end of the century and beyond (if the hospital still existed).

'What about him?'

Again, the head nurse leant in and lowered her voice. 'He's died.'

The chief executive had never met the man, but his name was commonly bandied about the management offices. Those who could remember him recalled a surly man who had kept himself to himself, never socialising with the rest of the team. He held short meetings and governed in a dictatorial way, rather than by committee. Many had liked this style, but it opened him up to extreme criticism when the embezzled funds were discovered, and it made his involvement in the scheme much more probable to many. He had been close to the disgraced financial officer, one of the few people to whom he talked outside of meetings, and although his hand in syphoning money from the hospital had never been proven in a court room, his guilt by association was good enough for most. He had been sacked as chief executive and had not been seen again in the health authority. He was reported to have retired to a seaside cottage in Cornwall, where he indulged his passion for sea fishing, taking with him many of the secrets about what had really happened.

'Can't say I was close to him,' continued Jennifer, 'but it's a shock.'

'Had he been ill?' asked the chief executive.

The head nurse shrugged her shoulders, 'Don't know.' She glanced around. 'Word is, he killed himself,' she said furtively.

The chief executive was shocked. 'Really?' she asked.

'The shame of what happened to him was ...' she trailed off, struggling to find the right words. 'He was a broken man after all that business and became a hermit, pretty much, down in Cornwall.'

'That's awful,' said the chief executive, distressed at what running a hospital could lead to.

30.

ERIC DROVE SLOWLY to the hospital, in no rush to face the working day. He had not slept and had a stuffy nose and a thudding headache. The dismay of the previous day's revelation played through his mind on a loop. He had been made aware, via a text from John Such, that the chief executive wanted to meet him. The text had said that she wanted to support him, so the meeting would be fine. This was some comfort to Eric. Nonetheless, he was dreading seeing her. He wanted to be alone and couldn't imagine how talking through the issue would help.

After parking his car in the half-empty car park, he made his way to the café. This would negate the need for him to make coffee in the communal tearoom. Several large groups stood in the café queue as he joined the end inconspicuously. He checked his phone. It was before eight o'clock, so he knew the offices would be quiet and he could slip in, hopefully unnoticed. He imagined his demise would now become a spectator sport; his colleagues taking entertainment from the failure of his career. There were unread messages on his phone. He would wait until later to read them – if he read them at all.

Two doctors with stethoscopes draped around their necks joined him in the queue. They started to talk about football before one of them ran off abruptly, having received a cardiac arrest message via his pager.

'Blimey, that's an early one,' the remaining doctor remarked to Eric.

Eric gave the faintest of smiles, recognising the comment

but at the same time indicating his unwillingness to enter into conversation. The doctor remained quiet. Eric ordered his coffee and left the café. In the corridor, two more doctors ran past him, one pushing a large machine, the lead of which was trailing behind, the plug dancing on the floor. The unpredictability of the hospital's business was disturbing to Eric and was the reason he knew he could never work on the other side of the management desks.

He reached his office, closed the door and sat down in his chair opposite the whiteboard. It was now completely blank. It would be a long time before he would write anything further on it. The pens lay in his drawer, which was locked. He noticed that his bin was unemptied but was in no mood to make a complaint to the housekeeping department. In previous times, a phone call to estates would have been the first job of the morning.

He switched on his computer and logged into the hospital intranet. He would have all the previous day's emails, currently unopened, to respond to. Outside his door, he heard people moving around. How long could he hide behind the door before he had to go out? He sensed that his colleagues would leave him alone. He had the meeting with the chief executive at 10 o'clock, and he would lie low until then, unseen but not unnoticed, using the next two hours to figure out what he was going to say to her. It seemed that he only had one decision to make: whether to resign on the spot or wait to be sacked.

His phone rang. He saw from the screen that it was John Such. He waited a moment, deciding whether to answer it. Reasoning he would have to face his colleague sooner or later, he pressed the large green button on the screen and put it to his ear.

'Hello,' he said.

'Eric,' replied the sub-chief executive, 'I just wanted to check you are OK.'

Eric remained silent.

'You made it in alright?'

'Yes', replied Eric, uncertain how to reply even to this most basic of questions.

'Good,' replied John Such. 'Listen, Eric, the CEO will support you, as will I. So, don't worry about meeting her later. It will be fine.'

Eric took a deep breath and mumbled a brief reply before hanging up. He looked back at the whiteboard. There were faint traces of red and blue ink, the only discernible evidence of the words which had landed him in so much trouble. When he had wiped the board clean the day after he had written the offending words, he could not have imagined the problems that would arise as a result of them. Of course, the writing of the words was not, in itself, the problem; it was their dissemination to a newspaper that caused his current predicament. He had asked himself repeatedly who might have taken the picture and sent it on for public consumption. It could have been any number of people in the office, but the likelihood of a work colleague doing it was not high. He had no true adversaries in the hospital. His nature, although intense and, as he would himself admit, on the unfriendly side, was not malicious, nor prone to creating enemies. He was a benign presence whom most tolerated, happy to accept his idiosyncrasies. He went along to the occasional office event (Christmas parties, leaving do's), at which he would stay for his allotted time, offend no one and endure the spectrum of bad behaviour into which these things typically degenerated.

He picked up a cloth and a spray bottle of alcohol-based cleaner, scrubbing the board until no trace of writing was evident. Then he went over to his filing cabinet and took out a list of all those working in management, filed under HR. He scanned the names, partly to consider whether anyone written on the sheet might have been the source of the leak, but mostly to reassure himself that he hadn't recently wronged anyone. He found no cause for alarm and reasoned that if it was one of his colleagues who had orchestrated the newspaper story, it was not out of revenge. He put the list back in the right place in the cabinet and sat down again. Over the next few days, however, he thought little about the possible identity of the person who had leaked the story to the press, focusing on his predicament from the point of view of its consequences, rather than its causes.

This contrasted with the chief executive, who had begun ruminating on the nature of the subterfuge and had already made it her mission to unveil the culprit, whatever it took.

31.

Life, illness, recovery and death all continued relentlessly within the hospital. The depths of the winter would soon be behind them. New shoots would spring from the thawing earth of the nature reserve, a new band of junior doctors would be unleashed on the wards, more board meetings would be scheduled. In Ward 19, Muriel Frank clung on to life. If she needed a reason to continue, then none was apparent to those who were looking after her. The nurses tended to her every need, and she had little choice but to accept their attempts, so far successful, to keep her alive. No one, not least the long-stay occupant of Bed 12, thought that improvement in her medical condition was possible, but the innate bonds of survival and the deeply held oaths of those who acted as guardians of her life meant that carrying on was the only path that could be followed.

Mr James Barabas, newly returned from a week's holiday in the sun of the Caribbean, arrived early to the hospital that morning. His first thoughts were for his long-stay patient. Indeed, he had thought of her every day whilst on the beach of the paradise island. His wife had booked the trip to take his mind off work, and had banned him from checking his work emails for its duration, so he had not had any form of update from his team about Muriel's condition. He wondered if maybe he would be greeted with good news for once.

He changed into his theatre blues, punched a code into the keypad of the operating theatre complex and headed for the coffee room. It was unusually quiet for that time of morning.

Several of the surgeons were away at a conference on laparoscopic surgery, being entertained at a ski resort by representatives of a pharmaceutical company who wanted to buy their souls. A few porters and scrub nurses scurried about, not taking much notice of him. He walked further into the depths of the theatre complex, past parked beds and dilapidated wheelchairs, before entering the coffee room. As he had anticipated, his consultant colleague, Mr Khalid Massoud, who had been looking after his patients in his absence, was sitting there, sprawled across two low chairs, feet on the table. He was nearly always in work when Mr Barabas got there.

'Jimmy boy!' he greeted Mr Barabas as he entered. 'Nice tan!'

'Thanks,' he smiled.

'So, how was it?' Mr Massoud sat up, taking his feet off the table.

'Yeah, great. Fantastic,' he replied, taking a seat opposite. 'The beaches are incredible. Beautiful.'

'Nice.'

They sat in silence for a few moments before, having exhausted the small-talk possibilities of a winter holiday, the conversation about work inevitably started up.

'What've you got today?' asked Mr Barabas, stroking his greying beard before taking off his glasses to clean them.

'Lap hernias,' replied the other surgeon, 'all blinkin' day!' He smiled at the prospect, revealing that this was not the hardship he had seemed to express.

A nurse, hidden behind a surgical mask, poked her head round the door. 'Mr Massoud, we're ready for you.'

The surgeon stood up. 'No rest for the wicked,' he said in a jolly fashion, before adding, 'Catch you later, Jim.'

Mr Barabas himself stood up. 'Before you go, Khalid, can I ask you if there were any issues with my patients while I was away?'

Mr Massoud thought for a second. 'No. I don't think so.'

'What about Mrs Frank, Ward 19?'

Again, Mr Massoud pondered this before replying, 'Which one is she?'

'Post-operative bleed after bowel resection, months on ITU,' he replied, surprised he had to remind his colleague.

'Oh yeah.' Mr Massoud shrugged. 'Fine, I think.' He smiled and added, 'No problems,' before heading off, tying the strings of his surgical mask in bows behind his head.

Now alone in the coffee room, Mr Barabas poured himself a cup of coffee and sat down. He had known Mr Massoud for years. They had come up the ranks of surgical training together and had been rivals, to some extent, vying for the plum jobs, the premier surgical rotations in the country. They had both ended up in the same department as consultants, which seemed an odd twist of fate, but they got on very well, and finding themselves working as colleagues was not unwelcome. Khalid had always been the more laid back, and, at the same time, the more charming. During training, some of the more senior consultants had thought him lazy, but in truth, he was efficient and did the job in half the time many of his grade took. He had a happy disposition, which made him popular on the wards and amongst the theatre staff. Scrub nurses competed to be in his operating team.

Mr Barabas found his thoughts returning to Muriel Frank. He would need to speak to his registrar to receive an update about her condition. Although it was in Khalid's nature, he was still taken aback by his colleague's lack of recollection of his most challenging patient. He wondered whether he had actually been to see her or whether he had left it to the juniors. He sipped his coffee and picked up a journal that was lying on the table: *Anaesthesia Today*. He scanned the list of articles. His interest was aroused by one, titled: 'Awareness in anaesthesia', and he was about to read it when Mr Massoud re-entered the coffee room, throwing his mask and a pair of rubber gloves in the bin by the door.

'Given the bloody fellow his breakfast!' he exclaimed, revealing the cause of the cancellation of the first case on his operating list. 'What a bunch of amateurs. Bloody Ward 15. Again!' He was forever moaning about the standard of care on that particular ward and had taken numerous steps (as yet unsuccessful) to make sure his patients were not admitted there. Still fuming, he resumed his position on the sofa, arms widespread, feet on the coffee table. 'I mean, what's the point? It's not like they haven't been a surgical ward for donkeys' years! Patients should be nil-by-mouth on the day of their op ... what's so hard about that?' He had said all this before and would say it again. In a few minutes, he would calm down and forget about it. The patient would be sent home and added to the nearly endless waiting list again. No big deal in the vast inefficiency of the health service.

Mr Barabas started to read the article. He lacked dynamism that morning, and was putting off the moment when he would confront the problems he had left behind just over a week ago. This was common after a holiday: a feeling of inertia, knowing that it was several months before the next break. How to keep going until the next holiday?

Mr Massoud's phone rang. He answered in a monosyllabic, business-like way, the call only lasting a few seconds. He stood up to get some coffee, spilling some on the floor after filling his cup excessively, then sat down again opposite his colleague. The lights flickered and in the distance an alarm started to sound. Two blues-clad women entered the coffee room and sat at the far end.

'That post-op woman on Ward 19?' said Mr Massoud, breaking the silence. Mr Barabas immediately put the journal down.

'Mrs Frank?'

'Yes. She's been in for months. Is that right?'

Mr Barabas nodded. He felt deflated just talking about her.

'What are you going to do with her?' asked Mr Massoud.

That was the question. What was he going to do with her? Early in her post-operative recovery (if that was the right word), he had thought he could manage it by himself and would get defensive, feeling a need to justify his decisions when anyone else tried to offer advice. Now, he was grateful if anyone could help him out of the mire.

He shrugged and replied, 'Don't know. What do you think we should do?'

'Well …' Mr Massoud began, choosing his words carefully, 'she has had several months of maximal therapy. It seems clear that she isn't going to do well.' He paused before adding, 'You've done all you can.'

Mr Barabas' gaze was fixed on the light switch on the far wall while his thoughts ran in all directions.

'Maybe it's time to pull out,' said Mr Massoud quietly.

32.

WITH AN ENORMOUS sense of dread and an uncertainty which had made him more uncomfortable than he had ever felt, Eric knocked on the door of the chief executive's office. She was talking on her mobile phone when she opened the door but smiled briefly and ushered him to sit down. Eric sat, his head bowed, his fingers interlocked. The chief executive was discussing issues relating to staff shortages on the surgical wards and was trying her best to end the conversation. Although Eric could not hear, he could sense the aggression of the person at the other end of the phone. There was a knock at the door. The chief executive, still talking on the phone, opened it, took a folder of papers from her secretary and, after gesturing to her in a signed code indicating she didn't want to be disturbed for ten minutes, closed the door. She brought the phone call to an abrupt end and sat down opposite Eric. She smiled again.

'Eric,' she began, 'how are you?'

Eric shuffled in his chair. He felt dreadful. Deep, dark furrows under his eyes indicated his lack of sleep, and his usually immaculately ironed shirt was crumpled and unkempt. His tie was stained with an oily substance just below the knot.

'Yes, OK. I guess,' he said, not meeting the gaze of his boss.

The chief executive allowed more time for him to express his opinion, but realising that this was unlikely, continued, 'Eric, we are here to support you through this. Clearly something went wrong, and we need to find out what happened.'

She paused. His face remained impassive.

'We're not holding you …' she continued, stumbling over her words, 'we're not blaming you for what happened.'

They sat in an awkward silence for a while. Beyond the office door people scurried around. Eric felt hot around his collar and loosened his tie. He sensed the chief executive was staring at him. He knew she was impatient for an explanation of his actions, to find out what possible madness had possessed him to write such a thing in full view of anyone who might enter his office.

Finally, he broke the silence. 'I'm really sorry for what happened,' he said, still not making eye contact. 'I take full responsibility for my actions.'

He expected her to reply with something affirmative, but instead she stood up, looked out of the window and addressed him with her back to him. 'Eric. Who do *you* think might have leaked this to the paper?' She emphasised the word *you*.

She turned round and their gaze met for the first time since he had arrived. Eric, unable to hold their eye contact due to his self-imposed shame, looked down at his hands.

'I don't know,' he said. 'I've been wracking my brain as to who might have.'

'Well, we need to find out. It's just not acceptable that this sort of thing goes on in the hospital.'

He nodded, his eyes still cast downwards. He could tell that, despite her soft tones and her words of support, she was angry. He was generally not good at reading emotions in others, but this was beyond doubt.

The chief executive sat down and clenched her right fist, thrusting it forward. 'I will find out who did this,' she said. Then, as if a switch had been flicked, her tone changed. Picking up the folder her secretary had given her, she started talking in a much calmer manner.

'As you know, there are concerns about a possible pandemic – crescent moon disease. The DoH has told all the health authorities that they need a robust pandemic contingency plan. It's a pain, but we can recycle quite a lot of the other plans we have made before. I'd like you to head up the hospital's strategy and draw up the blueprint for our response.' She paused. Eric remained expressionless. 'Is that OK?'

'Yes – fine,' he said, almost involuntarily.

'Great. We'll talk later,' she replied, indicating that their meeting was ending.

He stood up and made to leave. Before he opened the door, the chief executive repeated her support for him, although he couldn't help detecting the half-hearted nature of the sentiment. He left feeling more perplexed than when he had entered.

After returning to his own office, he reflected on the meeting. He had gone in determined to resign from his job but had ended up being told to head the pandemic response team. It made no sense to him. The chief executive was angry with him, of that there was no doubt. So why she had assigned this new job to him was wholly unclear. He opened the folder of papers the chief executive had given to him. He scrutinised the first few lines of the first page before his mind once again drifted back to his obsessive thoughts. He glanced up at the whiteboard on which he would no longer write. It was clear of any writing now, pristine and shining. The offending red and blue pens had been locked away.

33.

THE CLOCK AT the far end of the office was running slow. Although Aamaal Hossein knew from the radio news bulletin which played loudly in the room that it was already past midnight, the clock displayed a time of five to twelve. It was still yesterday by the clock's reckoning. Whatever day it was, she was exhausted, and her feet ached. She had worked for five hours on this shift and had been up since 7am working in the supermarket – carrying heavy boxes, stacking shelves, and enduring the dismissive disapproval of many of the downmarket establishment's clientele. Her husband had been feverish for several days but was resistant to any medical help. She had rung her doctor's surgery in her lunch hour to seek advice but had failed to get through. She was relying on her eldest daughter to keep him safe. On Friday, his condition had worsened, and this had manifested itself both physically and mentally. He had become more withdrawn, barely speaking. Decay had infiltrated his core. She knew that he was giving in to the illness, yet she didn't have the strength to challenge him or rage against his cruel predicament.

The lights in the office were dim and a gentle hum of electrical equipment was ever-present. The place was empty save for a co-worker who called her name from the other side of the office – the first person to acknowledge her that evening. They exchanged a few words in Urdu before each carried on with their chores. Aamaal carried a large black bin bag into which she placed the paper recycling from each of the bins in the open-plan office and the smaller individual offices. Spreadsheets, meeting minutes, policies, standard operating procedures – they all ended up as waste for recycling. Information was fleeting and reusable. Her bag was becoming heavy, and she needed a fresh carrier. Placing the full bag next to the door, she went to the store cupboard, which was situated next to the office where she had read those strange words written on the whiteboard on her last night shift. She stared at the door, which bore the label *Eric McDowell, Director of Transformation*. She would need to clean in there later; a prospect which unsettled her. For the moment she could put it off, doing all the other chores, leaving that room until last.

Having sourced an empty bag, she resumed her collection of the unwanted (and mostly unread) paper documents. She had been told to separate out coloured paper from the more abundant plain black and white printed sheets. The reason was not given, but she diligently added this to her list of tasks. She would agree to most things in order to keep her job.

An incoming text message was signalled by her phone. Despite it being past midnight, it was her daughter with an update on Aamaal's husband. Her daughter often stayed up for much of the night to care for her father and did so with a diligence and a maturity that others of her age would find hard to comprehend. The text message reported that her father was still very feverish but had managed to sleep for a while. It was brief and practical, similar to a nurse's handover. Aamaal sat down to compose a response. She hoped her daughter would be able to get some sleep that night. Aamaal was working the first of seven nightshifts, so it was going to be a challenging time for both of them. She paused, considering what to write, but ended up just writing *Thanks*. It was hard for her daughters, particularly the eldest who had taken on the mantle of a second, yet more present, mother figure. She should be working for her exams and enjoying her free time, rather than being bogged down in domestic drudgery.

Aamaal's own experience as a teenager had been similar in some ways. Her own mother had come to England in the late 1970s without a word of English. She had lived a life out of sight, rarely seeing anyone but her immediate family. Her children had become her voice and her view on the world. She had become so reliant that she was paralysed with fear at the prospect of any social interaction, so Aamaal had needed to take the younger children to the park, their doctor's appointments, their school plays. As a result of these experiences, Aamaal had been determined that her own children would be free to be children – but her husband's illness and their financial struggles had meant that this dream was not possible, and the cycle of the eldest daughter taking on the role of parent had begun again. It was destiny, and there was no way to escape it. Fate had beaten her.

She continued to collect the wastepaper. Emptying the final bin, she found only a single newspaper, neatly folded, almost pristine. She was about to place it in the larger bin bag when she froze. It was not the headline, but the picture which immediately drew her attention. Three words written in blue capitals on a shining white background. It was exactly the same picture as the one she had taken the other night, and which was stored on her phone. A picture she had intended, by means as yet undefined, to sell to the press and make enough money to give her daughter a few nights off by paying for a period of respite care for her husband. But the picture had already been sent to the press. Someone had beaten her to it.

She immediately took out her phone and opened the app labelled *Photos*. She found the picture and, ashamed of her guilt by intention and frightened of the consequences should she be found in possession of the image, deleted the photograph in an instant. It would be of no use now anyway. She sat down in a hard wooden chair, shaken by the incident, struggling to understand what had happened. A few days earlier, she'd had a half-baked idea to sell an incriminating picture to the newspaper but had put it off, partly because she was too busy doing her other jobs but also because she felt embarrassed, perhaps unclean, for considering such a thing. And now the idea she had conceived had been carried out by someone else? It was as unfathomable as it was disturbing. In her heart, she knew that she would not have been able to go ahead with it anyway. It would have been betrayal to an organisation which, despite its faults, provided her with an income. To follow through on her act might have helped her make some quick money, but it would not have been the right thing to do.

She looked at the paper again. 'KILLING OF FIVE: THE UNCARING FACE OF HOSPITALS' ran the headline. Shock gave way to confusion and then fear. She recalled her initial reaction to seeing the words on the whiteboard. And now here it was in the newspaper. So, the hospital was killing its patients.

34.

THE HOSPITAL SOCIAL club was an inauspicious venue for meeting people. The main room had once been the location of the sexual health clinic and was the reason many referred to the social club as *The VD Clinic*. The walls were off-white and showed the brickwork, and by the end of the evening streaks of condensation were often present, glistening in the dim light. The bar, which displayed a rack of half-empty spirit bottles and a single beer on tap, was a gnarled and cracked slab of oak which, legend had it, had been taken from a manor house in a neighbouring village as payment for clinic services when the lord of the manner had got into trouble with one of his many mistresses. Many similar stories arose within the place where people went to escape. A few tables and chairs were dotted around the central floor area, although most people stood while drinking, a reflection of the fact that they had too much to do to contemplate sitting down for any length of time. A single poster of a cult 1960s film adorned the wall, its frame battered, its perspex glass front cracked.

Matt Butcher had finished his shift and was already on his second pint of beer. He had arranged to meet his friend and colleague, Jared Frost, a fellow surgical junior doctor, for a quick drink before heading to the town's cinema. His colleague had rung to say he had been delayed by 'a bleeder' but would be there shortly. For the moment, he had the bar to himself. Sitting at a rickety table facing the dartboard, that lone instrument of entertainment, he checked his phone for messages, then placed it down in front of him. It had been a bad day. He had failed to take blood from three patients, and since this was his main job at the moment, he was deflated and downcast. How was he meant to perform complex surgery if he couldn't even put a needle in someone's vein?

He drank on. A few more people came and went, only two settling at a nearby table. He checked his watch. They had missed the film now, so he ordered another beer. He wasn't sure how wise this was given his early start the next day, but he wanted to talk to Jared and needed an excuse for his continued presence in the bar. The barman obliged, carrying out the transaction silently and without expression. Just after Matt had paid, however, Jared entered the bar looking flustered, the shiny black tubes of a stethoscope garlanded around his neck.

'There you are!' said Matt, smiling.

Jared approached the bar and asked for a pint of beer. 'That was challenging,' he replied to his colleague. 'We had to give eight litres of blood.' He stopped to take a large drink. 'As soon as we got it in, it came out again.'

They sat and he recounted the details of the major haemorrhage. Matt listened to the horrors which had unfolded on Ward 13. Like many novices, his overriding thoughts were whether he would have coped in such circumstances. During training for incidents like this, he was told that his instincts and his experience would kick in and that saving lives would become like clockwork. He wasn't so sure. The prospect of something happening to him that was similar to his colleague's experience was terrifying.

Jared took a long drink and finished his pint, his story exhausted (for now, although doubtless he would recount its gory details again and again). He got up to go to the bar, asking his friend if he would like another.

Matt was already feeling mildly drunk, but the desire to be sociable and also to forget his own perceived inadequacies made him agree to a further beer.

They continued to talk, cataloguing their triumphs and failures from the first few months of their new career. With rising alcohol levels, each became more reflective, more grandiose in their thoughts, more exaggerated in their assessment of their own abilities.

'So, was it worth it?' Jared declared after the anecdotes had dried up.

'What?' asked his colleague.

'The six years of medical school, the hard slog, the debts?'

'Oh,' said Matt, taken aback at the requirement for such an evaluation at this point in the evening. 'I guess so.' His glass was now empty, but he had decided not to drink any more. He looked at his colleague and he noticed, for the first time, an aura of confidence, bordering on smugness. Perhaps it was getting through his first major incident as a junior doctor that had allowed him to join the real club. Perhaps he had always had that confidence, and Matt was only now noticing the contrast between how confident he felt himself and how the person he had known for six years was acting. They had started medical school together, naïve and untutored. He remembered arriving in the lecture hall with two hundred other eighteen-year-olds who had passed the tests for getting into medical school. None had any real idea what they were letting themselves in for, irrespective of how much work experience they had claimed on their CVs to have done. Now they were all working, save the handful who had been kicked off the course or had bailed out, knowing it wasn't for them.

Jared continued to exude the confidence of one who had saved a life and fulfilled his childhood dreams. There was no questioning whether his career choice was the right one, at least for now.

Matt, the alcohol in his bloodstream making him disinhibited, asked his colleague, 'Don't you sometimes think it's a bit pointless?'

Jared raised his eyebrows and took a big breath of the stale air of the bar. 'What, medicine?' he asked.

'Yes, I mean … sometimes I don't know what we are trying to achieve.' He sat back in his chair, wishing he had another drink in front of him. He glanced over at the bar. The room had become busier now and the levels of chattering had increased. A queue of thirsty healthcare workers had formed.

Jared didn't know what to say and was in no mood to be deflected from the day's achievements.

'Well, we're trying to help people. Make them better,' he said, rather limply, harking back to the medical school interviews which he had had all those years earlier and in which he had been asked what his reasons were for choosing medicine as a career.

Matt sat forward. He needed to express what he had been feeling for the few long months of the job. 'We're keeping some of these people alive so they can just have more problems, more complications, more pain. And why?'

'Well, that's kind of what we are meant to do,' replied Jared, baffled that he needed to spell this out.

Matt was silent, confused in his thoughts, unable to express exactly what he felt. His colleague sensed his unease and decided it would be best if he left him to himself. Standing up, he put his glass down on the table and said, 'I'd keep those ideas to myself, if I was you.' And he walked out of the room.

35.

SERENA ALYOSHIN'S LETTER to the chief executive arrived in the midst of the carnage already unfolding within the management offices. Not only was the hospital under fire from all angles and the chief executive's position under extreme threat, but she had also started to suffer from debilitating bouts of dizziness. On repeated occasions when she stood up, she experienced a great pressure in her head, followed by a sensation of the world spinning and sparkles of light in her visual field. The symptoms were often so bad that she felt the need to lie down. She felt like she existed in a whirlpool, a vortex pulling her down. She had seen her general practitioner, who had discussed her stress levels. He explained that her stress was manifesting as a physical embodiment. She got the impression it wasn't the first time that day that he'd had that conversation. There was no getting away from it – the job was not good for a calm disposition and the preservation of sanity.

She read Serena Alyoshin's letter along with several other complaints that had come in that week, but that one in particular stuck in her mind, giving her a sense that it would prove more of a problem than all the others. All complaints were investigated and chewed over before a response was constructed. The medical teams involved were invited to provide their own angle on the criticisms levelled – usually at their alleged suboptimal care of a patient. Most complaints were resolved through a response from the chief executive (written by the complaints team in a well-defined template) which bordered on an apology, irrespective of whether there was a genuine case for a complaint, but which did not admit guilt. Ninety percent of complaints ended there. Some went further – to arbitration meetings or even court.

This particular complaint referred to the death of the complainant's father and the '*shocking manner*' in which Dr Smithers, consultant geriatrician, had spoken to her. The chief executive's interest was heightened by both the reference to a drug error and, more concerningly from her point of view, the mention of *The Herald's* newspaper story of a few days earlier. The letter was inarticulate and openly accused the hospital of deliberately killing the writer's father. It stepped into the libellous, as many of the letters did.

As the final arbiter on all manner of grievances, the chief executive often read the most scurrilous, inaccurate and offensive accusations, but she had to remind herself that the letters were from people who had lost loved ones and who were grieving, and it was better in these circumstances to listen and sympathise rather than take offence. Starting a fight was in no one's interests.

However, this was the first time the newspaper story had been referred to by a member of the public. Although the chief executive knew that the story was going to have a huge impact on the local population's opinion of the hospital, seeing it referred to in black and white was unsettling. The connection between the story and the death of an actual patient had now been made. She envisaged the next day's paper: numerous recently deceased patients, their pictures printed with short biographies, coupled with the accusation of institutional homicide. There would be no end of family members who would come forward. This was a story that would run. The destructive nature of current affairs reporting was unstoppable. Controlling the damage it caused was her main task for now.

She would need to speak to Dr Smithers to find out what had happened. As far as she was aware, they had never met, and she hadn't seen his name come up before in previous complaints. She was in no doubt that the patient's daughter had embellished and misinterpreted events, but there was likely to be a core of truth. There usually was. She picked up her phone to speak to her secretary and asked her to arrange a phone consultation before starting to read the remainder of the day's post.

Surprisingly, after only five minutes she received a phone call from Dr Smithers. He was clearly keen to speak to her, like a guilty man wishing to unburden the details of his crimes.

'I thought I'd ring now, if that's OK?' he began. 'Your secretary said you were free for a while.'

The chief executive was a little annoyed. Everything should be in its place and its allotted time. That was part of the strategy for keeping her head above the swirling water. He must have caught her secretary off guard, maybe using his consultant status to bully an appointment. Maybe she had felt sorry for him.

'Yes, fine,' replied the chief executive, hiding her annoyance.

'Thanks. It's a bit of a mess, I'm afraid,' said the doctor. She detected alarm in his voice, an anxious yet defensive tone. She found Serena Alyoshin's letter and surveyed it as he started talking. His next few sentences were jumbled, so she stopped him.

'Dr Smithers,' she said firmly, 'we are talking about Mr Alyoshin, who died a few days ago? Is that right?'

'Yes,' the doctor replied curtly.

'His daughter refers to a drug error ... the administration of the wrong drug,' she said. There was silence at the end of the line.

'Dr Smithers?' she continued, 'Is that correct?'

The doctor's nervous verbosity had been replaced by a quiet reticence. 'Well, yes,' he replied quietly.

The chief executive considered his words. This was all they needed. A footnote to the letter said that the daughter had already been in contact with *The Herald*, and that this was proof of the despicable policy of an institution which was meant to care for the sick and needy, not kill them (or words to that effect).

'Tell me exactly what happened,' said the chief executive, slumping back in her chair, her ears popping, her light-headedness returning and the room gently revolving.

After five minutes of a garbled explanation which was going round in circles, the chief executive stopped the doctor's account and thanked him, asking for a written account to be sent to her within the week.

She had heard both sides of the case, and the verdict seemed clear-cut to her.

She put her head in her hands, sobbing softly.

36.

THE BREWERS ARMS was a sprawling construction on the outskirts
of town. Its appearance was somewhere between old-world
charm and dilapidation. The main building was a mock Tudor
house with peeling white paint between the exposed black
wooden beams. Many thought it had a slight lean to the left,
which was, of course, exaggerated at the end of the evening.
It had a solid oak door, left open during business hours, above
which was a lintel expressing the Latin motto *Bibere humanum
est, ergo bibamus*; translated (infrequently by those entering) as
To drink is human, therefore let us drink. Since the pub had gained
a reputation for anti-social behaviour amongst its drinkers, this
was perhaps not the most apposite of advice.

As he approached the pub, John Such noticed the words and,
not having studied Latin at school, considered what they might
mean. Maybe *To err is human, to forgive divine*, he postulated, but
thought this an odd phrase to greet those entering the public
house. He would look it up later. Beside the door lay an old dog,
perhaps owned by the publican, which didn't appear to notice
those entering or exiting the institution. Its head was resting
on its front paws, its eyes barely open, its ears flopping to the
side. Its coat was grey and black, and it had a mangy and matted
tail. John Such decided against patting the dog, instead letting
it rest, although he suspected it would not have been troubled
by the attention.

He stepped through the door and into the main bar area
of the pub. He immediately spotted the group he was going to

infiltrate, if that was the correct description of the activity in which he was engaging. This clandestine action was a welcome change from the mundane nature of his day-to-day existence. He looked around the rest of the bar area, which was otherwise empty, save for two old men playing cards and drinking beers from pewter tankards. He wondered if he would ever get to a time in his life when he would have his own tankard to drink from in the local pub. A large log was burning in the impressive fireplace within the far wall, giving a welcoming warmth and a soft glow to the dimly lit room. He ordered a beer and headed over to the group in the corner.

There were seven or eight people spaced around a table upon which the banner of the Fox Defence League and a pile of pamphlets was lying. John Such approached the group boldly, stopped behind an empty chair and asked the man who was sitting beside it whether he could join them.

'Of course. Sit down,' said the man, who wore a checked cap and a heavy green overcoat.

The others in the group eyed John Such with a mixture of suspicion and surprise. He put his beer down on the table and smiled. 'I'm George,' he said, having decided on this alias before entering the pub. Several of the group put a hand up in greeting, and others took more gulps of beer.

'Welcome, George. Good to have you on board,' said an elderly man, apparently the leader of the group. He had an intensity about his person and an open laptop in front of him, and was clearly taking notes from the discussion. His beverage was tap water.

A young woman in a bright orange jumpsuit, which John Such thought was rather like those seen in American prison documentaries, leant forward and reached for his hand. 'Yes, it's great to have you here.' She smiled and immediately let go of his hand, resting back in her chair. John Such moved his chair back a fraction.

'How did you hear of us, George?' the elderly man continued.

John Such took out the flyer for the meeting that he had taken from the office's noticeboard and showed it to the group. 'I picked this up from your stall outside the hospital,' he replied. Whilst not strictly true, he had actually been given one on the first day of their protests.

'Great,' continued the leader of the group. 'We were discussing how we are going to increase the pressure on the hospital over the next few weeks. Make them understand the depth of feeling for this issue.'

John Such nodded in agreement and took another sip of his beer. He was unused to drinking beer, not being a common frequenter of drinking establishments, and he remembered the bitterness of the beer he had chosen from days gone by. The orange-jumpsuited woman leant forward again, reaching over the table to clutch the hand of the elderly leader at quite a stretch. This was evidently her way of attracting attention and was as unsettling as it was odd.

'Keith,' she said, holding his hand and his gaze intently, 'I am so pleased that we are making progress on this.'

She sat back again, having made her interjection. Even Keith seemed taken aback by her behaviour. The discussion continued. The main strategy, as far as John Such could make out, was to increase the level of picketing outside the hospital gates. There was a suggestion to write to the local member of parliament, but the consensus was that that right-wing holder of power was no more likely to defend the foxes in the hospital than repeal the unjust council tax laws. At one point, someone asked if any of those gathered had connections to the hospital; it was thought they could act as a foot in the door to influence the policy of fox elimination. John Such remained silent. He was unclear why they thought the hospital policy was to get rid of them, since as far as he knew (and he was ostensibly in charge of the problem) no decision had been made. The assumption in the current group seemed to be that the chief executive herself would drive horses and hounds through the hospital in the manner of a Boxing Day hunt, holding up the bloodied carcasses of the murdered animals in triumph. There was no discussion of the other side of the argument, as he had expected, but he had at least anticipated some sort of recognition that public health was a factor in the equation.

At one point, Keith asked John Such directly if he had any ideas for taking forward their cause. He was going to suggest a meeting of arbitration between the group and the hospital, before realising that he was the person they would be meeting, so he mumbled something about increasing their voice in local media outlets, specifically *The Herald*. At least that might deflect more attention away from the 'Killing of Five' issue, he reasoned to himself. This suggestion was met with indifference, with some articulating the opinion that the newspaper was merely a mouthpiece for the middle class. The discussion rambled on in more tangential and irrelevant directions. Several more rounds of beer were consumed, and members of the group came and went, mostly disappearing outside temporarily for a cigarette. After a while, the discussion became more heated and the woman in the orange jumpsuit became offended by some of the lines of argument. Descending into more farcical territory, Keith tried his best to keep order, but the conversation came to be more about personal insults than about foxes. John Such said nothing further and, after a while, made his excuses and left. He knew now what he was up against and was reassured.

37.

THE CHIEF EXECUTIVE, her thoughts fractured by the incomprehensibility of the recent events, had the feeling that she was being forced into actions she neither desired nor could control. Such unlikely happenings had led to the vilification of an organisation which she was expected to steer to greater efficiency. The problems were so far removed from her sphere of experience and seemed so uncontrollable that she felt her status as the leader of the hospital was crumbling. Six months, maybe less, was her remaining time in tenure – of that she felt certain.

Her obsession with seeking out the person or persons who had sent the malicious material (which had not been written out of malice by Eric, but had been construed as such by a scandal-hungry press, designed to generate outrage with which to feed its greedy clientele) was distracting her from her duties. The finance question was unsolved, debts were mounting. Before the newspaper stories had materialised, the risk of collapse of parts or all of the hospital had been high; now this seemed inevitable. She spent her days in a sleepwalk, her functions on autopilot, her emotions pared down to the bare minimum. What little she managed to achieve centred wholly on uncovering the culprit behind the newspaper leaks. If she were completely honest, the primary goal of this quest was not to discover the identity of the person in order to punish, but to understand the motives behind such an action. Why on earth would someone do this?

Others, too, spent much of their day contemplating possible reasons for this most damaging of scandals. John Such, whose disposition was calm and measured for the most part, was enraged at the affront to the hospital's name, an organisation in which he took great pride. Despite the nonsensical nature of many of the tasks he had to perform and the endless bureaucracy, he had a genuine and deep-seated belief that he was part of an important and fundamentally decent establishment, and that the soul of the hospital should be protected. With his friends, he joked about his work-life balance and often moaned about the more menial aspects of the job, as well as the people he worked for, but he couldn't see himself doing anything else. So, he had a genuine desire to catch the leaker, in order to look him or her in the face and explain the impact their actions had made to him and the hospital community.

It was an awful business, and the morale of the hospital was at an all-time low. Hasty meetings were called between the senior management and the local health authority. There was talk of the health minister making a journey up from London to ask for an explanation and formulate a proposal to quell the stories, but the pandemic plans, which were gathering pace, spared them that indignity. Jim Spier, head of the local health authority, made up for this, however. His relationship with the chief executive had been poor even before the current problems, and he had made no secret of hiding his displeasure at the direction in which she was taking the hospital. The newspaper stories gave him ammunition for a full-blown assault on the management style of the chief executive. When they had met on the day after the newspaper stories had seen the light of day, he had initially taken a conciliatory and reassuring tone (at least relative to their previous discussions), but this was merely a prelude, a warm-up. Longstanding threats to close down the hospital and merge it with the neighbouring hospital, whose virtues Jim Spier painted on a luminous and bountiful canvas, were repeated and now reinforced by the apparently proven incompetence of a management which could let such a thing happen. She sat through forty-five minutes of their most recent meeting, which was effectively a monologue. There was little she could say, and there was even less he wanted to hear.

When she was released from the meeting, and after escaping to the toilets of the authority's headquarters for a moment of solitude, she walked the mile or so back to the hospital along the brook, through trees which shaded the bright sun. Her mind was numb. When she had walked this route on other occasions, she had taken joy in the birdsong and the flowers; they had rejuvenated her after the stresses of whatever meeting she had just attended. But now she felt the world around her was artificial, not really there. It was difficult enough to attend to the mechanics of walking, to avoid low branches or rocks on the ground.

As she emerged from the riverside path, she entered the small housing estate sited there, following the winding footpath which skirted the back of the modern executive houses. The path was uneven, and the chief executive noticed for the first time, despite having made this journey on multiple occasions, that it was the tree roots pushing up from below which had disrupted the smooth tarmac of the path. Ridges and cracks crossed the black walkway, elevating small sections to catch the shoe or boot of the unwary walker. The path had been constructed, flat and even, no more than ten years earlier, but a force of nature, strong and quiet, had disrupted its solidity. That force was a tree which stood upright, unmoving, as it had done for decades before the path was made.

After leaving the path, she walked further on, past the security office and the nurses' accommodation to the back entrance of the hospital (thus avoiding the fox protesters). She braced herself for the deluge which was coming.

38.

WHENEVER HE THOUGHT about the relationship between the press and the local hospitals, Jim Spier, head of the local health authority, conjured up images in his mind of a slippery fish. He liked to keep one step ahead of all his adversaries, but knew that this was not possible in the case of the local hacks, who were waiting for any sign of a slip-up. Nonetheless, he had a series of strategies he would enact to counter any scurrilous story which saw the light of day. If he hadn't been so arrogant and self-important, some might have thought his attitude paranoid.

The current newspaper story about the 'Killing of Five', as it had been dubbed, continued to gain traction in all sorts of places, and it was clear that it had a longer time to run than he had originally hoped. He blamed the weak leadership of the chief executive, for whom he had little time. Ever since their first encounter at the start of her tenure in the hospital, he had taken a dislike to the woman. His deep-seated sexism, which he did little to disguise, coupled with his pompous nature meant that she didn't stand a chance, despite her efforts at conciliation. He was just too set in his ways, they had both concluded.

But the story was causing a considerable annoyance for Jim Spier. Regular phone calls with the Department of Health were scheduled, and even a visit from a delegation of officials from Whitehall was planned for next week to discuss a public relations exercise designed to make the story recede into history. Government had got wind of the bad press the health authority was generating, and it needed these stories to be quashed as soon as possible. He had considered sacking the chief executive but wasn't sure what good that would achieve and knew it might be seen as an admission of guilt. Anyway, he needed someone to act as scapegoat. She would do for now.

Regarding the local rag, *The Herald*, he had his sights on one journalist in particular. If someone had told him there was a more despicable specimen of an oleaginous aquatic beast than Mo Kane, he would find it hard to believe. In his opinion, everything the man did was shameless and brutally executed. He wrote such dreadful stories; ran buses through people's lives.

Jim Spier's hatred of the journalist had been cemented by an exposé of his business dealings and the alleged preferential treatment he had given to a company of surgical mask makers, in which he had invested heavily in years gone by. This had been published at roughly the same time that the embezzlement scandal at the hospital was coming to light. He had only just managed to cling on to his position at the time as head of procurement for the health authority. Mo Kane, now editor of *The Herald*, had pursued the story like a dog on the trail of blood, digging up any misdemeanour from Jim's past and laying it in front of a public looking for titillation, even in such an unlikely form. What rankled Jim Spier the most was that the journalist had the same traits and qualities as himself. The battle to determine the biggest fish in the sea was set up then.

In light of this, on opening up that day's newspaper, he was prepared for anything. In fact, he had predicted the line of attack the wretched journalist would use; he had found numerous willing families whose father, wife, mother, husband had died in hospital sometime in the preceding years and investigated whether their death might have been intentional: a part of the 'Killing of Five' policy which had, by the newspaper's reckoning, been in place for some time. The centre spread of the newspaper was subdivided into small squares, each of which displayed a photograph of the deceased and a precis of their medical care. There were sixteen examples in all, most looking old, frail and defenceless. He selected one at random to read: *John Simmons, 79, former post office worker. John was admitted to hospital with suspected peritonitis, but all tests were negative. His family say that he was denied life-saving surgery because of his age and have contacted* The Herald *to ask the question of whether John was killed by the hospital. They have previously put in a formal complaint to the hospital concerning his lack of treatment, but they were fobbed off by the over-officious system, which is designed to protect the hospital from litigation.*

Jim Spier put the paper down on his desk, open at the offending centrefold, face up. 'Is that the best you can do?' he muttered under his breath. Stepping out of his office, he summoned his personal assistant, whose desk was at an easy beckoning distance. She followed him obediently into his room, ritualistically taking a seat.

'Sally' he began, still standing. 'I want to send letters offering personal meetings with senior management of the hospital to all these families.' He pointed at the newspaper. 'We will also issue a press statement indicating an inquiry into every recent death in the hospital,' he continued. 'The chief executive herself will chair these meetings, and there will be an open forum for any aggrieved member of the public to express his or her opinion on the standard of care in the hospital. The chief executive herself will take full responsibility for the findings of the inquiry and will act upon the recommendations, no matter what they find.'

He paused to give time for Sally to take it all down. She knew the drill. She would type up a version of his orders, and he would distribute various tasks to his underlings to enact the latest counter-offensive. He continued, offering further musings, making it evident that his missives on the subject would be clear: this was the chief executive's problem to sort out (with guidance from him). Finally, he dismissed Sally and picked up the newspaper again, turning to the back pages. *Time for some deep-sea fishing*, he thought, although he would not be ensnaring the fish he most wanted to catch.

39.

TWO LARGE CRANES complete with haulage equipment had arrived at the hospital. Their mission to remove the old oak tree which had fallen at the southern end of the corridor had been hampered by further bad weather. Several men, clad in orange jackets and white hard hats, had already lopped off those branches which could easily be removed and set about attaching chains and ropes to the main trunk of the tree. The damage to the corridor structure appeared great, but a detailed assessment of the stability of the side walls would only be possible after the old tree had been completely removed.

Mr James Barabas had finished his morning ward round and was on his way back to his secretary's office when he spotted the complex operation being carried out. He was fascinated by the process, which was rather like an industrial-scale version of surgery; the removal of objects which shouldn't be there. The foreman of the group, who carried a walkie-talkie and a yellow toolbox, was directing the workers, who were slothful, reluctant. After a few moments, torrential rain sent them running back to their vans, and work was ceased temporarily.

Mr Barabas trudged on. His left shoe had acquired a hole and his sock was wet – a bad state of affairs so early in the morning. Lightning flashed outside and the rain drummed harder on the roof. The workers had made a good decision to retreat from nature's onslaught. He reached his secretary's office and was handed a pile of letters. He thanked his secretary and found a quiet corner of the office to read his post. He was in no mood for small talk. He was meeting up with the family of Muriel Frank in a few minutes to discuss her progress – or lack thereof. He would need to broach the subject of withdrawal of treatment.

His post was a mixture of letters of advice from general practitioners and promotional material sent by drug companies, peddling the latest drug or wound-healing bandage. He found it hard to concentrate, since the office was open-plan and noisy. After a few minutes, his secretary told him that the Frank family had arrived, and he followed her into the meeting room in which they were sitting.

There were three relatives: Mrs Frank's husband – a frail man in a wheelchair who, Mr Barabas guessed, had advanced Parkinson's disease; a younger man, whom he had previously met and knew was her son; and a woman who was introduced as Mrs Frank's daughter-in-law.

'I don't think we've met before,' said Mr Barabas to the woman. She was dressed like a lawyer, he thought.

'No,' she confirmed, offering him her hand to shake. He obliged.

The old man's left hand shook rhythmically. His head lolled forward as though it were too heavy for his neck to keep up, yet he managed to look ahead by directing his gaze skyward, his forehead carved in deep furrows. He chewed slowly on his lower lip, interspersing this with grimacing and licking his lips.

After they had taken their positions in the meeting room, Mr Barabas began to recount the latest aspects of Muriel Frank's medical care. He told them of her kidney function, her fluid balance, her wound-healing and all the other things they expected. They listened intently and politely, apparently hanging on his words, whether they understood or not. He knew they were learning little they did not already know. On balance, the surgeon concluded that it had not been a bad week, but that Muriel was not making the improvements for which he had hoped.

The elderly man, who had up to this point been silent, raised his trembling hand and in a faint voice said, 'Thank you, Doctor. I know you are doing all you can for her.'

Mr Barabas smiled at him and took his hand to shake it. As they interlocked hands, the daughter-in-law put her arm around the old man, crouching beside him.

'Arthur has great confidence that the medical team are going to get her better,' she said pulling her father-in-law towards her in the embrace.

Mr Barabas smiled briefly, unsure of what to say to this. It was so far from the reality of the woman's prognosis. He had been about to discuss the gradual withdrawal of treatment.

'Has Mrs Frank spoken to you recently?' he asked. She had certainly not said anything to him recently, although the nurses reported that she spoke to them. The younger family members looked at each other.

'She seems confused at times,' said the son, 'and maybe down in the dumps.' He seemed to be trying to convey a difficult concept without mentioning the specifics.

'What does she say?' asked Mr Barabas.

Again, the pair glanced at each other. 'Look, Doctor,' began the daughter-in-law, 'Mum is not doing well, *mentally*.' She hesitated before and after the word 'mentally', as though it were a forbidden word. 'But we keep her going.' As she waited for a response, the old man in the wheelchair, whom she still had her arm around, started to sob. She pulled him closer to her. 'It will be OK, Dad,' she said. 'She'll get through this, I promise.' Then she looked up at Mr Barabas, seeking his confirmation of the statement.

Unsettled that the conversation was not going in the direction he had intended, he resorted to his well-rehearsed patter for the patients who were not recovering well. 'Mrs Frank is an extremely ill woman,' he started. He needed to build up their understanding that the prognosis was dire, although he was not sure they were listening. He struggled to comprehend how they were so oblivious to the hopelessness of her plight. After a few minutes, the old man stopped sobbing, the woman stood up and the son's telephone rang. He immediately silenced it, but had been distracted by it. He declared that it was time for them to leave in order not to take up more of the doctor's valuable time. As they left, his parting words were, 'Thank you, Doctor – I know you'll do your best for her.'

40.

THE FOX COMMITTEE gathered in the late afternoon, just as its participants were considering home time. The few assembled members were those who could muster the enthusiasm for a cause that others thought futile and petty. They met in the hospital canteen, a source of coffee and cakes, which John Such purchased as an incentive for the attendees. He had decided against giving the presentation he had prepared, deeming it unnecessary. It was ridiculous, anyway, he had decided. Eileen Stewart, his secretary, was there to take minutes, and she welcomed the opportunity to escape the confines of the management offices for a half hour in the canteen.

John Such began by greeting the assembled group. To his left sat his secretary, peering over her spectacles at her laptop screen. By her side sat Tony Pilkington, an enthusiastic member of the transformational team, mopping up spilt coffee from the table in front of him. The group was completed by Marta Policek, head of public relations, who had arrived late, carrying stacks of paper folders. 'A small but elite band of thinkers,' was how John Such summed them up. He was kidding no one, but at least it raised a smile. The chief executive had wanted to attend, he said, but was in discussions with the local health authority concerning other matters. They all knew the matters to which he referred.

'I want this to be an open forum for generating ideas, so no agenda today,' he started – a statement which the rest of the group interpreted as a failure on his behalf to prepare for the meeting.

The discussion started fitfully. Stretches of uneasy silence were broken only by the faint tap of the laptop keyboard, which was an odd accompaniment to the meeting since, as yet, no one had said anything worth minuting. The ideas were chaotic and disjointed, like an improvised debate whose participants had forgotten the subject matter.

'These are all good points,' said John Such, trying to bring them back on track and at the same time recalling the information he had gleaned from his research a few nights earlier. 'We are walking a fine line between public health concerns and animal rights. We need to ensure the hospital is robust in guaranteeing hygiene to its patients, yet sensitive to the feelings of the local population.' He stopped, hoping someone would take up the baton. He looked at Marta to suggest a public relations angle, but she looked weary, and he suspected that she was not in the mood for spending her energy on this matter, given the other troubles she was handling. Tony Pilkington tried to get the conversation going, but after twenty minutes, mostly of clock-watching, the discussion fizzled out.

'Well, let's meet up again soon to take this forward. Thanks all. It's been constructive,' John Such concluded half-heartedly, convincing no one.

Eileen Stewart finished typing and closed the lid of the laptop after the others had left. 'That went well,' she said. John Such wasn't sure if she meant it.

'Do you need a lift home?' he asked her. His secretary lived a short distance away and usually walked to and from work, but on wet days he would sometimes give her a lift.

'Thanks, but I've got stuff to do in the office,' she replied, gathering up her things.

John Such watched her walk out of the canteen. He was now alone, save for the workers in the catering department who were cleaning up. They were not expecting any further business until the night-shift workers tramped in for their midnight feast. He stayed for a while, eating the last of the cakes and drinking his coffee while checking emails on his phone. He skipped over some of the more officious-looking missives. He typically only read the first few lines of most emails, anyway.

Distracted from the tiny screen of his phone, he gazed out of the window upon a pleasant green lawn surrounded by a low box hedge. The light was fading outside. They were past the shortest day, so every extra minute of daylight was welcome. He noticed a single mole hill in the centre of the lawn, which was otherwise well kept. Beyond the hedge he saw, among the other workers heading home, his secretary, head down, marching with a purpose. He was surprised to see her, given her earlier response to his offer of a lift. Perhaps she just didn't want to share a car with him. It was also unusual for her to be leaving so early, as she often stayed late in the office. In truth, he wasn't too sure what she got up to during her late-night sessions, but industry was to be applauded, not questioned. She turned the corner behind a brick wall and out of sight.

His coffee was cold, but he drank the remnants, feeling the need to replenish the caffeine levels in his bloodstream in any way possible. The first meeting of the fox committee had been pointless. Nothing had been decided, no tactic determined; nothing had been achieved other than the recognition that the issue was problematic. No doubt the chief executive would harangue him the next morning about the plan they had devised. Maybe she would even call him that night. He hoped not.

He opened the reminder app on his phone and surveyed the list of current topics he needed to work on. The list had grown over the past few days. There was too much to do and the priorities kept changing. No sooner had he commenced working on one strategy than another pushed its way to the top of the urgency list. His paymaster, dressed in her increasingly ludicrous outfits, was setting a new task on an almost daily basis. The fox problem was an absurd distraction. He would need to hand it over to someone else, but only when the chief executive had become so distracted that she had forgotten that she had charged him to solve the problem. Shuffling the problems around, keeping them just below crisis level (which was rarely possible) was the job of all senior management.

41.

THE EVENTS OF the past few days had, understandably, had a profound effect on Eric's mental state. His confidence, which had bordered on negligible before the newspaper stories, hit rock bottom. He became more withdrawn, shunning company. If he needed to leave his office, he would stand behind the closed door, listening to the noise on the other side, choosing a moment to make his exit in order to have minimal contact with his colleagues. His disposition had become more petulant, which acted as a further barrier to his colleagues, whose instincts were to comfort him, knowing the turmoil he was experiencing. Although he had no awareness of the fact, Eric was well-liked in the office. Several of the older women were maternally inclined to protect him. Or at least they tried. But he had closed himself up and had become an unsettling presence in the management offices. If he had turned up to work in penitential sackcloth, his colleagues would not have been surprised.

He persisted in his daily duties, however, diligently showing up on time and working his allotted hours. He skipped lunchbreaks (which he had done for some time anyway) to focus on the pandemic plans. The chief executive had been right in suspecting that giving him the task of developing the hospital's response to crescent moon disease would distract him from the newspaper scandal. He threw himself wholeheartedly into this new task, hardly stopping. Being so focused on it was a form of cognitive purging and was, Eric knew, the only way he could keep his thoughts from dragging him under. It had worked before on a smaller scale and needed to work again.

His first task had been to read the three hundred or so documents which had been written over the past few decades concerning major incident planning. Studying in-depth plans constructed to cover every eventuality was indeed pleasurable to Eric, whose whole life was carefully scheduled, day by day, hour by hour. Being afraid of risk, he found comfort in the detailed risk mitigation proposals which had been carefully contemplated and meticulously developed. All sorts of disasters had been considered: fire, flood, acts of terrorism. The list grew, year on year. Missives from the Department of Health necessitated that provisional plans were in place for even the most unlikely scenario. He read about mass poisoning, radioactive leaks, and infestations of tropical arthropods (which related to the arrival of large numbers of black widow spiders in boxes of bananas a few years earlier). There were several about pandemics, which had been written in response to previous threats.

A significant recommendation of most of the plans was to set up a committee to guide the enactment of policies and the deployment of resources. This was a problem for Eric. Now, more than ever, he shunned meetings, seeking any excuse not to attend. The idea of setting up and chairing a gathering of six or seven people was so anxiety-inducing that he dismissed it, focusing on other aspects of the planning, skirting around the notion of teamwork. Betrayal visited on him by a fellow human being, the one who had invaded his space and published his thoughts, pushed him further into solitude. His most recent workplace appraisal had summarised his perceived shortcomings: *Apart from his diffidence and his preference to work alone, Eric has no obvious faults.* He thought this was a fair reflection of his character. The current crisis had pushed him further down that path.

The document outlining what was needed to prevent the potential winter flu crisis of 2003 from overrunning the hospital was the largest, extending to over two hundred pages. He wasn't aware whether, in fact, it had proven to be such a problem, having not started working at the hospital until a few years later. Crises are easily forgotten in institutions fuelled by calamities. What struck him about the 2003 flu planning document was the doom-mongering language. It portrayed the landscape of flu-ridden Britain in apocalyptic terms. Water supplies, electricity, waste disposal services were at risk. Even to Eric in his current state of mind, this seemed a little far-fetched. Intriguingly, the proposal also called for the immediate cessation of all cancer therapies should the number of cases of flu in the hospital exceed a certain number. This was a radical idea, and one which would not even be mooted in contemporary healthcare planning. Prioritising one disease over another was always a difficult path to steer.

During his reading, he took notes about the various approaches, looking for common ground. He had determined broad strategic headings: finances, resources, staffing *et cetera*. He looked up at the whiteboard opposite his desk and for a brief moment considered writing these headings on it, but instantly dismissed the idea. The plans would be firmly secured away each night: paper documents in a locked drawer, computer files encrypted to the nth degree.

He checked his emails. He noticed one from the chief executive which had been forwarded from the Department of Health. It concerned the latest incidence figures of crescent moon disease. Curiously, cases had dropped, and the projection was now that a pandemic would be averted. The health minister had downgraded the risk to serious (from severe), and the funds for pandemic planning available to each health authority would be reduced in line. Nonetheless, the email continued, preparation of detailed contingency plans must continue to allow the country to be ready for this and other threats at any moment.

Eric smiled for the first time in weeks, relieved that he still had the task to work on.

42.

THE TALK AMONGST the secretaries, working in close order in the management offices, was of subterfuge. Six months earlier, Eileen Stewart had joined their ranks as assistant to the sub-chief executive, a role which, whilst not coveted intensely, was seen as one of the better jobs in the department. John Such was easy-going, a nice guy who treated people well and was not demanding. In contrast to the personal assistant to the chief executive's job, the stress levels were manageable. Several internal candidates had applied for the post but had been beaten to it by Ms Stewart. Her background was obscure. On direct questioning, she told the others that she had come from a big corporation out of town, and left it at that. This encouraged speculation in a band of workers who, because of the mundane duties of their jobs, sought out indelicate narratives, either true or fabricated.

Her nature was aloof, which added to the air of mystery concerning her background, and her unwillingness to engage in frivolous talk set her apart from the other secretaries. That this separation didn't seem to bother her widened the gulf and, other than superficial greetings on a daily basis, interactions were purely professional. The managers liked her, however, and she quickly took on increasingly important roles, notably secretary to the hospital board. Her secretarial colleagues resented the elevation, which came with a pay rise. They were a close-knit group before she had arrived and, as often happens, uniting again a common cause or person brought them closer together. Some even stopped saying hello to her in the morning. Her presence was not welcome, and her behaviour since starting – namely her indifference to joining in – was the major source of disgruntlement. She became the topic of many lunchtime conversations.

Jackie Booth and Jan Bullimore, two of the longest serving secretaries, sat, out of anyone's earshot, in the corner of the canteen. Their theories concerning the true identity of Ms Stewart were well formed; they had fed each other their own speculations every day for the past few months.

'I've been dying to tell you,' said Jan, unwrapping a large pile of sandwiches encased in a reusable wax bag. Jackie looked at her colleague, eager for the latest.

'Yes.' Jan glanced about her. 'My son was on the computer yesterday, and he looked her up.'

'Oh yes?' Jackie sipped her coffee, settling back in her chair. 'Seems like she used to work at *The Herald*.'

'Really!' Jackie replied. 'What did she do for them?'

Jan took a bite of her sandwich and chewed before replying: 'Not sure. He showed me her business webpage thingy …' She gesticulated an act of typing on a keyboard. 'But it didn't give many details. All seemed a bit vague.'

'So, is she spying on us for the newspaper?' Jackie asked, coming to a conclusion as quickly as she did over most of her theories.

'Well, it's a thought, isn't it?'

They stayed for a while in the canteen, eating and chatting, reinforcing their half-baked ideas by the act of repetition.

When they arrived back in the management offices, passing by the desk of Ms Stewart, they both felt a new sense of wariness. In time, they would warn the others.

Elaine Stewart was typing up the latest minutes of the finance planning meeting. Her concentration was resolute. She had, up to this point, remained more or less unconcerned by any hostility towards her. Although aware of the tittle-tattle which surrounded her presence, she was not unduly distracted by it. She had a job to do. She knew her colleagues viewed her with distrust. Staying late to complete her work was, she suspected, the most heinous of her acts because it showed the others in a poor light. However, she was aware that something had changed since the pair had returned from lunch. An uncomfortable quiet had replaced the busy industry of the secretaries, like a storm cloud about to break. Every so often, whilst typing, she looked up and noticed that Jan was staring at her, and made no attempt to look away when she stared back. It was clearly a statement intended to indicate that Jan was on to her; that she knew what was going on.

For the first time since she had started in the hospital, Elaine Stewart felt anxious, distracted. She had a hard exterior and an even harder centre. Very little got to her, but this newfound disapproval was now eating at her. She had a mission to uncover social injustice, to defend the oppressed. And now these people had taken against her, their opprobrium based on the newcomer's attempts to upset the natural order of their working. She felt the need to tell them that she was on their side.

Jan Bullimore stood up, walked over to Jackie's desk and whispered something in her ear. This was a more concerted effort to unnerve Elaine. She understood that if the true circumstances of her employment were known to these people, then she might have been a worthy subject of their vilification, but she couldn't understand how they had come to any conclusion regarding the reason for her presence. She had been very careful not to give anything away. Of course, they might have come to the wrong conclusion, but whatever it was they had worked out, she was now the subject of their disdain. She typed some more and then felt the need to get out of the office. As she stood, she felt all eyes upon her. Gingerly, she walked the few steps to the door, feeling a sense of relief on entering the lobby and then the corridor. From there, she headed outside to a bench bordering the central green lawn. She was cold, since she had not taken her coat, but she felt she would rather be there than in the atmosphere she had just left.

What was she to do? The ruse in which she was participating was folding much more quickly than she had anticipated. Did they know of her real purpose in the hospital? She took out her phone, summoned up her text messages and started to compose a message. *Mo*, it commenced, *I think I've been rumbled!*

Mo Kane, editor-in-chief of *The Herald*, read the text and immediately texted back: *Can we talk now?*

43.

AAMAAL HOSSEIN WATCHED her husband as he slept. He was so pale, she thought; his face had changed, disguised with a ghastly gauntness. His mouth was open a little, emitting a faint wheeze, his lips trembling as he slept. She had been away from home for a night shift and on returning this morning had noticed such a difference in him, indeed had struggled to recognise the man she had left just a day ago. Her daughter had kept her informed of the latest changes, but his condition had still come as a shock.

By his bed, blood-stained clothes and towels were strewn. Dutifully, she put them in a pile, ready to be washed later. On leaving the bedroom, she peered into the room of her elder daughter. She was lying on her bed, resting after a bad night, but she opened her eyes as soon as she felt her mother's presence.

Aamaal entered the room and sat down on the bed next to her daughter. She stroked the hair of her sleepy child, peering into her dark eyes. She had seen such terrible things in her young life.

'Mama,' said the child in a soft voice. Aamaal smiled and continued to stroke her hair. 'Hold me.'

The two embraced. Mother and daughter bound by the strongest, most terrible of emotions: the unfaltering love and devotion of a daughter to her parents, and the guilt of a mother who had no choice but to allow her daughter to bear the burden.

From the next room, Aamaal heard coughing, followed by a deep groaning sound. She tightened the embrace with her daughter momentarily before getting up to attend to her husband. Her daughter fell softly back into her bed.

Aamaal re-entered her dimly lit bedroom. The noises had stopped. She was not sure whether he was asleep or unconscious. His breathing was laboured, and so she propped him up a little on his pillows. She was shocked at how easy it was to haul his body up the bed. He was lighter than her youngest child now. This repositioning had the desired effect, and he looked more peaceful. She sat with him.

After a few minutes, her daughter came into the room. She was dressed in pink-patterned pyjamas and blue slippers. She yawned as she entered.

'How is he?' she asked, long since past the point of expecting any positive news.

'He's resting,' said Aamaal, in as comforting a tone as she could muster.

Her daughter sat on the floor by the side of the bed, resting against the cold radiator. She should be attending school later that morning, but would have to give it a miss again. It was six-thirty in the morning. The world outside was waking up, ready for the new day. Already the noise from the traffic outside the flat was building up as people hurried to their places of work.

'Mama. Would you like me to make you a drink?'

Aamaal smiled and shook her head. 'Rest,' she said. 'Go back to sleep.'

Aamaal's daughter didn't move, nor did Aamaal expect her to. She was staring at her father, not daring to ask the questions to which she most wanted to know the answers. Aamaal would be back at work in six hours. Barely time to do the washing, the cleaning and the other household chores that needed doing. The prospect of sleep was a long way off. Her fatigue was all-consuming.

Her daughter stood and picked up the pile of bloodied clothes that her mother had placed next to her. 'I'll wash these,' she said.

Her mother resisted, taking them back, letting a vest fall to the floor. 'No, Bibi, that's my job. Please rest.'

Stalemate having been reached, the daughter resumed her

position on the floor by the bed. Aamaal wanted to get up but lacked the strength.

'Mama,' Bibi asked softly. 'Shouldn't Papa go to hospital?'

Her mother was silent for a moment, and Bibi wondered whether she had fallen asleep. In time, her mother took a deep breath, looked over to her husband and said in a whisper, 'He's not going to that place. I can't allow it.'

44.

THE ISSUE OF the foxes had started to haunt the chief executive. At night, she would lie awake while thoughts of their whiskered snouts ran amok in her mind. If she dozed off for a few minutes in the small hours, she would stir in her sleep, imagining the elusive beasts pawing outside the bedroom window, going through the bins and creating carnage on her freshly mown lawn.

The Fox Defence League had stepped up their activity, picketing the hospital gates all day and all night. Saving the foxes had become an obsession for those who otherwise had no purpose or calling; so much so that the issue of the foxes was threatening to assume a greater importance than any of the other issues facing the hospital. To some extent, this might have been perceived as a blessing for the beleaguered chief executive; it took attention away from the issue of the 'Killing of Five'. In some way, there seemed to be an even greater sense of shame in the hospital persecuting furry animals than in it apparently causing the deaths of five chronically ill patients.

She avoided the pickets at all costs and set her mind on ways of placating the animal lovers who bayed for her blood in much the same way as a hound might lust for a wounded fox. She decided that the fox committee should take on increasing importance. The dilemma of protecting the sick from potential zoonotic illnesses versus the inhumanity of destroying defenceless wild animals was debated at length in the pages of *The Herald* and amongst the workers in the hospital. The fox committee (emerging from its early inertia) commissioned a SWOT (strengths weaknesses opportunities threats) analysis of the presence of foxes and planned to reconvene when this had been successfully completed. To add to the complexity (at a time when it was looking likely that the only conclusion the fox committee would be making was to come out in favour of full protection for the fox), the anti-fox lobby was gaining ground. Reports were surfacing of foxes attacking babies in prams and entering through unlocked windows to bite infants as they slept in cribs. An old story from Mexico concerning a savage fox which was estimated to have killed twenty children emerged, with the headline in *The Herald* running 'FOXES KILL TWENTY'. The story turned out to be over thirty years old (and was untrue), but the details mattered little.

It was not surprising, therefore, that one cold March morning as she arrived at work, the chief executive came across one of the beasts crossing the car park, nonchalant and unperturbed, stopping casually to cast a glance in her direction before slowly trotting off to a hole in the fence. The chief executive took it as a sign, and from that moment vowed to take up arms against the plague of vermin that was haunting her.

45.

IT WAS DARK by the time Matt Butcher finished work. He had intended to finish several hours earlier but had been delayed by a series of events which necessitated his presence. One of his colleagues had called in sick, and the shortage of cover on the surgical ward had resulted in overtime. He'd had nowhere else to be anyway and no plans for the evening, so he had agreed to stay on.

His more senior colleagues had suggested to him that filling the gaps was expected of him. They had done the same when they were at his stage of their training. It was the natural order. He had given up noting the number of times he had been told that surgical training was much harder in years gone by; there had been nothing like the European Working Time Directive to protect the last generation of trainee surgeons. Newcomers like him had it easy, he was told. Shifts had started on Friday morning and ended on Monday evening. No questions asked. His consultant was forever opining that the surgical consultant in ten years' time would lack the experience to perform anything but the simplest of operations. Thus, working time regulations were stretched to the limit, rules ignored, and the experience of the trainee surgeon was perpetuated.

He understood the reasons on both sides. It was true that the number of operations a novice surgical trainee would perform during training was about a third of that which the older consultants had performed. Yet the expectation of people coming into hospital was that much higher, the range of treatments that much greater. In the old days, if a mistake had been made in the middle of the night by a tired junior doctor, it had been easy to cover it up. That was no longer the case, and there was no excuse for exposing patients to the risk of error because of the excessively onerous working patterns of junior doctors. From Matt Butcher's perspective, it meant that the life of a trainee surgeon was harder now. When they were at work, their duties were more intense and more open to scrutiny. Shortages in the rotas meant they filled in gaps with no compensation, and the 'wasn't like this in my day' attitude of the old codgers who presided over their destiny was soul-destroying. He only had to look at the senior trainees to see the hardships they continued to endure in order to reach the top of the pile.

He was glad to have finally been released from duties that evening and decided to go for a walk. He lived in a small flat a few hundred metres from the hospital, so he dropped off his work gear, changed into more comfortable clothes and put on his walking boots. Even though it was dark, he decided to walk up the hill which bordered the eastern side of the valley. Over the other side of the hill, on the main road which bypassed the town, was a pub. He would stop there to have a drink if the mood took him.

The rough stone path leading up the hill was more difficult to traverse in the dark than he had reckoned with. Ambient light from the town guided his footsteps for the first part of the walk, but after a certain distance, he had to resort to the light from his phone to illuminate his path. He continued but was not really sure what he was trying to achieve. It was bound to end in failure, and there was no way he would reach the top without a serious accident. It was cold now, the temperature just above freezing point, and he had visions of sustaining a broken leg and dying of exposure on the dark hillside. He turned around and, after a while, was comforted by the lights of the town. It had been a silly idea to attempt the walk. He reached his flat again but changed tack and headed towards the hospital to seek company in the social club. It was likely that someone he knew would be there. The quickest way to the social club was to cut through the hospital via the open section of the corridor and go through the back entrance. At the midpoint of the corridor, he bumped into his colleague, Madhu, who was the senior surgical trainee in the hospital – the next to be anointed as a consultant.

'Matt,' said the surgeon, dressed in theatre blues complete with surgical mask around his neck, 'I thought you were with us today.'

The junior doctor immediately felt a sense of guilt. 'I was just filling in for sickness.'

'Oh,' said Madhu. 'We're still really short.'

Matt noticed Madhu look down at his boots. They were wet and caked in mud. *Hardly the look for a young professional*, Matt imagined him thinking.

'Anyway, are you up for the night shift?' said Madhu, confidently, almost rhetorically.

Matt Butcher hesitated. Was he really asking him to work the night?

'Look, Matt. If you want to get on in this career, you've got to step up and work whenever you're needed. The bosses notice this kind of thing. They like people who are dedicated to the job.'

'Erm … I don't know. I was just going to …' He tried to think of an excuse, but nothing came to him.

'Mr George is on tonight. He's head of the training school. It'll be major brownie points.' Madhu was practised in sealing the deal.

Matt looked down at his boots once again, wishing he had taken his chances on the hillside. He had no excuses he could think of. 'OK then,' he said. 'I'll be there in twenty minutes.'

'Good man,' said the older surgeon, turning around and heading off back to the operating theatres.

Matt Butcher sighed. At that moment, he realised that a career as a surgeon was not for him.

46.

A DUCK SWAM serenely across the pond outside the chief executive's office. As it glided, a V of ripples followed, spreading out to the bank. The chief executive watched and contemplated the duck as it performed several circumnavigations of the water without any particular purpose and with no degree of interest in its destiny. She thought that she had never seen this particular duck before. Its emerald-green head was particularly iridescent, and its plumage seemed to shine more brightly than others in the rather motley collection of wildfowl which frequented the hospital grounds. Maybe this new duck was a sign that things were about to look up.

Her reverie was broken by the ping of a text message. It was Eric, transformational director or director of transformation (she forgot exactly what his title was). It seemed that the BBC were to run a piece on the 'Killing of Five' controversy. Eric had got wind of this and, given his unbearable sense of guilt over the affair, wanted to meet immediately. She hadn't seen him for a few days but thought it best to talk over this latest development, even though little was likely to change; the film was undoubtedly in the can. Nonetheless she replied and confirmed a time of 4pm for a *debrief*. She knew that using this word would make Eric feel better.

There was just over two hours to go before the allotted meeting. Eric would be punctual to the second, there was no doubt of that.

She was still angry with him. Despite the instincts of others in the senior management team, she laid the blame for the debacle at his door. If he hadn't have written those ridiculous three words on his office whiteboard, they wouldn't have been in such a mess. Strangely, she didn't feel as much animosity towards her sub-chief executive. He was the one who had made the flippant remark at the board meeting. Yet uttered words vanish as soon as they have been spoken. Anyway, it was in response to the ridiculous suggestion Eric had made. Whatever had he been thinking?

She thought back to the board meeting. Someone had leaked the minutes to the press, which had documented the discussion and the offending idea for reducing costs. Of course, they had dismissed the concept immediately, and she hadn't thought of it again until the newspaper story broke. She sat down at her desk and opened a list of files on her computer. She found the minutes for the board meeting and reread them:

The CEO led a general discussion of the methods they could employ to achieve an overall, department by department, reduction in costs of ten percent. A variety of possibilities were considered ...

She skipped the next lines to read the part that had caused the trouble:

Eric M discussed the breakdown of our expenditure per patient and pointed out that in each department of the hospital, approximately five patients utilise up to ten percent of the costs. There was a discussion concerning whether there were any practical implications relating to this fact.

The chief executive wouldn't have gone as far as to say there had been a discussion about this. It was, as far as she recalled, dismissed out of hand almost immediately. John Such's silly comment hadn't been minuted, as she would have expected. The minutes were fairly innocuous anyway. She couldn't imagine that anyone would have called them out unless there was a specific agenda. In conjunction with the whiteboard picture, they made a story, but the minutes alone were not really a problem. Which all came back to the question: who had done this, and perhaps more importantly, why had they done this? Someone who was at the board meeting? Someone who had been sent the minutes?

Someone who had access to the offices, presumably late at night when they were empty? There couldn't be that many on this list.

She looked out of the window again. The iridescent duck had departed. A light drizzle fell amid the gloom of the afternoon. She recalled those who had been present at the board meeting, thinking about each in turn. When she came to John Such, something connected. He had been at the meeting and was often in Eric's office. He was the last person people would suspect. Nice, kind John Such. That, in itself, made the possibility more interesting. Furthermore, he was second in command. Perhaps this was an attempt to overthrow her as chief executive. A calculated coup as the motive?

47.

MR BARABAS HAD discussed similar issues with countless other families before, yet the discussions with Muriel Frank's family were proving challenging. There were many factors compounding his problem, not least his guilt over causing the problems, albeit unintentionally, in the first place. The newspaper stories weren't helping. They added an air of anxiety to all clinicians in the hospital, who had one eye on public perception while considering the imprecise art of the physician. It was grinding down many of the workers and, although most patients and their families retained a respect for and confidence in the medical teams, there was no doubt that the stories in the press had knocked the workings of the institution and forced its workforce onto the defensive. The ramifications of this were wide-reaching. The decision-making process of medicine was dependent on so many factors, some controllable but most uncontrollable. The unpredictability of illness dictated that decisions were made based on risk-benefit analyses linked to years of experience. Any decision for an individual patient had to be tempered in the light of parameters concerning not only their personal circumstances but also the health of the whole population. There was no doubt that having the papers breathing down the necks of the workforce had upset the balance. Many decision-makers became more cautious, which had the consequence of delaying decisions. This, in turn, caused the clogging-up of beds that other patients needed. Practising defensive medicine was not in the best interests of a hospital that depended on risk-taking for its continued survival.

With all these considerations weighing on his mind, Mr Barabas met the family of Muriel Frank for the second time in a few days. Their last meeting had established some of the boundaries for her care. At least, he hoped they had. He wasn't sure they had taken much in. He had asked to meet her son and daughter-in-law without Mrs Frank's husband, who seemed less able to comprehend his wife's prognosis. The couple came to the meeting on a cold Friday morning. They arrived late, owing to the closure of several roads leading into the hospital on account of more haulage vehicles being needed for the tree clearance project. Mr Barabas ushered them into the room, telling them not to worry concerning their tardiness.

He started by going over old ground: the operation, the haemorrhage, the days on the intensive care unit. This was, he hoped, laying the groundwork, reemphasising the dire predicament their mother faced. They listened courteously and waited for him to finish before asking questions, which were, in essence, the same questions that they had asked before. The same unanswerable questions, pitched with the hope that if the question were asked often enough, the desired answer would be forthcoming. It was often a hard slog for the surgeon, employing a strategy of attrition; using words which were not completely devoid of hope but which painted a poor prognosis in kind words. Usually, it got through and the questions changed. Muriel Frank's family was different. Their blind optimism was unshakeable. He would need to be more blunt.

'Look, I've got to be honest with you,' he said, blank-faced. It was a statement that he knew would indicate to most people that bad news was on the way. 'Your mother is very ill, and it seems unlikely she is going to get better.' He paused to provide a chance for this to sink in.

The son stroked his chin, then rubbed gently below his right eye. 'But she might?' he asked quietly.

Before he had a chance to console himself in false hope,

Mr Barabas continued. 'No, I'm afraid she won't. We are just prolonging her difficulties.' He avoided the use of the word agony at the last moment, leaving the sentence awkward. The sentiment was still clear.

'Well, I think,' began the son, flustered by the gravity of the discussion. His wife, who was sitting in the adjacent chair, put her arm around him.

'So, what are you saying, Doctor?' she asked, looking him in the eye.

Mr Barabas leant forward and drew his hands together in a clench. 'We will have to start to determine a ceiling of care.'

'What does that mean?' asked the son, gazing forward, crossing his arms over his chest.

'It means that we will treat her for certain things in order to keep her comfortable, but if she becomes more unwell, we may not … it may not be in her best interests to go down certain treatment routes.'

The son looked confused, so Mr Barabas clarified. 'So, for instance, if she becomes very unwell again it would not be a good idea to send her back to the intensive care unit.' He paused to determine whether they had understood. It was a challenging concept: blurred lines and judgement calls.

'So, you're going to stop treating her?' asked the daughter-in-law, tilting her head to the side as if awaiting his response.

'No. We will treat her if she gets an infection or a blood clot, or if she needs more fluids. But we have to draw the line at certain types of treatment.'

'And what line is that?'

Mr Barabas felt they were finally getting somewhere, so continued. 'If a treatment is not likely to be beneficial in the long run, then it would be wrong to give it.' Again, he paused, giving them time for this to sink in. 'We will continue to look after her and make her comfortable,' he added for reassurance.

The son and daughter-in-law were quiet, contemplative. They asked no further questions.

'Thank you, Doctor,' said the son, shaking the surgeon's hand as he left the room. 'We'll think about what you've said.'

Mr Barabas nodded and smiled. There wasn't much for them to think about; that was the way it would be.

The daughter-in-law left the room behind her husband, but did not offer her hand for shaking. Nor did she offer her thanks.

48.

THE MEETING BETWEEN Elaine Stewart and her editor occurred late in the evening in the offices of *The Herald*, just off the high street. The darkness of the streets and Elaine's appearance – collar turned up and hat pulled down – added to the clandestine atmosphere of the affair. The pretence of secrecy was still needed, despite the suspicions of the secretaries in the hospital management offices.

The offices were on the first floor of a terrace of buildings, just above an estate agent, accessed via a discreet and battered door which led onto a narrow staircase. The place was in need of renovation, evidenced by the smell of damp and the cracked plaster on the walls. Mo Kane sat behind his desk, dishevelled from a long day's work, craving nicotine – which he had decided to forego in his latest attempt at a healthier lifestyle. He barely looked up as Elaine entered, concentrating on finishing his sentence on his oversized laptop. The story would need to go to press in less than an hour. Elaine took a seat, pulled out her phone and checked the latest messages: nothing of any consequence.

'I'll be with you in a second,' said Mo, still typing on his keyboard. The heaviness of his finger strokes made a shower of dull thuds which reverberated through the solid wooden desk.

'There,' he declared after a few more minutes, finishing his latest output.

Elaine put her phone back in her pocket and sat to attention. This was the first time they had met since the incident with the secretaries.

'As we discussed on the phone, Mo,' Elaine said, getting straight to the point, 'I don't know how long I can keep this up for.'

Mo Kane put his hands on his head and leant back in his chair. He said little in meetings. This was a tactic Elaine had observed since they first met: let others talk, spill the beans. People didn't like silence and were compelled to fill it.

'What do you think, Mo?' Elaine was impatient. She no longer cared for the kind of operation in which she was now embroiled, and, if she were honest with herself, putting aside the thrill of the chase, she had felt out of her depth from the moment she'd got the job in the hospital. Undercover investigations were not her preferred method of journalism. They were unclean, a form of trickery.

Mo Kane opened up the newspaper in front of him, seemingly making a point of taking his time. He pointed at an article. 'The story is running well.' He tapped the page, then closed the newspaper, discarding it onto a pile on the side of his desk. Elaine took from this that her boss considered it the end of the matter – the end justifying the means.

She became annoyed. She had known before she entered the offices that this would happen. It was just a matter of how long before she lost her temper.

'What are we looking for now?' she asked. 'You've got the story.'

This was not entirely true. She had been sent undercover to expose concerns about financial irregularity and mismanagement of budgets. *The Herald* had been the paper which had revealed the embezzlement scandal several years earlier. Since then, the editors had kept a close eye on the story, expecting more revelations. Not only had the previous chief executive been suspected (but not convicted) of being part of the scam, but it was likely others knew about it. They had received a tip-off recently that something similar might be about to break. The topic was hot at the moment, linked to a national story about bank accounts in Caribbean islands used to syphon funds from a variety of national institutions. The 'Killing of Five' exposé had been a bonus; not directly linked to the misappropriation of funds, but an indication of how the hospital management was planning to balance the books. Or, at least, that was how it was spun.

'Look, Elaine,' said the editor lugubriously, 'we're near exposing more about the embezzlement. If we could uncover some more names, more evidence of the corruption at the heart of that place, we'd strike gold.'

He paused and scratched his head. 'That was our biggest story of the last decade.' He pointed to the wall behind him, at the framed front page of the newspaper that had broken the story. 'The gold medal of journalism!' He sniggered as he said this, but Elaine detected a semblance of pride in his words.

Elaine sighed. She wanted to explain to her boss the wider picture, the consequences of the path he was taking, but knew it would fall on deaf ears. He would not understand that if the scoop he desired (whether true or not) was published, it would ruin the hospital: people would lose their jobs, the sick would need to travel to other units further away, a community would be disrupted. It was all very well exposing the truth to protect against corruption, but it seemed that the current strategy was mostly destructive.

Mo Kane stood up and walked to the window, which looked over a small courtyard, dark save for a faint light emanating from the downstairs window. 'Keep going,' he said.

She shrugged her shoulders, knowing they didn't have much more to say to each other. Mo would get restless soon and turn his attention to something else. She got up and left, descending the stairs before exiting back into the street. The night was cold.

As she trudged home, she reflected on the meeting with her editor. When she had started at the hospital, she was keen to find the truth, to reveal whatever wrong was occurring in the interests of investigative journalism. But having worked there for several months, her attitude had changed. She had been an outsider in the offices, which was her choice and her method of working. She hadn't formed a personal connection with the workers and was not emotionally bound to them. Nonetheless she could see the situation from their point of view: the imperfections and their ways of working, which were dedicated to a goal, flawed yet vital. They didn't deserve the newspaper's attention. She regretted sending in the story about the 'Killing of Five'. It had been a cheap shot.

49.

HAVING PROMISED TO deliver an open, honest culture within hospital senior management, the chief executive, not even a year into her post, now presided over an atmosphere of mistrust and suspicion. Increasingly adopting a mentality of isolation, she considered her next moves with extreme caution, revealing little and reducing her interaction with members of her team. Financial planning had all but ground to a halt, so mistrustful was she of those she felt would trample over her to gain the upper hand. This was a dangerous policy, given that the very existence of the hospital was at risk if the savings targets were not met. Even if she fought off acts of treachery and retained her job, she knew there might not be a job for her to do for much longer.

At the heart of her suspicion was John Such. Kind, gentle John Such; everybody's friend. She had never experienced the sort of problem now facing her. Building collegiality was the cornerstone of her management style, but currently she didn't know what to do. She thought about confronting her deputy with her suspicions. But if she were to allege such double-dealing, she needed proof. It had the potential to make things worse – much worse.

She went over to her filing cabinet and pulled out the sub-chief executive's personnel file. She looked over his *curriculum vitae* for any connection to *The Herald*. Finding none, she read his references provided by his previous employers. He had worked in a local chemical plant as head of quality control for the production of polycarbonates. His previous boss had found his work to be exemplary. His ambition was highlighted: *John will reach the top of his chosen profession; of that I have no doubt.*

There was a knock on the door and, as though the forces of destiny were driving the crisis to a head, John Such entered. He smiled and raised a hand in greeting. The chief executive noted his air of calm, in contrast to her own mood; either he had nothing to hide, or he was a good actor.

'Boss,' he said, 'how's it going?'

The chief executive sat down and beckoned her deputy to do the same. She shuffled some papers on her desk, considering what she would say. She glanced at her diary and noticed that the two were scheduled to meet at this time. She had forgotten this, but it explained his presence.

'Fine, John. Thanks,' she replied, composing herself. She noticed that she had left his personnel file out on the shelf next to the desk. It looked anonymous enough, so it would not reveal her suspicions.

'We're meeting about finance management?' John Such said, breaking the awkward deadlock.

'Yes,' she replied, trying to think of an excuse to get out of talking to him. 'Look, John. Can we postpone this meeting? I've just got ...' She deliberated on her options. '... a lot of paperwork to get through by this evening.'

John Such nodded and got up. As he was about to leave, he turned back to face her. 'If there is anything I can do to help ...' he started, leaving the sentence open.

This simple, well-meant offer enraged the chief executive. Her mind screaming with the illogicality of her distrust, she was, by this point, convinced of his hand in the newspaper leak. The way in which he smiled while conducting his treacherous acts was too much for her to shrug off. John Such paused at the door, awaiting her response.

'Was it you, John?' she snapped at him.

John Such recoiled.

'Was what me?' he asked, screwing his face up a little.

She looked at him, puzzled as to whether he was truly innocent or just continuing the pretence. His gaze remained resolute.

'The leak? The newspaper leak?' she retorted.

John Such looked stunned. 'What?'

The chief executive regretted asking as soon as the words had come out of her mouth. It had been a foolish thing to do, and she knew now (as she had known even before the idea had fermented in her head) that it was a preposterous accusation. John Such appeared truly hurt at the allegation.

'You think I went to *The Herald* with the story that the hospital was considering killing its patients?' he said, his voice incredulous. 'Why would I do that?'

The chief executive stood and raised her hand, as though asking for the discussion to stop, for her last remark to be wiped from the record. The stream of her troubled consciousness came out in a garbled manner. 'Look, I'm sorry John. It was wrong of me to say that. It's a crazy idea. I'm just so confused. The stress is getting to me.'

The sub-chief executive shook his head. 'OK,' he muttered in a barely perceptible voice before leaving the room. Alone, the chief executive walked to the shelf, picked up her deputy's personnel file and threw it across the room. The pages fluttered to the ground, landing a few paces from her feet. She banged her clenched fist on the table before sitting down, burying her face in her hands.

The chief executive's woes continued to mount. Alienating her allies was part of her journey to self-destruction – a journey she felt unable to abort.

50.

ARTICLES CONCERNING THE hospital continued to be published by *The Herald*. It was a concerted attack on a struggling institution. No mercy was granted, no let-up to allow time to recover before the next onslaught. Stories concerning foxes had now given way to a litany of articles about improper deaths. Anyone with a grievance, unfounded or not, took the paper's bait to tell their story of how their loved one's death had been hastened by the deeds of the organisation they had previously trusted. The editor, for reasons unclear to those around him, saw this as a crusade. Even those who had worked at the paper for years and were hardened to the reality of newspaper publishing started to question the unrelenting negativity. After all, the hospital was a place they would rely on in years to come, if they didn't already. This was a dangerous game to play, with life-or-death consequences. But any insubordination was glossed over in the search for the big story and ever-increasing circulation figures.

The gulf between actual events and their reporting created a new narrative: one which was difficult to fathom, which created widespread uncertainty, and which generated conflicting emotions. There are two sides to any story, no doubt. But, in newspaper reporting at least, one side steams through, trampling the delicacy of the other, discarding humility, picking a fight where no need exists.

Reading about the death of Mr Alyoshin in *The Herald*, Barnaby Smithers entered into that world where the boundaries of truth were blurred and doubts in his mind concerning his hand in the affair were rampant. *The Herald* had embarked on a peculiar sort of storytelling, he thought. The ridiculous, farcical stories of the fox had given way to a more malicious storyline. Yet they were feeding off each other. Those in the hospital tried as best they could to ignore them, hoping that the patients and their relatives would see through the salaciousness of the tales, maintaining their trust in the institution and their relationships with their doctors. This was crucial to the functioning of the health service.

Seeing his name in the newspaper, however, made this much harder. He would be in an outpatient clinic later in the day and, undoubtedly, many of the patients attending would have read the article. He imagined the conversations over breakfast: *Have you seen this about Dr Smithers? We're due to see him today. Do you think it's safe?* It was likely someone would mention it. He suspected that most would support him, but others would ask for transfer of their care to another consultant. That was understandable.

He read the article again. Serena Alyoshin, the daughter of the patient who had died after receiving a drug that should not have been prescribed to him, had been given free rein to express her feelings; the desolation of the bereaved child. He remembered that she had been estranged from her father and had hardly ever seen him; he knew that her outpouring of grief was far removed from the reality of their relationship. Much of the article was fantasy, but the truth of the significant drug error gnawed at Dr Smithers, even though it had not been his mistake. He had handled their meeting badly. He had observed an indifference in the daughter and assumed that she wasn't interested in what had happened to her father. He should have phrased his explanations in a better way: one that would not have led her to the doors of a newspaper willing to denigrate the hospital in whatever way it could.

But all this was in the past, and he would have to deal with the consequences. He rang his wife to discuss the article, to get her perspective on the issue. Maybe it wasn't that bad. Maybe he had misinterpreted the attack on his own professionalism because of his insecurities. She was supportive, naturally, and told him that it would blow over in time. She reminded him that he was a good doctor, and, anyway, he had not been the one who had made the mistake. His only crime had been to tell the truth, she said. She talked in terms of integrity and courage, and he was reassured, at least for now.

Later that morning, he met a consultant colleague in the canteen, after the latter had texted him a supportive note and offered to meet. *There but for the grace of God* was the sentiment of their meeting. The unburdening was helpful, and he was able to face the afternoon clinic.

Only one person who attended the clinic mentioned the article, although he suspected most of the others had seen it. It was a woman in her nineties who was consulting him about her reduced mobility. She had been a patient of the hospital for decades, first being seen forty years earlier for a leaky heart valve which – she had been told in the blunt manner of those times – needed replacing if she wanted to live more than a few years. She had refused at the time and had lived an active life until her recent deterioration, when age had finally crept up on her. She took pride in telling the story every time she attended the hospital. This repeated description wasn't through a sense of blame, however – it was more a fable about the choices everyone would be faced with and the difficulty of predicting the future. She held no grudges against her initial cardiologist, to whom she referred in affectionate terms.

She had read that morning's *Herald*, as she always did, and after the examination of her gait and the strength in her legs was complete, she gave her opinion of the article. 'I saw your name in the paper today, Doctor,' she said, while her daughter helped her to put on her shoes.

Dr Smithers stopped typing on the keyboard and looked at her.

'Complete nonsense, of course,' she said, 'I've every faith in you, Doctor.'

He thanked her for her words. It was kind of her to say them, even though she had not met him before today. He discussed the plan of investigations he would order to try to determine the cause of her poor mobility, and she left, wheeled out by a grateful daughter.

What was the faith his patients had in him? Blind faith? His experience from the patient safety committee had told him that he was unable to provide reassurance that his treatments were completely safe. So, on what premise were they basing their faith? Was it a faith that arose when the alternative is much worse than not believing? That morning's article had created in him a huge doubt in everything he did. It would take some time to repair his confidence – if it could be repaired at all.

51.

THE RAIN FELL in violent outbursts, as it had for weeks. No sooner had an area of ground dried than it again became a patchwork of puddles. The hospital, being constructed of low-level buildings with flat roofs, forever echoed with the drumming of rain, which threatened to breach the ageing structure. The walls became damp, water seeping in from outside, and leaks from the corridor's roof were noted at regular intervals along its length. The damage to the southern end of the corridor caused by the fallen tree was exacerbated by water damage. Temporary shelters constructed to protect the fallen masonry were no barrier to the downpours, such that the site around the tree fall was now a quagmire. Work was halted and the cranes which had arrived to clear the site sank deeper into the mud.

The rain had one positive effect, though. Sightings of foxes declined, and it was as though the creatures had tired of the incessant storms and decided to move to drier climes. Perhaps it reflected the fact that visitors to the hospital spent less time outside, so noted them less. Whatever the reason, the fox problem slipped lower down the agenda.

Eric had arrived at the management offices early. He had avoided the worst of the weather, dashing from his car to the front entrance of the hospital when the rain started to become heavier. However, just after leaving the car park he had managed to misjudge his step, his left foot landing directly in a brown puddle. Reaching the haven of the hospital corridor, he noticed that his shoes and the bottoms of his trouser legs were spattered with droplets of mud. His left sock was wet, and he had no spares, so he would be uncomfortable for the whole day. He reached his office and, notwithstanding the discomfort of his wet foot, immediately started to work on the pandemic plan. The Department of Health had sent daily updates reflecting the current trajectory of the crisis. That day's figures suggested the flattening of cases was continuing. Full-scale panic was to be avoided. He was pleased that he could make plans without constant demands for immediate action. The chief executive had stopped asking for regular updates. She was so preoccupied with other matters that he barely saw her. He was thankful to her for letting him work on the project in peace.

He had been working for an hour, generating a robust standard operating procedure for surgical services in the event of pandemic cases swamping the intensive care unit, when there was a knock at the door. He had been so immersed in his work that it was with some annoyance that he opened it. Before him stood Elaine, secretary to the sub-chief executive. She looked a little bedraggled, the mascara around her right eye running and her hair more out of place than usual.

'Can I come in?' she asked, since Eric showed no sign of inviting her in unprompted. He nodded and she sat down in the chair opposite his desk. Eric resumed his seat and folded down the lid on his laptop.

'John has asked me to get together the finance spreadsheets for tomorrow,' she started.

Eric shrugged. 'Ask Elise. She's in charge of the accounts,' he said, not sure why she had asked him.

'She's away, and there's one file I can't locate. The third quarter of last year. It isn't on the server.'

Knowing that a missing file would upset Eric's sense of order, she persisted. 'There is an anomaly between the balance carried forward for vascular surgery and the final balance for the year.' She paused. 'So, the missing spreadsheet is crucial to explain the figures.'

Eric opened his laptop, his sense of order upset by the missing file, and started to type on the keyboard. She waited patiently for him to finish his search of the files on the server.

'Yes', he concluded, 'you're right. It's not there.'

He looked puzzled and immediately started to type again on his keyboard, as though a new idea had come to him. After a while, he shook his head and rubbed his chin. 'That's strange.'

Elaine continued to press. 'What shall I tell John?'

'Again, this is really an issue for Elise, as she files the accounts.'

Elaine lowered her voice and sat forward, resting her hands on the table. 'Eric, can I confide something in you?'

Eric nodded uneasily in assent.

'There is something odd about the accounts. I've been going through them for the finance board and can't make them tally.'

Eric shrugged and continued to type at his keyboard, delving into its hard drive in the search for the missing file. After a few moments, he stopped and looked up. 'As I say,' he replied robotically, 'you'll need to speak to Elise.'

'Yes, but she's away, and I just wanted to know whether this had been flagged up to you?'

Eric went back to typing, ignoring this last question. Elaine left. A seed of doubt had been sewn in the mind of the director of transformation.

52.

JOHN SUCH HAD decided to cycle to work. The sun was bright, and the rain had relented. His route took him up the side of a hill and across a narrow stretch known locally as Goat Pass before descending into the valley. The first part was hard work, a relentless slog until his thighs burned with lactic acid build-up, but the view from the top was magnificent, particularly on a day like this. Even though he had ridden this route often during the years that he had worked at the hospital, he still marvelled at the glory of the valley and would often stop to admire it. The hospital seemed so small from this vantage point, tucked away, way down below, the scant buildings huddled together. The road that fed into the hospital was already clogged up with cars, the tiny vehicles moving like a line of snails. He inhaled the fresh air of the hilltop and made his descent to the valley floor.

The day's schedule included the second meeting of the fox committee. Any semblance of structure to the proceedings had gone, and there was a feeling amongst the few members who had bothered to turn up at the inaugural meeting that they were just going through the motions. The fox problem was a distraction from the main issue, and they all knew it. Why the committee continued at all was uncertain, save for the notion that the hospital had to be seen to be acting to repel any threat. John Such didn't mind dedicating time to it, however, as it distracted him from his current main worry, which was his increasingly challenging relationship with the chief executive. Her behaviour, of late, was unpredictable and the accusation that she had made against him was as irrational as it was upsetting. They hadn't spoken since the outburst. He had expected at the very least an apology, even a text message that evening, but her silence had been complete. He understood that she was under immense pressure, but her actions were not those he would have expected. The newspaper stories had put the whole hospital under a cloud, and it was a time for strong leadership, more than ever. Yet the chief executive was withdrawing deeper into her own world, shutting herself off from her former allies. He decided he would approach her today to clear the air, even though he felt it was her responsibility to make the first move.

He arrived at the management offices after having showered and changed. It was the birthday of one of the secretaries, so balloons and a banner were displayed near the door, next to a table of buffet food and a large chocolate cake bearing the figure *50*. After agreeing to attend the lunchtime gathering for the celebrations, he went to his desk, picked up a folder of papers and his laptop, and headed for the meeting room at the far end of the offices.

Elaine, his secretary, was already sitting in the room, typing on her laptop. She acknowledged him as he entered and then continued to type. John Such sat down. The potential meeting with the chief executive was weighing down his thoughts and he felt gloomy. He would need to get it over and done with that day.

Elaine stopped typing and turned to John Such. 'I don't think we'll have much of a committee today,' she said, handing him a piece of paper. 'Pretty much everyone has cried off. I'm just waiting for Tony to get back to me, but word is he's had to take time off today.'

He was neither surprised nor disappointed. The fox committee was now irrelevant in his mind. Ever since his attendance at the pub meeting and with the pressure of other events building up, he had decided that the only course of action would be to tolerate the foxes and let the story die down. Having pest controllers slaughtering the beasts was the last thing they needed.

'What shall we do?' asked Elaine, shutting her laptop.

John Such tapped his fingers on the desk. 'Elaine,' he said, 'I need to see the chief exec today. Do you think that will be possible?'

She wrote the request down on a piece of paper and said, 'Yes, I'll try and arrange it. Was it about anything in particular?'

John Such frowned. He disliked discussing his petty squabbles but needed to confide in someone.

'It's about the newspaper stories.'

'Oh yes?' she said, putting down her pen.

He shook his head. 'The chief exec thinks I'm the one who leaked the minutes and that photo.'

'Really?' she said. 'Why does she think that?'

'I don't know. She doesn't seem herself at the moment. She is having all sorts of strange ideas.'

'I can't understand why she would accuse you, though. Do you think she's trying to deflect attention away from herself?'

John Such looked at her, puzzled. 'What do you mean?'

'John, can I be open with you?' she asked, awaiting no reply. 'Since starting here and working on the minutes for the finance committee, I've noticed some … unusual activity.' Her pause before the word *unusual* indicated that she had chosen it deliberately, carefully.

John Such raised his eyebrows. 'Go on.'

'Well, some of the files are missing, and there is a big gap in the finances for surgical specialties which can only be accounted for with reference to missing files.'

'What are you saying, Elaine? Someone is cooking the books?'

'I don't know. It's not my place to question this, but something odd is going on.'

'And you think the boss might be involved in this?' asked John Such.

'I just don't know, but ...' she broke off, and smiled before changing the subject. 'Anyway. I think the foxes will live on for another day!'

John Such smiled back, then studied her face momentarily. Who exactly was she? He had never before encountered a secretary like her.

53.

MR JAMES BARABAS, specialist colorectal surgeon, had been summoned to meet the chief executive. The reason for the meeting was not known to him, although he had an inkling that it related to surgical budgets, which were a significant headache to the hospital accountants. There were rumours that a big hole in the budget had appeared. Whether this was caused by incompetence or foul play was not clear. The local health authority was so concerned, given its history of financial irregularity, that it had already employed an independent firm of auditors to investigate the department's budgetary affairs. Given Mr Barabas' role in procurement of surgical supplies – gloves, scalpels and the like – he had already spent hours with the auditors explaining the purchase decisions he had made.

The meeting took place in the chief executive's office. She looked tired; her eyes were dark, her face unemotional. Mr Barabas had only met her once before, at an interview panel for a new consultant, back when she had only been in post a few weeks. He had thought her very efficient, workmanlike, not one for small talk.

True to form, as soon as the surgeon was shown into her office, she got straight to the point. Picking up a printout of an email, she surveyed the first few lines. 'I've had a concern raised by the family of one of your patients.'

Mr Barabas felt his heart rate quicken. It was unusual for complaints to come, without warning, directly from the chief executive. There was a process which would allow him time to reflect and compose a response. Being confronted out of the blue was disconcerting.

She continued. 'I believe Mrs Muriel Frank is a long-stay patient of yours. Is that right?'

Mr Barabas swallowed hard and nodded. 'Yes,' he mumbled, anxious to hear why the chief executive was questioning him about his problematic patient.

She glanced back at the paper in her hand. 'They say that you spoke to them recently about her treatment.'

'Yes, that's right. Her case is very complex. I've kept in regular contact with the family.'

She handed him the piece of paper. 'They seem to be concerned that you are not going to treat her any more.'

Mr Barabas looked at the paper. It was from Mrs Frank's daughter-in-law, who had identified herself as a solicitor in a local law firm.

'As you know,' continued the chief executive, not giving him enough time to finish reading, 'the hospital has been under attack in the papers. Several unsavoury – and, I must emphasise, untrue – accusations have been made.'

Mr Barabas continued to read the email whilst listening to her words.

'I discussed a ceiling of care with them,' he said. 'Their mother is a very sick woman, and her prognosis is dire. She had a serious post-operative complication and has been in hospital for months. The treatment we are giving her is in her best interests.'

The chief executive listened, smiled.

'Of course,' she interjected, 'I am sure you are doing all you can.'

The surgeon felt his anger rising. 'They talk about wishing for her to have all possible treatments, including returning to ITU if needed.' He held up the piece of paper. 'Well, that wouldn't be appropriate. It would cause unnecessary suffering to Mrs Frank.'

The chief executive considered this. Her face was drawn, and a vein in her temple appeared to throb.

'Even so, Doctor. I think it would be best to abide by the wishes of the family.'

The surgeon was starting to get annoyed. 'Why? Because of the newspaper stories? Is that it?'

The chief executive, keeping her repose, not altering the tone of her voice, replied, 'Things are delicate, and we must maintain the highest of standards in the hospital.' She then added, 'As I'm sure you will, Mr Barabas.' She stood up, indicating that she had said all she had to say.

Later that day, Mr Barabas, benefiting from some free time due to the cancellation of a patient from his operating list, sat in the corner of the theatre coffee room. He was alone and couldn't get the conversation with the chief executive out of his mind. She had effectively interfered with the management of his patient for the sake of the hospital's reputation. That was a dangerous route to go down. The hospital's reputation was built on the efficient implementation of clinical skills, including making the right decisions for all the patients who walked through its doors. The chief executive was asking him to make a treatment choice to pacify those who had read nebulous stories in the newspaper. How would the hospital function if they adopted this policy? He was firm in his resolution that he had to do what was best for the patient and thus ignore the conversation he had had with the chief executive. Yet, the whole of Muriel Frank's management had been so challenging that he no longer knew what the right thing was to do.

Down the corridor on Ward 19, Muriel Frank's life ground on.

54.

THE FOG WAS particularly dense just after sunrise, shrouding the arrival of the day. From her window, Aamaal surveyed the small patch of ground directly outside. It was blanketed in white frost, delicate yet harsh. Further out, she could see the faint outlines of trees but little more. Condensation had formed on the window, dripping onto the sill and from there down the stained walls. She wiped the damp away with the sleeve of her dressing gown, not caring that the wetness would seep through and make her cold. From the bedroom, the coughing had long since stopped, and nothing distracted her from her now trance-like state. She was observing the world around her but was not part of it. Occasionally she heard a baby's cry or the noise of arguing from an adjacent flat. Outside, the rumble of cars had started up, muffled yet increasing in volume. The day was starting up after the long night. She embraced these distractions, an aside from the cruel silence she had endured for the past few hours. Life was continuing outside the walls of her tiny flat.

She heard faint stirrings from the bedroom of her younger children, but they became quiet again after a moment, as though they sensed the desolation of the morning. They would ask no questions whilst going through the motions of the morning ritual. A cat screeched in the hidden terrain beyond the distant walls. A siren wailed. And throughout, her daughter sobbed, trying not to be heard.

He was dead. It had happened sometime in the night, although the transition from life to death was not clear-cut, and the moment of his departure from the world was only noted with any certainty in retrospect. His breathing had been barely perceptible for hours, the fine margin which separated life from death too subtle to perceive. Both wife and daughter had been by the bedside, clinging on to each other as the man in the bed slipped away. They had both known that this night was when it would finally happen.

The daughter, having put the younger children to bed, had taken up the vigil with her mother. She had not brought up the possibility of calling an ambulance again. Instead, she sat, silently, supporting her mother and the decision she had made. Now it was all over.

Aamaal's life, so dependent up to that point on the union between partners, was torn into two parts. She had not made any decision without the consent of her husband for so long. And now he was gone, so how could she decide what to do with the dead man beside her?

She was struck by the confusion of the new reality which faced their family. No longer were they waiting for something to happen. Now it had happened, she had no idea what the next step was to be. There was no point in calling an ambulance now. Her husband was dead, and she needed to tell someone; someone who would remove the body, prepare for the funeral. There must be paperwork.

As though this were now a matter of supreme urgency, she sat at the family computer and looked up the macabre subject, one which she had no desire to look up, one which she had not, up to this point, envisaged having to deal with. Through her tears and her muddled mind, she worked out that she should contact her general practitioner, but the phone line was closed until 9am. It was only 7.30.

She would need to wait.

55.

THE HOSPITAL RAN on principles which resembled those of a military institution. The hierarchies were well entrenched, their observation necessary for its efficient running. The generals of senior management sought to project a more caring and inclusive atmosphere, but the final say lay with them, and the direction of policy, much like the decision to launch an offensive, fell within the jurisdiction of the commander-in-chief, the chief executive.

The rules and policies of the hospital were forever shifting, however, and there were few reliable solutions available to guide its leaders battling overfull wards and threats of new and deadly diseases. Indeed, the different priorities of the managers and the clinicians led to conflict. The clinicians had their own code of practice, a morality which was often at odds with the managers. The managers had money at the heart of their rulebook, which defied the actions of the clinicians, causing regular challenges to their moral codes. It was an unhealthy cycle.

At the bottom of the hierarchy were the administrators and the secretaries, the foot soldiers. Their collective memory and their adaptability were unmeasurable resources without which the hospital could not function. Good secretaries knew their way around any problem. Just as a sapper could defuse a bomb before the generals had even suspected one, this group of underpaid workers diverted all manner of problems. Their presence was a requirement for the running of the hospital, their absence unthinkable. Yet, despite their importance, their voice was rarely heard. In the midst of the chaos which engulfed the management, now more than ever, the secretaries were expected to do their jobs like children from years gone by – seen but not heard.

And so, Elaine Stewart, known by the secretaries for some time as an infiltrator from the local paper, continued to work. She had become increasingly unhappy about her role in the hospital. Not only was she shunned by her co-workers, but the rationale for her presence in the hospital was increasingly unclear. She was aware that the other secretaries suspected, indeed knew, the reason for her being there. Rather surprisingly, however, their concerns had not filtered up the chain to the senior managers. She was certain that John Such, her boss, was unaware of the rumours which were circulating. The disconnect between the structured echelons of the organisation had seen to that. She could, therefore, continue to unearth information concerning the financial dealings of the hospital, and, despite her misgivings on the ethics of her mission, she was making progress. There were indeed anomalies in the documentation of finance meetings and in the implementation of the necessary checks and balances. Whether this was mere sloppiness on the part of the accountants or an attempt to cover up an act of fraud, she was not yet sure. It seemed to hinge on finding those records for a financial quarter which were currently missing. She had sought this information in the guise of the secretary to the finance board (thus not attracting undue attention) in the usual areas but had come up with a blank. That, in itself, was a story. Her editor had urged her to unearth more. The absence of information, and thus the implication of guilt, was not as useful as definitive evidence proving misdoings. The problem now was that she didn't know where to look. She had arrived at the conclusion that the inefficiency and, it must be said, the incompetence of hospital management was the reason for the missing information, so the suspicions of embezzlement were unfounded. Yet the spectre of previous disgrace loomed, and her editor's eagerness to expose further scandal drove her to continue, albeit increasingly half-heartedly.

As she sat at her desk, typing up minutes, organising meetings, answering queries, she felt the eyes of the office were on her. Jackie Booth and Jan Bullimore were the ringleaders for the process of her marginalisation. They had alerted the other secretaries to her treachery, and now many would not greet her and would actively go out of their way to avoid a chance encounter. Her isolation was to be expected once suspicions were aired. It made it no less uncomfortable, however. She found it hard to understand the reasons why their concerns hadn't filtered up to the managers. She imagined those higher in management didn't want to indulge the petty tittle-tattle of the workers, whose priorities and prejudices they didn't comprehend.

Jan Bullimore, the most senior of the secretaries, controlled the shots. She held a power over the others, notably Jackie Booth, which meant her way was the way of the office. She took the decisions on the organisation of the offices, from work patterns to coffee cups. She had never trusted this newcomer to the office. She had been uneasy with the way Elaine had wangled her way into some of the more senior jobs, which should have been given to those who had served in the office for years or decades. This newcomer's manner was brusque and her background mysterious.

Jan met with Jackie for their lunch break. They had walked to the café, skirting around the blockades in place around the damaged corridor. The roof and walls of the southern portion were unstable, and attempts to repair it seemed to be making it worse. Mud and rubble were expanding rather than being removed. It was turning into a major constructional challenge.

Once at the café, the pair of secretaries took their place in the corner, unwrapped their lunches and settled down for their half hour of chat and gossip. Jackie was unsure how they should proceed regarding Elaine's motives. She was keen to warn the senior executives of their suspicions, but Jan suggested caution. It was not proven that Elaine was working for *The Herald*. Jan thought that any approach by them to the managers would be seen as malicious gossip, which the management would use against them in years to come. Anyway, they probably wouldn't listen.

'John Such,' said Jackie, chewing on her flimsy sandwich. 'He's a decent man. He'll listen.'

Jan took a drink of water and wiped her mouth on her sleeve. 'I don't know, Jackie. He seems to have been taken in by our Elaine. She can do no wrong in his eyes.'

Jackie nodded. 'Yes, you're probably right. But the rest of that lot are even less likely to take us seriously.'

'We could tell Eric!' said Jan in irony, causing the reaction in her colleague she had expected. But out of the joking there emerged the realisation that they had no route to the managers to tell them their concerns. They would keep their suspicions to themselves. Whatever truth came out in the coming days, weeks and months would be discovered by a leadership which didn't hear their voices. If that caused further problems, then so be it. It wouldn't stop them talking about the scandal of it all, nonetheless.

56.

IT WAS WELL-KNOWN that Jim Spier wore a hairpiece to conceal his baldness. To many, this was illogical, since he was trying to hide something all knew about. A little over two years earlier, he had gone from being bald one day to having a thatch of hair the next. It wasn't even a realistic wig. The colour of the artificial hair didn't match the remaining hair on the sides of his head; the top was a shade of russet brown, the sides a dull grey. People who had not met him before couldn't help but marvel at its absurdity on their first encounter. However, he wore it with a sort of blasé indifference which indicated that he must have convinced himself of his extensive and natural hirsuteness.

Aside from what was happening on top of his head, Jim Spier did little to maintain his physique. He was morbidly obese, his abdomen bulging over a too tight belt, his shirt buttons straining, the flesh below his belly button often breaking through the covering of the garment. His face was ruddy, no doubt the result of nights of excessive red wine drinking, and was traversed by thin, purple lines, a network of broken blood vessels. He walked with a limp, often exacerbated by the flare-ups of gout to which he was prone. In short, he was a caricature of modern middle-aged decay. In contrast, his mind was sharp and focused. He had reached a position of power, head of the local health authority, which he believed was a stepping-stone to a senior position in the Department of Health. It was only a matter of time, he reasoned. He needed to keep his head down, balance the books and deliver the Department of Health's long-term plan (or not, since that was generally accepted to be unachievable). Therefore, the scandal which was escalating in one of the hospitals under his authority was of concern. If he couldn't suppress the newspaper stories quickly, then he might be seen in the corridors of power to be weak, thus negating his next career move. He needed to be decisive.

Sacking the chief executive was unlikely to be enough. He had decided even before the 'Killing of Five' issue that he would need to get rid of her. Concerning that matter, he had no hesitation. He had very little time for the woman and had taken against her the first time they had met. He had been on the interview panel which appointed her and had reluctantly agreed to employ her, predominantly because there was a paucity of other options. Anyway, he had already been hatching a plan to close down the hospital, so had decided that appointing someone whom he viewed as highly inappropriate for the job might serve him well in his long-term Machiavellian plan.

In the months following her appointment, she had done little to make him change his mind concerning her leadership skills. Their relationship had been cold since the moment they had met. His disrespect blossomed and he made no secret of his intention that her days as chief executive were numbered.

The feelings he had towards the chief executive were entirely reciprocated. He suspected she was behind the recent accusations of sexual discrimination which had been made against him. He would, in former times, have shrugged such things off as minor inconveniences, but the newfound enlightenment of contemporary times gave a prominence to such allegations over and above that which he considered appropriate. They were another reason for him not to be promoted. If only the old rules still applied.

But the problems in the hospital ran deeper than one person. In front of him, on his solid oak desk which occupied the centre of his spacious office in the health authority headquarters, was the report on the potential closure of the hospital. Marked

CONFIDENTIAL by virtue of a bleak red stamp, it had been commissioned by the Department of Health and was only for the eyes of the select few. The chief executive might have had an inkling of the machinations of the health authority but was not yet party to the arguments laid out in the pages of the document.

Greater emphasis on community care was the current direction of thinking of the Department of Health. Old behemoths consisting of wards, stuffy clinics and operating theatres were not the modern way. The hospital could make way for smaller, more efficient community units. The public would support improved access to medical care, the report stated, quoting from the various focus groups which had worked on the issue of relocation of hospital services. In addition, the real estate value was huge, and the sale of hospital land, at least in the short term, would enable debts to be reduced. After spending several hours with the minister of health on a train to London, Jim Spier had discerned that he was keen on the proposals. Four cans of beer into the journey, he had learned a great deal about overall government policy, which he toasted with several more rounds of drink at the pub at the end of the line.

In his defence, Jim Spier would maintain, he had given the chief executive a lifeline. If she were to find a way of reducing overall costs by at least ten percent, then there might, just might, be a way to save the hospital. He had felt this was unachievable, given the historic debt and the rising costs of health care. Even he had not imagined that the crisis in the hospital would be escalated so spectacularly. How the chief executive had managed to steer from savings targets to national scandal confirmed his view of her management skills.

He put down the report and looked at the diary appointments for the day. The chief executive would come later in the day, and he would watch her squirm her way through half an hour of his questions. He had not decided when he was going to tell her about the likely closure of her hospital. He would keep it from her for a little while more. He was enjoying the sport of it.

57.

Matt Butcher had stopped shaving for work and now had a two-week growth of stubbly beard on his chin. Its presence was remarked upon by the ward staff with an unsubtle irony. They directed him to shave it off, for his own sake. Even he acknowledged that it made him look unkempt, and yet an inertia towards looking smart, driven by his ruminations on the futility of his career, negated the picking up of his razor in the morning. It was enough for him to turn up at all. His clothes were crumpled and not that clean; his shoes scuffed, the sole peeling off from the main body of the left shoe. He was never late, however. He methodically set his alarm and attended the set place of work with the assiduousness he had felt as a medical student attending his lectures or his ward placements. The desire for routine was ingrained in him. Just not this routine.

Mr Barabas had not commented on the appearance of his junior doctor. It was up to him how he looked, as far as he was concerned. He was not an old-school consultant type who would take a junior colleague aside to inform him or her on the proper way to dress. He had enough on his mind to be concerned with matters of sartorial elegance.

The two met up just outside Ward 19 for their regular ward round. Since Matt Butcher had started working at the hospital, all the ward rounds began on Ward 19 and all began with Muriel Frank. He noticed how anxious Mr Barabas always appeared before the ward round. This time was no different. The stalemate of her medical care would consume the first twenty minutes before they moved on to more mundane matters. Matt Butcher imagined that if he were to return in several years' time, the routine would be the same.

Before they entered the ward through the heavy double doors which swung aggressively on their hinges, Mr Barabas enquired about the latest news on his long-term patient.

'Stable,' replied Matt Butcher. 'Renal function about the same, fluid balance is fine, haemoglobin is OK.'

Mr Barabas nodded. 'That's good news,' he said, rolling his sleeves up in preparation for entering the ward.

Matt Butcher hesitated. 'Can I ask where we are heading with her?'

'What do you mean?' asked the senior surgeon, stopping mid-sleeve-roll.

Matt Butcher considered whether to probe further into the direction being adopted by his senior. This was not the done thing in medical circles. He was emboldened, however, by the realisation that surgery and maybe medicine as a whole was not to be his long-term career. He had little to lose.

'Well, we have this conversation every ward round and nothing changes. Are we trying to make her better or just not make her any worse?'

He had said it, albeit rather inelegantly: that gnawing doubt in his mind, which not only pertained to this particular patient but to a large spectrum of medical practice. At the same time, however, he had shocked himself. He had never spoken to a consultant in this way before. The decision of the consultant was sacrosanct. That was how it always had been.

Mr Barabas turned to the junior doctor.

'Are you questioning my decisions?' he asked, glaring at the junior.

Matt Butcher stood his ground. After all, he had not signed up to the grotesque hierarchical decision-making process in which he was now bound. He scratched his chin, which was itchy due to the unaccustomed hair growth.

'Well?' Mr Barabas broke their silence, staring at the young man who was now looking down at the floor.

'Listen,' continued the surgeon, 'we will treat the patient in the way that I see fit. I make the decisions and you carry out whatever I ask. Have you got that?'

The junior doctor, feeling the rage of his senior colleague, nodded his still-bowed head before gesturing to enter the ward. Mr Barabas pushed open the heavy doors, one sleeve still unrolled, and entered the ward. He approached the ward sister, who was carrying a box of surgical masks, and instructed her to join him for the ward round. She immediately grasped his mood and meekly complied, putting down the box and following him. Matt Butcher trailed behind, his thoughts raging, his resolve split directly in two.

'Right, let's see Mrs Frank,' Mr Barabas barked at the two of them. 'Before we do …' he stopped outside her door and directed his gaze to Matt Butcher, '… before we do, let's be clear. We are going to keep treating this lady with the full range of medical options. If she deteriorates, I want intensive care to take her back. All medical problems will be treated with full and active treatment.' He stopped. His jaw was trembling. 'Is that clear?'

The sister, who was not party to the context of this tirade, and Matt Butcher, whose thoughts were running wild with the possibilities of dissent, both nodded.

'Let's see her and behave professionally,' added the consultant, pushing open the door.

His anger continued throughout the whole morning. The ward staff were on edge, steering clear of any controversial subjects, not asking him any questions other than the banal. Matt Butcher said little for the rest of the day, continuing his duties as calmly as he was able. He had broken the rules and questioned the judgement of his senior colleague. That had given rise to the fury vented on him and the rest of the ward staff. Yet, he was convinced that he was acting in the interests of the patient by questioning the management plan. The surgeon's reaction was over the top, of that there was no doubt. He had no idea that Mr Barabas' increasing level of anger was predominantly a consequence of the discussion he had had, only the day before, with the chief executive.

58.

THE FOXES HAD all but gone from the hospital, their presence now receded into memory. The newspaper stories were confined to the archive, having given way to larger, more tangible stories of disgrace and humiliation. Like the remnants of a defeated army, occasional beasts, either alone or, rarely, in pairs, were seen skulking in the backdrop of the hospital like an afterthought. People now paid little attention to them. The ones which were seen seemed wary of any contact with their human counterparts, their previous boldness replaced by suspiciousness. They were seen only at night, occasionally traversing the car parks or disappearing into a hedge. They looked leaner, more battered, and walked with a weary air, or even, if one were to personify the creatures, a sense of resignation to their fate. Not that any sort of decision had been made concerning their presence. The fox committee had not decided one way or another. Priorities had changed, and that was that. Neither side of the debate, those arguments pro-fox or those anti-fox, had succeeded, neither had failed.

The chief executive had stopped thinking about them. Her erstwhile dreams of the furry beasts had been replaced with a greater threat to her position and indeed her sanity – Jim Spier. He occupied her waking and her sleeping hours. Her dreams of foxes going through the bins around her house were now exchanged for images of the bloated leader of the local health authority, his overwhelming unpleasantness filling her mind. In one such reverie, she imagined him enthroned in her office, behind her desk, barking orders at her, while she ran around complying with his every whim. He was a hundred times more threatening than a fox, and a thousand times more repulsive. She knew that the nature of the job was firefighting – once one problem had died down, another needed quenching. At present, however, the conflagrations were spreading unchecked, her attempts to repel them increasingly impotent.

John Such, on the other hand, rather missed his fox project. It had been a distraction from the other difficulties he had to deal with, and, since the outcome didn't really matter (in his eyes), he was not stressed by the meetings or the preparation surrounding the issue. He had enjoyed reading about foxes. Perhaps it was a manifestation of his frustration that he hadn't gone into nature conservation as a career. He would have preferred that line of work, no doubt. Yet its prospects, opportunities and pay were uncertain, so he had chosen industry and then hospital management as a safe option. As a result, his migraines had been escalating in their frequency. It was not helped by the continuing mistrust which had built up between him and the chief executive. Although she had, rather belatedly, apologised for her accusation, he sensed that she still harboured a deep scepticism for his motives, believing him to be plotting her downfall. He was not alone in observing a change in the chief executive. She was displaying several paranoid tendencies, so much so that he and others had been concerned over her mental health. Some tried to help her, but any attempt by other members of management to help her offload her worries was shrugged off.

And what became of the fox protesters? Their presence in the hospital grounds slowly slipped away, in parallel with the beasts they were aiming to save. All that remained was the oil drum which was never lit, or even filled with fuel. The public relations team had to hire lifting equipment to remove it, since its owners were not known. The winter of vulpine discontent had not materialised. Flyers were undistributed. Meetings in *The Brewers Arms* were cancelled.

Oddly enough, John Such spotted the leader of the Fox Defence League in the hospital one day. He was dressed smartly in a three-piece suit and a bright red tie and was sitting in the waiting room of the main outpatient's department. John Such half-expected to see the rest of the crowd: the woman in the orange jumpsuit and the others, but the man sat alone. He looked anxious and forlorn, as though nervously waiting to receive some news. John Such was in the outpatient's department to discuss a new efficiency drive to reduce waiting times, so spent much of the morning in the offices next to the waiting room. As he was leaving to return to the management offices, he noticed that the pro-fox leader was still there. Now, however, the woman in the orange jumpsuit was sitting next to him. She was dressed as before, and the contrast between the two was striking. They held hands as the old man sat, expressionless. Perhaps some good had come of the fox protests, thought John Such.

59.

ATTACHED TO A half-empty bag of saline, fluid dripped irregularly in a plastic chamber, from where a transparent tube led straight into a vein. Flow within the tube was regulated via a machine which controlled the rate of hydration and warned against the presence of any impurities. Frequently a kink in the tube set off the alarm, that harsh indicator of impending medical demise. So often did it sound that the alarm was silenced for much of the day, rendering it redundant. At intervals of six hours or so, the nurses changed the bag of saline, and the process was repeated.

Matt Butcher studied the plastic chamber and the slow drip. It had all but ground to a halt. The silenced alarm had been warning of the perilous rate of flow for several hours. It could be ignored no longer. There was no getting away from it; the latest cannula delivering fluid into Muriel Frank's veins was failing, and it would need to be replaced. The prospect filled the junior doctor with dread. In an attempt to remedy the situation, which he knew would prove fruitless, he moved the patient's arm, placing it into different positions to see if it would increase the flow of fluid. Then he removed the dressing from the site around the cannula and gently wiggled the plastic apparatus to determine whether this would unblock the tube. It was all to no avail. He resigned himself to further likely-futile attempts at cannulation.

He trudged out of the side room and into the storeroom near the entrance to the ward. There was found the necessary equipment for the procedure upon which he was about to embark. In front of him, racks of medical supplies were piled up in drawers labelled with such bizarre names as double-lumen Foley, bougies, Swan-Ganz. The vocabulary of medicine was a covert code. He grabbed a blue tray and started to assemble what he needed. His actions were slothful, filled with an apathy which accompanied a feeling that he was going through the motions of failure. He had tried to cannulate this woman on several previous occasions and had always failed. He would ask one of his senior colleagues or even the anaesthetist to do it, but only after he had stabbed randomly at a patch of flesh. He knew they wouldn't come unless he had attempted it first. Mr Barabas' newfound zeal for treating his most problematic patient had dictated that the fluids and other life-preserving potions being given to her must continue under all circumstances. Maybe he should ring Mr Barabas himself and ask him to carry out the procedure, if he was so keen on it. The heated exchange from earlier that morning cast a shadow on the rest of the day's work.

Having gathered the necessary equipment, he returned to the room. Muriel Frank was sitting up in bed. It was the first time he had seen her in this position; usually she was supine, her head turned away from the door. He couldn't recall seeing her face before. Rather unnervingly, she appeared to be looking at him – the first contact the two had shared beyond the monologues he had spoken at her. As if a reflex had kicked in, Matt Butcher smiled at the woman on the bed. There was minimal response, but he approached the bed, her gaze following him.

When he was at an arm's length, he stooped down so as to be at her eye level. He looked at her face.

'Hello,' he said, doubting whether she would be able to process his words. He was taking out his pen torch to check the response of her pupils to light in order to assess her level of consciousness, when she replied.

'Hello,' she said in a soft yet definite voice.

Matt Butcher, startled by this response, dropped the pen torch, which clattered on the floor and rolled under the bed. Had she really spoken? He looked around the room for the nurse, but she had left a few minutes earlier to empty some noxious fluid down the drains of the sluice.

He tried again. 'How are you?'

This time there was silence. He must have been hearing things. Perhaps he had wished a response rather than actually heard one. He picked up the blue tray with the tools for the attempt to cannulate a vein. He placed it by the bedside and washed his hands in the large white sink at the side of the room.

Still troubled by the imaginary greeting, he approached the patient again, opening and then laying out a pair of sterile rubber gloves. Again, he heard a soft sound coming from the woman. She had shifted her gaze so that, once more, she looked him in the eye. He couldn't make out what she was saying.

'What's that?' he asked, coming closer to her. He looked at her lips and turned his right ear a little towards her mouth. He was straining to hear.

She repeated, faintly, but unmistakeably, 'I don't want it.'

He took a step back. 'What?' he asked, then clarified: 'What don't you want?'

Muriel Frank looked down at the blue tray which contained the instruments for the latest assault on her skin, and Matt Butcher understood. He also realised that by the blue tray she meant the whole scope of her treatment. This was a woman who had endured months of this treatment and who had now expressed herself where no expression of consent was thought to be possible. She had communicated her wishes. Her voice, so hard to hear, needing every measure of energy to summon up a few words, was heard. He had thought her beyond words, beyond choice, and now this assumption condemned him.

'I'm so sorry,' he said, casting aside the blue tray, grasping her hand as if imploring her to remove his shame.

60.

WHEN JOHN SUCH finished management school, he had been excited by the prospect of making a difference in public service. Now his attitude verged on cynicism. The machinations of this dysfunctional organisation had driven him to question his calling. What troubled him the most was that he had no idea as to how the situation in the hospital had descended to such a level. Mistrust, paranoia, and unfriendliness had spread through the fetid atmosphere. Workers had stopped talking to each other, had ceased meeting after work for a drink and now ate their lunches alone. Of all the work groups, the secretaries, typically barometers of the mood of the hospital, demonstrated the malaise at the heart of the organisation in all its bewildering disrepair. They formed factions which sniped at each other, spread rumours, and excluded anyone with a conciliatory attitude. His own secretary, Elaine Stewart, had been a catalyst for the fracture of a healthy working environment. He understood the reasons why she might have antagonised the others: she was focused and rejected small talk, she asked questions with a dogged determination, but above all, she kept herself to herself. She had only worked for him for a few months, so her effect had been dramatic. When she had been appointed, he had thought her overqualified. She had a business degree and experience in marketing, but the reason she had given – that she wanted to work flexibly to care for her elderly mother – had been accepted by those on the panel. As time had gone on, however, John Such had become increasingly uncertain as to her true motives for taking the job.

He had got wind of the rumours circulating about her, and, having first dismissed them as sour grapes amongst the longstanding secretaries who felt their influence usurped, had started to take them more seriously. As much as he didn't want to believe it, there was a good chance that she was the person who had leaked the minutes and the picture to the newspaper. She had taken the minutes, after all, and she often stayed late in the offices, so she'd had ample opportunity to go into Eric's office to take the photograph. No one would have questioned her going in anyway, even in the middle of the day. In addition, she had been asking a lot of questions about the finances and had all but forced her way into being the secretary to the finance board. If she were feeding stories to the papers, then exposing further evidence of shady dealing in hospital finances would be a major scoop.

For hours, he could think of nothing else. His thoughts spun around upon themselves into a web of superficial truth, fabricated on little but supposition. He needed to talk to someone about it. Perhaps if he aired his suspicions, their ludicrous nature would be exposed, and he could move on. In other times, he would have spoken to the chief executive, but given their recent conversations and the strange manner that she now displayed, that was not a viable option. He decided to talk to Eric, who would surely put him right in his cold and unemotional way. He had noted that his colleague had been happier for the past few days, distracted by pandemic planning, which consumed his waking hours.

The two arranged to meet in the canteen at the end of the day. John Such had managed to extract the director of transformation from the latest standard operating procedure document, version sixteen, or whatever it was he was working on. Although Eric was diffident and found it hard to show emotion, John Such knew that Eric saw him as a friend, an ally, and that Eric needed him on his side in the increasingly hostile working environment which had grown over the past few weeks.

They met, bought drinks: a coffee for John Such and a cold drink for Eric – who explained that ingestion of caffeinated drinks beyond the hour of 3pm would not allow him to sleep – and sat in the corner of the room.

'Will it ever stop raining?' asked John Such, looking out of the murky window. He knew that this would be enough small talk for Eric, so got to the point.

'Eric,' he began, 'there's been a lot of talk about the identity of the person who leaked the minutes of the board meeting.' He stopped short of mentioning the photograph of Eric's words which had appeared in the newspaper, giving the impression that it was the meeting minutes rather that the infamous blue words which were the bigger problem. He could see Eric's unease at his mentioning this. He had immersed himself so effectively in other matters that he had been able to put the issue out of his mind for a few hours.

'Look,' said John Such, 'I don't want to bring this all up again, but if we find out who sent the story to the papers, then we might be able to …' He paused. He wasn't really sure what they might be able to do. 'We might be able to get some closure on the matter.' He wasn't convinced by this but hoped that Eric would see the benefit.

'So, who did it?' asked Eric, who seemed indifferent to revealing the identity of the perpetrator.

'Well,' replied John Such, sipping his coffee, 'suspicion has fallen on Elaine, my secretary.'

He waited for a response. He knew Eric wasn't into gossip and hearsay but wanted to gauge if this would garner a response from him.

Eric shrugged his shoulders. 'And what evidence is there to say that?'

'She had access to the minutes – indeed, she wrote them. She was around the offices, often late into the evening.' It seemed flimsy evidence now he mentioned it.

'And why would she do it?' asked Eric, unimpressed.

That was a good question. It was her unusual way of working, her overqualification for the job and her divergence from the norms of the other secretaries which fuelled his suspicion, as it had fuelled the suspicion of her own colleagues. He was being sucked into their prejudices. This was akin to the witch hunts which had occurred so famously over in the Black Witch Hills all those years earlier.

'I don't know,' he conceded. 'Forget I said it.'

They sat in silence for a while, John Such feeling as foolish as the chief executive had most likely felt when she had accused him of the same crime.

'Keep this to yourself, Eric,' he said, gulping down his coffee and burning his mouth.

61.

FAINT SHAFTS OF sunlight broke through the grey sky on the eastern side of the valley. To the west, the weather was changing to a more welcoming prospect; the early morning rain having departed, leaving behind the slightest of rainbows. The valley was quiet. Occasional dog walkers performing their early morning duties plodded muddy paths, appearing from small copses or from behind high hedges. Outgrowths of evergreen trees, in contrast to their spindly deciduous cousins, grew strongly in the lower reaches of the valley, protected from the wind. And underfoot the mud persisted, expanding to provide the basis of all footpaths.

Into this landscape stepped the chief executive of the hospital. Unaccustomed to hill walking, her footwear was inadequate, and her coat was too heavy and over-padded to provide comfort later in more strenuous terrain. The idea of walking the route over the valley into the neighbouring village had come to her yesterday while reading – or, in truth, failing to concentrate on – the latest missive from the Department of Health. Seated in her chair behind the battered wooden desk, her thoughts had strayed beyond the piece of paper to the window and from there to the hills, which were just about visible over the low-built walls of the hospital. She had projected herself far from the confines of the office to the top of the distant mount, the wind in her hair, all her problems compartmentalised to the box which was the distant tiny construction, the hospital viewed from afar. The distance between these two destinations was vast.

She walked on, slipping every few paces in the deep, sucking mud. She was not bothered by the uncertainty of her footing; the placing of her feet into the moving earth was enough to provide her with a sense of release. At one point, her foot became stuck in a deep channel traversing the footpath. Her ankle twisted and her contralateral knee gave way, causing her to fall sideways, muddying her trousers and placing her hands deep in the slimy brown earth. She stood up and extracted her foot, wiping her dirtied hands on her coat. Further on, she entered a field, usually the home of cows which she would often see from the car when she drove to work each morning. She had never walked in the field before. The cows were presently housed in the cowsheds for the winter and now the field seemed barren, large clods of earth scattered between irregular patches of scant grass. The going was easier in this field, the mild frost of the previous night creating a hardness underfoot. She headed for a gate, a break in the hedge, which indicated the start of the climb up to the summit of the hill. The track now was stony and narrow, bordered on each side by a ragged hedge. Small burrows were dotted at the base of the hedge, homes to the creatures which occasionally scuttled across the path, unsafe out in the open. Walking became more strenuous, and the chief executive became hot under the multiple layers she had donned that morning. She was sure of her footing, though, and marched purposefully upwards. She passed a large barn at the point where the path levelled out. From inside, she heard the lowing of cattle and the deep, yet harsh, mechanical sound of machinery. A tractor was parked haphazardly across the path, and she skirted it, careful not to get stuck in the deep furrows the tyres had made. The day was getting brighter by the minute. A beautiful blue sky was now on the horizon and the winter sun, cold yet welcome, shone from her left. Birds began to sing.

Up she climbed. The hedge enclosing the path grew sparser before eventually petering out. The track now crossed open fields. The way to the summit was clear and she saw for the first time a large rock at the top of the hill, a way-marker and a comfort for the weary climber. The full extent of the valley was becoming clearer now. The river which had cut out the ravine in prehistoric times meandered forcefully below. The chief executive sat down on a level slab of rock by the side of the track. She would catch her breath before attempting the final climb. She took off her coat which, on closer inspection, was splattered with mud, little of the floral design now discernible beneath the brown stains. The sun shone brightly now and although the air was cold, she felt an inner warmth from its rays. She was happy to have taken the day off to escape from the deepening crises which were engulfing both her and the foundations of the hospital. She had left her phone at home, so no one would disturb her. This was her wild time, her time for recalibration. It had been John Such who had inspired her to take up this walk. Having always been a city dweller, she rarely felt the need to get outdoors into the countryside. Hearing the sub-chief executive's stories of sojourns into the wild had activated an interest into whether this might be a solution, or at least a help, to her increasing anxiety. He had spoken to her of birdwatching and rambles deep into the heart of the county and how it helped him to set his priorities. She had thought it worth a go.

Thinking of this, her most recent encounter with John Such came into her head. She had been foolish to address him so and bitterly regretted the loss of trust which had ensued. She doubted they would ever get back to a functional working relationship again. He had been her main ally and she had lost this bond. Indeed, alienating the man whom many viewed as the most loyal and reasonable in management was a dreadful turn of events, and one which would surely hasten her demise.

Her demise. That was what she was looking at. When she had started the job as chief executive, she knew the hospital was on a knife edge. Careful management was needed to steer the organisation through the latest Department of Health reforms, not to mention the toxic clutches of the local health authority's leader. He had been waiting for any calamity to blame on her and, as a result, diminish the standing of the hospital. She had not figured out his reasons for this approach, nor his end game, but imagined it to be one involving her being cast aside and taking the blame for the ills of the hospital.

A few drops of rain started to fall, and she put her coat back on. She pressed on upwards to the summit. The rain became harder for five minutes before stopping. She encountered no other walkers *en route* to the top; the solitude of walking was her newfound elixir.

Eventually, she reached the summit. She stood by the large rock, upon which had been attached a plaque showing the local landmarks which could be seen. She looked in all directions, in awe of the panorama, showered in a gilded light, before her gaze fell on the hospital, now diminutive and insignificant. This is what she had come to see. This was the purpose of her journey: to view her world from afar; to determine its significance in the context of the grand view from the top of the hill.

62.

SECURITY WITHIN THE management offices was as lax as ever, despite the recent leaks. Secrecy was not in the remit of the hospital; openness and transparency were strategic principles. In the great benevolent organisation, a utopian dream of healthcare for all, filing cabinets lay open and computer documents remained unencrypted, regardless of evidence of flagrant double-dealing by one of their own. Thus, Elaine Stewart continued to mine information late at night in the empty, unprotected offices. She persisted in her goal of unearthing financial irregularity, hovering between two opinions: either there was major fraud and a cover-up, or the organisational framework of the hospital was so haphazard that files were lost with alacrity. The more she delved, the stronger her conviction regarding the latter became. Not that sloppiness was the intended way of working; disorder was more attributable to the ever-changing and mounting demands on the finance department, coupled with the illogical method of dealing with accountancy which had been decreed by the Department of Health. In short, most of the financial transactions were virtual ones and dependent on numerous opposing factors. Money was shifted around from one computer file to another with abandon. Losses and gains – black figures and red figures – were theoretical; spreadsheets showed movement of imaginary money (that is to say, money which didn't really seem to exist) from one pot to another. If a saving needed to be made in order to meet a target, the money was transferred from one pile to another. The most bizarre aspect of the accounts was called Quality Improvement Tariffs – a system of rewarding departments for achieving a certain goal (typically

218

self-declared by a department as one which they were on track to achieve anyway). However, the financial incentive was applied from funds already in the department. It was little wonder, Elaine mused, that the accounts didn't make sense. It was a never-ending game of Monopoly.

Thus, trying to understand the intricate and unique machinations of financial dealings made it harder for Elaine to unearth wrongdoing. She had been instructed to continue her investigation by an increasingly zealous editor, eager to see the completion of the scoop he so desired. Her search took her back to Eric's office. Of all the senior management team members, he was the one who kept an ordered filing system. She could easily find hard copies of all the necessary documents (if they existed) in his filing cabinet, which was unlocked and neatly subdivided. So, when all was quiet and the last of the staff had gone home, she entered his office, pulled up a chair and went through the files. Even if she were to be challenged, she had a reason to be there; her underhand methods had an alibi.

She was looking for the file which had eluded her and was missing from the computer servers; the file that detailed the surgical budgets from a certain quarter of the year. The quarter before and the quarter after showed a huge difference, and sight of the missing spreadsheet would explain (or not) the discrepancy. She fingered her way through the filing cabinet with its neatly arranged subsections and brightly coloured subject dividers. Here too, however, the quarter in question was absent. She sat back and looked around the office to determine whether there might be another location for the missing document.

She heard footsteps outside the door and the noise of the door being pushed open. Elaine Stewart looked up and before her stood the cleaner, clad in a blue tunic, mop and bucket in hand.

'Sorry,' said the cleaner, stopping in the doorway.

'It's OK,' said Elaine, 'I'm done here. Please come in.'

The cleaner entered, placing the bucket to the side of the door. It clanged on the floor, spilling part of its content as the fluid sloshed from side to side. She stood, looking at the escaped liquid, clearly unsure whether to clean up or wait until Elaine had left. A nervous dynamic had been set up between the two.

Elaine had seen this cleaner on several occasions. She had said hello to her but not interacted in any other way, each worker having their own job to do. She thought the woman had a melancholy air to her which appeared to be weighing on her more this evening than on previous nights. Her head was bowed, and her eyes were dark with a sorrowful intensity, so much so that Elaine felt compelled to enquire about her wellbeing.

'Are you OK?' she said with true concern. Her words made the cleaner bow her head more deeply, closing up into the shell of herself. 'My name's Elaine,' she continued. She looked for acknowledgement but saw a rapid yet furtive glance in her direction. She smiled. 'Well, I'll let you get on.' The cleaner gave the briefest of smiles, then nodded. She came further into the room, taking a cloth from the pocket of her tunic.

Elaine made to leave. She would need to come back later when the cleaning had been finished. 'It's always neat and tidy in here,' she said, smiling, attempting to reassure the cleaner. This time the cleaner looked at her blankly, pathos displayed on her pallid face. 'Look, are you sure you're OK?' said Elaine firmly. 'Is there anything I can do to help?'

The cleaner looked to be fighting back tears. 'No, thank you,' she replied.

Elaine left, closing the door behind her. She returned to her desk, troubled by the encounter. She was not sure why. It was not because she had been caught in Eric's office. There was no way the cleaner could have suspected anything out of the ordinary. There was something deeper. Perhaps an evolving awareness of the complexity of personal interactions within the hospital. There were so many people who depended on the place for their livelihood, not to mention those who depended on it for their life. She typed some more on her computer but couldn't get the image of the distraught cleaner out of her head.

63.

THE CORRIDOR WAS closed off in its entirety. A sign at each entrance read: *Closed for repairs. Do not enter.* A series of elaborate diversions had been set up to direct people to the wards and offices that had previously been accessed via that route. Long tents ran parallel to (yet some distance from) the crumbling corridor, covering walkways in a fashion which reminded many of a hastily assembled military field hospital. Inside the tented passageways, mud and darkness combined to create a new unholy atmosphere. Temporary lights were strung along the sides and fluorescent markers were taped to the walkway to guide the walkers and trolleys. After a day or so, these markers became invisible, caked with mud and debris from the stomping of those coming in from the inhospitable weather; the very conditions that had made everything so difficult from a construction viewpoint.

Since the moment the builders and architects had arrived to repair the damaged section of the corridor, a whole series of calamitous events had arisen which had culminated in the corridor being closed off. The main concern was the discovery of traces of asbestos within the broken structure, bringing about a new public health scare. Builders in cranes were replaced by officials in protective suits and breathing apparatus. Environmental officers flowed in and out of the hospital gates in their white cars, carrying all manner of devices and gadgets to protect them from an invisible menace. Since asbestos had been a common building material at the time of the corridor's construction, it was assumed that much of the structure contained the toxic substance. Further tents were erected over the crumbling structure in the style of a forensic procedure; they looked similar to those which would hide a body at the scene of a crime. After a day, the hospital resembled a refugee camp with its collection of canvas marquees and its ever-increasing number of vehicles which chewed up the lawns and turned everything around them into a quagmire.

The corridor became a sorry sight. What had been the talking point of the hospital was now its shame. Apart from the collapsed section at the far end which had been the result of the treefall, further parts of the corridor started to slide into disrepair. The midpoint from which the main hospital wards were accessed had started to deteriorate badly and the floor cracked such that a minor sink hole appeared. The roof of the corridor had been removed at that point after having been deemed unsafe, so the elements had wreaked devastation on the structure. Even so, the speed of decline was astonishing; in just a few days, the corridor was barely recognisable as the busy highway it had once been. At an alarming pace, the team of workers and the weather had combined to destroy the central artery of the hospital.

The chief executive, behatted in a bright yellow helmet, the plastic inner digging into her scalp, had been called upon to inspect the damage. She wore a tight face mask which had been fitted using a special machine to ensure no damaging particle would enter the sanctum of her lungs. Her guide was the head of the local construction firm, who was trailed by health and safety teams armed with clipboards and eager to warn of the slightest of transgressions. He spouted facts and figures concerning tensile strengths, amalgams, aggregates and conglomerates. She nodded, not out of understanding but because she lacked the energy to interrogate his words. Whatever the massed groups of experts considered to be the best course of action would be the one they would go for. She was just rubber-stamping, like a politician inspecting the site of a natural disaster: the collapse of a mine or the ruin of a bridge.

The delegation stopped near the tree fall. The large yellow

crane had sunk deeper into the mud and appeared more like an art installation than a functional piece of machinery. The likelihood of it doing any work soon was low. Metres of red and white tape were wrapped around the metal hulk, extending to the fallen tree and the broken walls of the corridor. Signs warning of the danger of impending collapse were everywhere, although the collapse already looked complete. By the side of the tree, a large pile of rubble had appeared, harvested from the breakdown of the structure and set aside for future use, even though the prospect of rebuilding was a distant hope. The chief executive sighed. The man talking in engineering jargon who was leading her had fallen silent for a few moments. A strange solemnity came over the party as they all stood viewing the breakdown before them.

'So, in summary,' the man in the white hard hat said, interrupting the moment, 'the working party has recommended demolition of the whole structure in line with engineering reports and health and safety inspections.' He paused to check the chief executive was taking it in. She mumbled something in the affirmative from behind her mask, and he continued.

There was little else that could be said. The corridor had to go. Just the act of demolition was going to be a major enterprise which would take months and a massive effort. She couldn't bring herself to think about the cost. The reality was that the financial situation of the hospital was no longer something she had any control over. The spreadsheets she inspected on a daily basis were now documents of some alternative world, a series of numbers which bore no relevance to reality.

The rest of the party moved on. The chief executive stayed, surveying the scene. It was similar to events at a funeral: the spouse of the deceased being allowed time alone with their loved one. Yet, she didn't love anything about the hospital anymore. If the whole place had collapsed, there would be no tears shed. She walked on and joined the group.

64.

DR BARNABY SMITHERS, so shaken by the printing of a newspaper article bearing his name, resolved to tighten up his medical practice. The learning of medicine through apprenticeship causes a hazardous relationship between tutor and pupil, and is one in which the tutor takes the blame for the mistakes of the apprentice. Allowing others to prescribe drugs in his name was at the root of the difficulties he now faced concerning the death of Mr Alyoshin. He determined that he would need to oversee the junior doctors in a more proactive way, not allowing changes to the management of patients without his agreement. This would significantly increase his workload. Every Friday he ran a clinic alongside the medical registrar. He or she would see the patients by him or herself and usually, but not always, discuss the management of their patients with him. The amount of oversight he provided varied depending on the seniority of the doctor running the clinic, with senior registrars – those about to become consultants – needing little. The newer ones would discuss everything down to the finest detail, which caused the clinics to overrun. If he were uncertain whether the junior doctor had grasped the true nature of a patient's medical history, then he might need to see the patient himself, thus adding to the late running of the clinic. After the death of Mr Alyoshin, he had decided he would need to see everyone and check everything more thoroughly. The Friday afternoon clinic nurses would not be happy, since it would mean it ran over until the late evening. He saw no other option.

There was much about the practice of medicine which was increasingly troubling Dr Smithers. Despite a move away from old-style paternalism in medicine, the concept was still prevalent, albeit in a weakened form. From the point of view of many patients, having someone knowledgeable and experienced making decisions was comforting and necessary. However, from the medic's standpoint, this could lead to dilemmas and conflict. Clinicians who thought too much about the responsibility this brought tended to veer away from a career making life and death decisions and head for specialities where such judgements were not required. Thus, the hospital wards became concentrated with personalities who felt confident making decisions on behalf of other people, and, some would say, those who felt they knew better than others. It was no different from, say, a car mechanic, who would have a better idea as to whether to scrap a car or to take the effort and cost to repair it. At least, that was what the confident medic would say, at the same time as acknowledging that the stakes were naturally higher in the case of medical decisions.

Occupying the middle ground – making judgements which were felt to be the right ones, yet respecting and seeking the opinion of the patient – involved walking a difficult line. It took only the smallest of shift in momentum to end up off track. So, Dr Smithers found himself doubting his experience and wondering if he had made – or would in the future make – the correct call in matters of life or death. And yet mostly, he wasn't making life-or-death decisions. For the most part, the difficult decisions were whether to treat or not treat, rather than decisions over life itself. Everyone veered towards death, with those presenting to the hospital often nearing the final stages of life, particularly in the field of geriatric medicine. At the very end, most medics were not so arrogant as to think they had much power over reversing the final outcome, at least for the majority of patients. Death marched on. A simplified viewpoint might be that Dr Smithers and his colleagues tinkered around the edges of oblivion, prolonging, buying time. If he thought deeply about it, then that might not be too far off the mark.

He was reminded of a consultation he had conducted with a woman in her eighties shortly after taking up his consultant post. She had been fit and well up until developing a condition which was easily treatable, yet which if not treated would cause her death in a few months. The woman had elected not to be treated for the sole reason that her dog had recently died, and she saw no reason to carry on living. He remembered thinking that this was such a trivial reason to succumb to death. He suggested she got another dog and had the treatment. There was no persuading her and she left, never to be seen again. Dr Smithers, newly promoted to consultant and in his mid-thirties, had been shocked at the time, both at the seemingly flippant attitude of the patient, but also at his inability to provide what he thought was the optimal care for the patient. It had troubled him deeply that he couldn't make the woman see the error of her ways and that he had failed in his duty. As time went on, however, he understood the fragility of the desire for life. In countless others, he comprehended the need to evade unbearable decisions, to reach the end of the journey. The old woman whose dog had died had lived her life and saw no reason to continue with it. That should have been enough.

Yet for every patient like her, who had made peace with their final outcome, thousands fought hard against their illness. It was sometimes his job to tell them that the end was near and there was nothing that could be done. Take Mr Alyoshin. He'd had months to live before the cancer would invade all his organs, causing them to shut down in a slow and, in all likelihood, painful death. One consequence of the drug error was that this outcome had been prevented. His end had been quick and painless. Was that a good death? Random acts and fate had combined to steer his life's voyage, and the drug error had been another step in that journey. It was, perhaps, no different to the random act of one cell deep within his lung, the genetic code of which had instructed it to divide uncontrollably and take on cancerous properties.

Of course, this was nonsense, Dr Smithers told himself. The act of medical negligence had killed the man. Thinking otherwise was the slippery path to all kinds of heinous acts.

65.

FILLING TIME WITH only the dull routine of the day, Muriel Frank sank deeper into despair. Curiously, she had noticed a newfound vigour in the actions of the doctors and nurses treating her. The lacklustre approach to administering her fluids and drugs on time which had crept in over a few weeks was gone. Previously, she had often gone for half a day without fluids being pumped into her veins (for the most part due to the repeated failure of the doctors to put a tube into her veins), which made her feel nauseous and brought on a pounding headache. Drug timings were random and often missed. The attention from her doctors had waned with little more than a cursory inspection of the various machines to which she was attached. For the past few days, however, she had noticed the visits from the consultant had increased in frequency and duration; attention was given to ensuring drugs and fluids were given on time. She had even had a procedure to insert a tube into a major vein deep in her neck – a long line, she had been informed – so that the daily fiasco of stabbing her arm would not be necessary.

No one had discussed with her the reason for this new interest in her wellbeing. Her family, on the occasions of their visits, had mentioned that the doctors were 'going to do all they can' – as though they had hitherto been practising in half-measures. Such was her difficulty in speaking that she was unable to have detailed discussions about her care with them or with the medical teams, other than to nod approval or attempt refusal. She assumed that someone else was consenting to the treatment she was receiving. Her family had told her not to worry about a thing, which she took as faint comfort. The slow hand of fate was moving the pieces in her game of destiny, of which she was merely an onlooker.

The nurses fussed around cheerily, seeing to her every need, but at least they treated her with a degree of civility, talking to her, enquiring about the latest ache or pain. In contrast, the doctors seemed much more focused on the charts at the end of the bed, the degree of swelling in her ankles and the flow of urine into the bag that was hooked over the railings by the side of the bed. She was the central character in a pantomime where people acted around her in a stereotyped way, performing a succession of actions which impacted on her future, speaking a series of asides to the man in charge: Mr Barabas, consultant surgeon, Fellow of the Royal College of Surgeons, untouchable and aloof.

Only ten minutes earlier he had been in with his entourage, barking orders, receiving deference. Questions were asked, some rhetorical, most unanswerable. So long as the responses were those he expected to hear, all was well. The court of the consultant surgeon was indeed sacrosanct. Nurses scuttled more frantically, finding jobs which would negate the need to be present for the duration of the ward round. Junior doctors waited anxiously for the latest order, their mandate of subservience in the name of healing.

Today, however, the junior doctor, the one to whom she had recently spoken to decline his further attempts at cannulation, was combative. There was a frisson between him and his master. They had addressed each other in strained terms, still professional, yet displaying the deep contempt each had for the other. Words were few, barbed, and confined to those necessary to convey the message. The younger doctor accepted what he was asked to do through a barrier of reticence.

Muriel Frank, an observer of their dispute, had no idea of the central part she took in the drama. To her, she had little significance to them, was a nuisance; one who needed a little plastic tube repeatedly to be inserted and one for whom daily notes were written, the documentation of a life in decline.

The other character who was central to the drama sat in her office, oblivious of the goings-on in the side room of Ward 19. The chief executive had never met Muriel Frank, nor was she likely to. She had no interest in the nitty-gritty of the woman's care, but the overriding principle of Muriel's management was central to the survival of the hospital. Or at least she thought that to be the case. Any more scandal regarding patients dying out of neglect or, worse still, some form of euthanasia, would be terminal to the reputation of the hospital. She had instructed several consultants to pay closer attention to their more perilous patients to ensure any accusation of mistreatment could be avoided. Some had taken this as an affront to their professionality but saw the bigger picture as soon as the threat of their name being emblazoned across the headlines was pointed out to them. That would do such damage to their private practice.

66.

ACCUSATIONS, RUMOURS AND counteraccusations occupied the small talk of many within the hospital. John Such, rising above these matters, struggled not to be drawn into divulging anything more concerning his suspicions. He had talked to Eric, but that was like talking to a brick wall. He was, by now, convinced of the guilt of his secretary. One of the night cleaners with whom he had no more than a vague acquaintance had told him that Elaine spent a considerable amount of time in Eric's office of an evening and into the early hours of the morning. She was clearly snooping for something. The pieces of the jigsaw fitted together. Or was he bashing them together where no match existed? He needed to tell the chief executive but knew that this might be a difficult conversation given their recent history in matters concerning the newspaper leak. Although the majority of her time was now occupied with overseeing the destruction of the corridor, she remained preoccupied with unearthing the culprit behind the leaks.

The two met, the chief executive effusive in her welcome, noticeably different in her manner from their previous encounter. She asked her secretary to bring in coffee and biscuits, a peace offering to make up for the aforementioned unpleasantness.

'So, John,' she started, 'how are things with you?'

John Such smiled briefly and nodded. Not being one to hold grudges, he was determined to forge a new professional atmosphere. After all, the hospital was at crisis point, and there was a genuine threat to both their jobs.

'I'm doing OK,' he replied. 'And you?'

The two exchanged further pleasantries before getting on to the matter in hand.

'I'm concerned that Elaine, you know … my new secretary,' he clarified after he detected a lack of recognition in the chief executive. She nodded.

'I think she might be behind the newspaper leaks.' The chief executive sat up on hearing this.

'What makes you say that?' she asked meekly, scratching her left forearm nervously.

John Such could see that she was uncomfortable. Perhaps he shouldn't have brought it up. Perhaps he was acting as foolishly as she had acted when accusing him.

'Maybe I'm wrong,' he muttered, wishing wholeheartedly to retract his accusation, just as she had done a day or two earlier.

The chief executive stood up and walked to the window. She surveyed the scene outside: churned up lawns, dumper trucks parked indiscriminately, piles of rubble and tents in the process of falling down.

'This is such a terrible mess,' she said, referring to the newspaper stories and all that had followed, although she could have been referring to numerous other recent occurrences. She continued to stare out of the window, addressing him with her back turned. 'I just don't know what to do about it.'

John Such was silent. He was still angry following her hurtful accusation but knew that she was trying to open up to him. Turning to him, the chief executive continued, 'Do you think it was that woman?' she said, getting back to the original conversation.

John Such shrugged. 'Who knows?' he replied quietly.

The chief executive sat down again, straightening some papers on her desk. 'Does any of this matter anymore, John?' she asked in a tone that was forced, against her nature.

'Well, I guess we need to root out anyone in the team who is acting against the interest of the hospital,' he responded, although he wondered if perhaps she expected him to capitulate with her.

There was no response from the chief executive.

'Look,' he continued, 'if Elaine is feeding information to the papers, then we need to stop it immediately. This is causing untold harm to the hospital, and with the health authority breathing down our necks, we are on thin ice. I'm really fearful that we will all go under if we don't get on top of this.'

He felt like he was talking to a boxer in a corner, urging her to go out for the final round despite losing all previous rounds on points.

Suddenly she smiled and, as though a switch had been thrown, sat up to attention. 'Yes, you are right, of course,' she said decisively. 'We'll fight this. Together.'

She extended her hand to John Such in a gesture of truce. He shook it, and the two connected once again.

'You know what I saw today?' said the chief executive, now a different persona to the one who had greeted John Such when he had entered the office only five minutes ago.

John Such shook his head. 'What?' he asked.

'A fox … a blooming fox!' she chortled. 'Right outside the window, sniffing around in all the debris out here. No doubt the workmen had thrown their sandwiches into the pile of rubble.'

John Such smiled.

67.

MATT BUTCHER FINALLY made it up to the summit of the hill which bordered the eastern side of the valley. An unexpected day off had given him the opportunity for leisure time, and he had decided to explore the local area. He thought back to his previous attempt at the climb, late one evening, which he had abandoned due to the dark and to the treacherous nature of the terrain. But now it was a fine day, the late winter light brighter than on previous days. He had set off after a good breakfast, packing provisions for the day ahead. He had planned once again to walk up the eastern hill and from there to walk the half mile across the moor to the pub in the village of Old Efterton. He had calculated that by the time he reached the pub, which was known throughout the region for its fine cuisine, it would be lunchtime.

At the top of the hill, the panoramic view of the valley unfurled before him. He saw the town, the main road snaking alongside the river and, of course, the hospital. It was an unexpected sight, since the dominant feature which could be seen from such a distance was the rows of canvas tents, dirty grey blending into the surrounding ploughed-up brown earth. Diminutive vehicles dotted the scene, looking redundant and out of place. The bright yellow crane adjacent to the fallen tree trunk was poised for action, its lifting apparatus angled towards the obstacle it was due to remove. To the left of the tents was a temporary car park, now full of multicoloured oblongs, shining in the misty light. The main hospital buildings now seemed insignificant compared to the building works. From this vantage point, the scene was of a construction (or, more appropriately, destruction) site rather than of a place to cure the sick. The only activity was mechanical; glinting steel and earthworks.

He pressed on, leaving the view of the hospital behind him, and after a short time reached the level fields and the footpath leading to Old Efterton. The village was small, with an old-world style so favoured by tourists who sought a glimpse into simpler times. There were few houses, but they presented a solidity of stonework capped with dull orange roof tiles or fading thatch. In the central village street, a shop selling everything of necessity in such parts, a tearoom with frayed lace curtains, and the pub, his destination, were the only hospitality establishments. The pub was double-fronted with two large windows, one on either side of the solid black door, which was slightly ajar. The name of the pub: *The Harridan*, was painted in large old font above the lintel. A sign featuring the grotesque character referred to in the pub's name swung from a gallows-like structure next to the door.

He pushed the door and entered. Inside, the warming aroma of fermented hops greeted him, which at once made him think of ordering a pint of beer. This olfactory reflex was exclusive to his visits to public houses; he never felt the desire to drink beer at home. He approached the bar and stood, one foot on the rail which ran along the bottom of the bar, his hands palm-down on the shiny bar top. He could see the bartender, who was busy attending to some barrels in the yard, through the open door behind the bar. Waiting patiently, he looked around the room. It was a gloomy place, the decor dark and the windows small. On the wall were a series of framed prints featuring witches in various outlandish garbs, a reference to the name of the inn. A large painting above the fireplace, now dormant, showed a coven of three witches, seemingly referring to Macbeth's famous trio. It was illuminated from below, which cast dark shadows of the frame up the wall.

The bartender appeared and accepted the order of a pint of

beer. Matt Butcher took a menu which lay on the bar and perused the offerings. It was standard food fare, yet at an inflated price to cater for the passing tourist trade. The bartender returned with the drink, which was received gratefully by the thirsty walker, who continued to study the menu. To the side of the bar in a dingy corner, Matt Butcher noticed two men drinking and tucking into a meal of fish and chips. On closer inspection, he realised it was Mr Barabas and Mr Massoud, consultant surgeons from the hospital. He should have taken the fancy BMW in the pub's car park, registration BAS1, as a warning that they were there. It was all he needed. He had no desire to talk to work colleagues, since his sojourn over the mountain had been designed as an escape. He turned his back away from the two, certain that he had not been spotted. Would they recognise him anyway? He was just a junior doctor, one of many, a minion in the grand hierarchy of medical circles. He gestured to the bartender and ordered steak before heading over to an empty table at the opposite end of the inn, behind a wooden screen.

His last encounter with Mr Barabas had been fraught. He had broken the age-old dictum which stated that senior consultants should not be questioned. It was a form of infallibility presiding over the decision-making of all hospitals. He had not been back at work since the encounter with his consultant colleague and the subsequent encounter with Muriel Frank. The emotions were fresh in his mind, as he had had little time to process them. Part of the reason for taking the trip over to the other side of the valley had been to clear his head, to make sense of what had happened. The reminder sitting in the same room was unwelcome.

He supped more beer and sighed deeply. In the gloom of the pub, there was little else to concern him, so his thoughts turned to events on Ward 19. He was most troubled by the interaction with Muriel Frank in which she had refused further attempts at cannulation of her veins. It was his umpteenth encounter with her, yet the first in which he had heard her voice, her opinion.

That was his failing. He had assumed her beyond conscious thought, so had not sought out her opinion. She had been an object, a body to be kept alive. He was vaguely aware that the nurses spoke to her, but had dismissed this as fantasy, not wishing to challenge his own conceptions. In hindsight, he was mystified as to why this would be. He had been sucked into the machinery of surgical management, viewing the body as a series of pipes and rods which needed to be cleaned out or nailed together. This was the ethos he had entertained ever since medical school, the days of cadavers and endless facts about death and dying. Perhaps it was a mechanism of survival; a way not to have to contemplate too deeply the horrors of illness. Perhaps it was just arrogance. The moment Muriel Frank had spoken to him, coupled with the words and behaviour of Mr Barabas, had changed him, of that he had no doubt.

His steak came and, at the same time, he noticed that the two senior surgeons, having finished their meals, were leaving the inn. Mr Massoud laughed loudly and slapped his colleague on the back as the two disappeared through the door.

68.

THE DAY OF the official unveiling of the *Star of Thanks*, the artistic tribute to health workers, had arrived. Previous concerns over protesters causing a spectacle outside the hospital had gone but had been replaced by much larger problems. The original site for the ceremony was now a broken-down structure containing mud, rubble and the risk of asbestos poisoning, so the unveiling would be performed in the canteen. Whether the actual art installation would fit under the low ceilings of the canteen was a cause of worry for the artist. She had contacted hospital officials on several occasions after she had heard of the relocation of her creation but had got the sense from them that her artistic concerns were of little importance. Emboldened by a spirit of duty, she pressed on with making the best of a bad deal. Duly, on the day before the ceremony she arrived at the hospital with a van containing the *Star of Thanks* in pieces to be assembled on site. She was greeted with such an eyesore, however, that she was no longer sure she wanted to present her work to the public in such a place. It really was as though a bomb had gone off. She inspected the canteen where, she had been told, the artwork was now to be housed, but found a dingy and damp room tightly packed with tables and benches and an assortment of foul-smelling machines churning out a variety of brown liquids.

The artist despaired. However, since the piece had been commissioned and, more importantly, paid for, she had no choice but to construct the installation in whatever form she could. A hospital official, introducing himself as 'Fitz from procurement', had been sent to the canteen to help her, and between them they pieced together the yellow statue. Fitz, having no concept of what it was meant to look like when assembled, struggled with its construction. In addition, the artist was taciturn and grumpy because she considered the hospital officials to be disrespectful of the work. She mumbled continually about the insult of making her erect it in such an environment. When they came to piece together the final fragments, it became apparent that the ceiling was indeed too low, so the artist had to bend the frame on which the papier mâché had been applied, making the top spike of the star curl forwards at a strange angle. The artist, having lost all sense of integrity, no longer cared, and resigned herself to the imperfection of creativity. It looked nothing like her original design, and its resemblance to a star was minimal. People not knowing what it was supposed to look like was probably for the best, she reasoned.

They worked until late, and the next day both the artist and Fitz arrived for the ceremony. A host of local dignitaries pitched up, crammed into the communal room, which had been closed for the breakfast, the tables and benches stacked against the walls. Both Jim Spier and the chief executive were there, ready with speeches and words of encouragement. John Such, who was standing at the back taking photographs, noticed that the chief executive's shoes were caked in mud. Jim Spier was the first to speak, his words coming out with a hiss as a result of the hastily requisitioned and faulty microphone. He spoke of seeing the artwork (which he barely looked at) as a sign that the hospital would rise up from its troubles and give new life to the community, or something like that. The chief executive listened in disbelief, in full knowledge that his words were the opposite of his intended actions. As he handed the microphone over to the chief executive, he winked and touched her arm which put her off what she was intending to say. Instead, she merely thanked the artist, cut the ribbon which was loosely placed on the sculpture, and shrunk back into the background.

John Such took photos of the various dignitaries in front of the *Star of Thanks*. He stood next to the photographer from *The Herald* but didn't speak to him. The presence of representatives from the newspaper was infuriating to the hospital management, yet was tolerated in the hope that it might provide a positive story about the hospital for once.

Looking at the monstrosity that was the *Star of Thanks*, the chief executive was fairly certain they would spin the story into bad news. The main problem, she thought, was that it didn't really look like a star. She wasn't sure what it represented; maybe a dead canary? The campaign to give thanks to health workers during difficult times was well-meant and had given a morale boost to the hospital's workforce. Children placing images of gold stars in their windows, simply and innocently made, was the main aim. The spectacle occurring in the ruins of the hospital was hijacking good will and appeared tacky. *They couldn't even get this right*, thought the chief executive, noticing that *The Herald*'s photographer was packing away his cameras ready to leave.

After the last of the luminaries had left, John Such went over to talk to the chief executive. She had been talking to the artist, who was now busy repairing a section of the artwork which had been damaged after Jim Spier had tripped over the wires keeping it in place. The chief executive was still upset at the manner in which Jim Spier had handed the microphone over to her. 'That went well, I think,' said John Such, not sounding confident.

The chief executive shook her head. 'That man!' she muttered, clenching the fist of her right hand as if ready to impart a blow to the very concept of overweight middle-aged men in management. He was winning a battle she had no desire to fight. Combative and weighty, he didn't mind on whom his aggression was foisted. The thrill of fighting was half the excitement.

'He's a bad lot,' said John Such, showing solidarity with his boss.

'That's an understatement,' she replied, still agitated. 'I don't know what his game is, but it's looking bad for the hospital.'

'Really?' he asked, an urgency to his voice.

'I tell you, John, even before this wretched business in the papers, the hospital was on its last legs. We haven't even talked about the ten percent savings question since this fiasco began. That's been thrown out while we firefight all the other nonsense,' she replied.

John Such shuddered. The chief executive was not one for scaremongering.

'But the hospital has to survive for the community.'

'I wouldn't count on it,' said the chief executive, quietly and without feeling.

The two colleagues were now the only ones left in the canteen. Behind them, they heard a crashing sound as the *Star of Thanks* crumpled to the ground like a collapsed soufflé.

69.

THE CHIEF EXECUTIVE knew that she wouldn't have to wait long for her next encounter with Jim Spier. The following day was the board meeting of the local health authority. She walked from her home to the headquarters, that fine stately home on the outskirts of town. Her route took her though the wooded riverside path and up to the elevated glade from where she could see the house in all its splendour and opulence. The going was hard by the river, the path churned up by the combination of heavy rain and dog walkers. Planning ahead, she had worn boots and over-trousers, carrying her work clothes in her rucksack. She looked a sight and dreaded to think what her style consultant would make of her. She wouldn't bother seeing her again anyway, so what did it matter? The superficiality of the consultant's stance was intolerable, and the chief executive would be glad not to have to deal with her again.

At one point on the path, a small tributary of the river had appeared *de novo*, crossing the walkway, such that a leap was required to continue. Missing her footing by a fraction, her back foot landed in the stream, causing water to enter her boot, soaking her sock. A shudder of cold came over her as she extracted the boot from the underlying mud. As uncomfortable as it was, she knew that a wet sock was the least of her troubles.

The difficulty of her journey and the need to change her clothes resulted in her being the last person to enter the meeting room. She checked the clock and was reassured that she had made it with a minute to spare. The chairman called them to order and began the meeting as soon as she had sat down.

'We're all here now, I think, so let's begin,' said Pras Lolpara, chair of the board, looking over his low-slung glasses at the assembled group, then looking at the agenda before him.

'Firstly, apologies. As you can see, Jim is not here today. He has been called away to an urgent meeting with the Department of Health, so has sent Fraser to deputise. Welcome, Fraser.' He nodded at a young man bearing red acne scars on his face and dressed in a tight-fitting suit. Fraser smiled back.

The chief executive, her gaze directed to the papers in front of her, gave a jolt and looked around. She hadn't noticed that her tormentor wasn't in the room when she had entered. The imaginings of her sleepless night, which she had spent worrying about their next encounter, would not come to fruition. But the sense of relief in his absence was short-lived when she considered, in her now deeply paranoid mind, the reasons for him having urgent meetings at the heart of government. She knew that his absence would inflict further psychological blows on her fragile psyche. Whatever he did, he now held her firmly in his power, like a cat pressing its paw down on a wounded bird.

Fraser had been sent to deliver the latest musings from the health authority's reshuffled priorities. Jim Spier's deputy was being moulded in his image, a frightening prospect for future generations. He had breezed through public school, redbrick university, management school and the health service's accelerated management scheme which made clones of civil servants who were not afraid to deliver bad news or unpopular policies in the interests of progress. The fact that this new breed of managers had never worked in the lower echelons of healthcare, as nurses or allied healthcare workers, for example, was viewed in negative terms by the majority of those who had risen through the ranks and knew what was going on at ground level. This scepticism was ignored by the newcomers, since they had been tutored in the best way to manage and had several university degrees to prove it.

The agenda dragged on. Shortly after tea break, Jim Spier's

report on reorganisation within the health authority was distributed to the attendees in the form of a two-sided piece of paper, bullet-pointed and typed in a small, hard-to-read font. Fraser was given the floor and started to go through the salient features of the report.

'Firstly, apologies that you were not sent this before, but it has only just been completed,' he began, focusing on the paper in front of him. *That's a lie*, thought the chief executive. She knew that this method of introducing controversial topics at the last minute, halfway through a meeting, was intended to reduce levels of scrutiny.

'The audit into the sustainability of our local hospitals has raised a number of important points.'

The chief executive was only half-listening; she was frantically looking down the list of bullet point to decipher the messages therein. She heard words such as 'sustainability' and 'cost-effectiveness' interlaced with the management consultant jargon which Fraser had acquired during his extensive training. At the bottom of the page, she read the final recommendation: *Merger between two acute healthcare hospitals*. This would mean that one of the two hospitals in the region would close, and services would be transferred to the other. Given that this was a decision that would be overseen by Jim Spier, the chief executive had no doubt as to the fate of her own hospital.

The speaker rambled on, but the chief executive found it hard to concentrate. She was imagining the possibilities of a new job, a new life. An enforced change was likely to be coming. She could move away from the region, put the whole sorry episode of managing the hospital behind her. She had options, she told herself.

The chair of the board shuffled his papers noisily, becoming agitated as Fraser skirted around the issues.

'Fraser, can I interrupt you? As time is short, can you summarise the main recommendations for us?'

Fraser looked at the chair, affronted at the interruption. He checked his notes.

'OK. Well, the bottom line is that we need to amalgamate services to reduce repetition of work. The two main hospitals should merge to a single site. That site will be developed to cater for the needs of the expanded services and the other hospital site sold off to generate capital for investment.'

The chief executive exchanged a glance with her counterpart from the neighbouring hospital. It was his or her power which was being taken away.

The room went quiet. Most were expecting something like this, but to see it in black and white in front of them and delivered so dispassionately by the acne-scarred individual just out of management school brought home to them all the certainty of what was about to happen.

Pras Lolpara broke the silence and asked the question – an obvious question, yet one for which most present had had little time to prepare, the enormity of the answer being so far-reaching. 'So which hospital is to close?'

Fraser raised his eyebrows and subconsciously shifted his gaze in the direction of the chief executive.

70.

Seated upon the crest of an ancient burial mound, Eric contemplated his future. Underneath him, centuries-old men and women were interred, victims of the injustices of former times. Feudal laws and pestilence had been their challenges; random acts of whimsical men or the spread of unseen plagues. His challenges were less tangible, but no less virulent. The complex order into which society had evolved led to questions and disputes which were a world removed from The Danelaw, whose subjects lay in repose beneath him, freed from the horrors of their time.

The valley was covered in a dense, low-lying mist, and a muffled rumble from the nearby road hung in the air. The grass of the hillfort sparkled with the early morning dew. Eric shivered. His ears, exposed to the elements, had gone beyond the point of cold and were now burning. He thought back to a medical talk he had attended in the hospital. He had arrived early for a management lecture and caught the end of a presentation from a local pathologist, in which he described the final moments of the man who had ended up on his slab. The unfortunate man had fallen into a river in the depths of winter. Having managed to drag himself out, he had become severely hypothermic and, being in the middle of nowhere, had been unable to find shelter or dryness. The pathologist had described the unusual phenomenon of those who had gone beyond the stages of hypothermia who, imagining themselves to be burning up, took action to cool down. The paradox of the terminally cold meant that the man was found completely naked on the coldest night of the year. It was hard to imagine that such a thing was true. Strange things happened.

Eric rubbed his gloved hands together and pulled his woollen hat down lower to cover his ears more effectively. In the hedges which bordered the edge of the Carthen Ridge, a network of white, lacy cobwebs was visible, highlighted by the frost. Three large black crows sat atop the skeletal outlines of the trees further off towards the valley. A further crow glided in the air above him, watchful for any activity on the ground below or the threat of a larger bird. At the base of the hedges, rabbits scurried in and out of passages and hollows, minimising their time on the exposed turf.

He had come to the hill fort that morning before work to clear his mind. The beauty of nature and the acknowledgement of the past put his current predicament in its place. Like those who studied far off galaxies in order to confirm their own insignificance, Eric found the calm of ancient landscapes to be a leveller. His thoughts still played in his head, but they were tempered by the environment. He would need to set off for work shortly, he thought, surveying the view in front of him once more. In the hospital he would again be confronted with the latest policy shifts. His role as director of transformation had been all but forgotten as he focused on the pandemic planning. He was nearing the end of ensuring all the documents and operating procedures were in place should another pandemic happen. The threat of crescent moon disease had abated, and the Department of Health had downgraded the threat to the status of: *Be vigilant*. The chaos of healthcare management equated this to: *Forget about it for now*. He needed to finish what he had started, however, and was glad to have had the project to focus on while so much else was going on.

He now spent less time thinking about the newspaper leak and the image of his writing which had appeared on the front page of the papers. Whether it was acceptance or denial, his strategy for reducing the angst the incident had caused was working. Others seemed more vexed by the issue. The chief executive was going out of her mind. Eric saw little of her now: she was either holed up in her office or working off site. He was glad of that, since he detected a high degree of animosity from her. He sensed her assumption of his guilt, despite her reassuring words. He had felt vilified from the moment the newspaper had printed the story, so had gone out of his way to avoid her. She didn't request his presence or his reports anymore. He wondered whether she had lost the spirit for survival. He wouldn't be surprised if she were to announce her resignation in the very near future.

Casting his mind back six months or so to when he had first met the chief executive, he thought about how the situation could not be more different. He had been heartened by her enthusiasm and her attitude. As a boss, he had liked her. The chaos which had unfurled over the past few weeks was as unthinkable as it was unpredictable. It was now evident that Elaine Stewart, the mysterious secretary who had appeared and broken the mould, was responsible for feeding the board meeting minutes and the damning photograph to the papers. Whether she worked for *The Herald* or had merely been opportunistic was unclear. John Such had laid out the evidence, and Eric had no reason not to believe him. Oddly, the discovery of the culprit had left him cold. On the day of the newspaper story's publication, he had wanted a form of vengeance. But as time went on, he placed less emphasis on revealing the identity of the perpetrator. It mattered little. What had happened had happened. Fatalism was the only state of mind which had got him through. Feeling bitter and hard done by was counterproductive.

Above him he noticed that the circling crow was now mobbing a buzzard occupying the same sky. The larger bird was threatened by the crow and dodged its attacks by tacking and jibing high above the ridge. The crow vocalised its disapproval of the bird of prey and, as if it were a call to arms, the three crows in the tree flew up in reinforcement. The buzzard was outnumbered and swooped lower to escape the attack. Their mission accomplished, the four crows then flew back to the tree and settled.

Eric, his feet numb with the cold, stood up and headed back to his car for the journey to work.

71.

Mo Kane and Elaine Stewart met in a coffee shop on the edge of town. It was quiet for a Friday morning, groups of mothers who would usually gather there after the school run having been denied their morning meeting due to a teacher training day. The coffee shop itself was one of a large chain, branches of which could be found in every high street across the land, offering a wide range of drinks and pastries at inflated prices but with comfortable chairs.

Elaine had arrived first and ordered herself a large coffee, not feeling able to wait until her colleague's arrival due to a headache which indicated caffeine deficiency. He was often late, running on a schedule which was, to Elaine's mind, unnecessarily hectic. She sat down and drank the reviving liquid, checking her phone for the latest information for the day: a series of messages in her inbox, mostly inconsequential. Before long, the dishevelled figure of Mo Kane appeared. He gave the impression to those around him that he had no time for sartorial matters. He was happy to go along with the ruse that he spent all day and all night at his desk, breaking rarely and certainly not having time for domestic chores such as ironing clothes. In reality, he spent much of his time in betting shops and amusement arcades, a vice all at *The Herald* knew about, but none mentioned, keeping up the pretence of his unadulterated industry. He lived a chaotic life and an impoverished one, thanks to his addiction to losing money in improbable transactions. No one knew where he lived or whether he had a partner. It was irrelevant to ask. He was a newspaper journalist, and now editor, and that was that.

Mo Kane sat down. He had purchased a Danish pastry topped with purple jam, on which he started to munch greedily, spreading flakes of pastry on his lap and the floor around him. Elaine waited politely for him to finish. The clock in the corner of the room displayed the time of half past nine. He was on time, at least.

'Elaine,' he said after dispatching the last of his breakfast, 'what's the latest?'

Elaine put down her coffee and stroked her chin. 'I'm not getting that far with the finance records,' she said. 'They simply don't make much sense.'

Mo Kane raised his eyebrows: 'What do you mean?'

'Well, the filing system is so bad, I just can't find the right files. There is something fishy going on, but I'm not sure whether it's just incompetence.'

Mo Kane sat back in his chair and more crumbs fell to the floor. 'What about the missing finance meeting's minutes? Have you found those?' he asked.

Elaine shook her head.

Mo Kane made a low mumbling sound, clearly of disapproval, and then fell silent. Elaine wasn't sure there was much more to say. She wanted to get out of the hospital. She had no desire to continue what she saw as a fruitless and destructive process, digging up dirt where none should be dug. She had resolved to tell him today that she was not prepared to do it anymore. The silence amplified her discomfort.

'Look, Mo,' she began, sitting forward, 'we've known each other for a while now, and I've always tried to do my best for the paper. I just don't think I can do this anymore.' She took a further gulp of coffee. 'It's not working. I really don't think there is anything in the idea that there is embezzlement going on now. There is no evidence.' She stopped, waiting for, but not expecting, a response. 'I really want to make it work. I am really grateful for the opportunity you gave me to work on this, but I've got to …' She hesitated. 'It's got to stop,' she said quietly, looking down at her coffee, half-empty on the crumb-dusted table.

Mo Kane, expressionless, took a deep breath and stretched his body, raising his arms high above his head, before slumping back once more. He grimaced, pouting his lips, then interlaced his fingers, getting ready to speak.

'Move back to the killing story,' he said decisively, after some thought.

'What?' Elaine snapped, not hiding her dismay at the suggestion. 'What do you mean?' she asked, even though she knew exactly to what he was referring.

Mo Kane remained impassive. 'It is a great story, and it can run. Why not?' he asked.

Elaine was annoyed at the flippancy of his decision-making. 'And what exactly do you want me to do? Drag the doctors and nurses through some jumped-up allegations? It was a cheap shot in the first place.'

Mo Kane stood up, indicating his reluctance to hear her protestations any further.

'We are in the business of selling papers. That's it. If you don't like it then you know what you have to do.' And with that he left.

Elaine was left to finish the remainder of her drink alone. She was not surprised by the actions of her editor. His reputation was for abruptness and rudeness. She worried that she hadn't handled the situation well, since she was keen to carry on working for the newspaper – for career reasons but mostly for financial reasons. The job she had obtained in the hospital would soon be over; she would leave before they were able to prove any substantial wrongdoing. And then where would she be? *The Herald*'s management (which was, in effect, Mo Kane) would sling her out as soon as they were done with her. If she didn't play their game, she was of no use to them.

She looked back at the clock. Their meeting had lasted less than five minutes. She knew she was through with Mo Kane and his unscrupulous ways. She had been foolish to think that her foray into investigative journalism would result in some good. It had had the opposite effect. It had just made the staff within the hospital unhappy and paranoid, and it had made her feel like an outsider. The whole experience had been a disaster. She finished her coffee.

72.

RESISTING THE URGE to walk away, to never set foot in the hospital again, the chief executive arrived at the management offices the next morning. Her professional life had become so full of turmoil that she vacillated between subjugation and struggle. In the former scenario, Jim Spier would win, and she would walk away from the place before it dragged her further under. In the latter, she would fight for her job, her career and to steer the organisation in the direction she desired, ultimately leading it from the mire in which it now found itself and onto greater success. She had read somewhere that in times of crisis, the mind goes into self-preservation mode. Blinded to the array of negative outcomes, a person focuses on the mundane, achieving small victories: doing the laundry, catching a bus, arriving on time for a meeting. In time, the threat of disaster either goes away or engulfs the person, in which case the fall-back position is to reject the cause of the crisis and settle into the mindset of not wanting to continue fighting anyway. The humdrum allows for an excuse to be made, a get-out clause that life continues despite everything.

She wasn't ready to give in, however – not just yet. Her fighting spirit was emboldened by the need to win the battle of the two hospitals. She felt deeply that the hospital should survive. It was the right choice for the community and the staff. And, anyway, this was what she was programmed to do, to fight the big battles and to win.

Jan Marling, her secretary, entered her office after the chief executive had taken off her coat and switched her computer on. She brought coffee and problems, a list of firefighting issues to be tackled that day, ready to be ticked off or, mostly, postponed until another day. Whatever was on offer, the agenda had changed dramatically, once again, with the threat of closure now being a very real prospect.

Jan put down the coffee and took a seat.

'How are you this morning, Jan?' the chief executive asked. Jan smiled and replied that she was fine.

'And how is Tony?' The chief executive knew that Jan's husband had been sick recently but was not sure of the exact nature of his ailment.

'Yes, he's on the mend. Thanks,' replied Jan, looking at her list in front of her, eager to get started on tackling the current issues.

The chief executive smiled. 'That's good news,' she said.

'I've got today's meetings and phone calls here,' said Jan, brandishing a sheet of paper. The chief executive took the paper and placed it on her desk.

'Before we start, Jan,' she said, 'have you heard about the possible merger of the two hospitals that was announced at yesterday's board meeting?'

'Yes, I had heard talk of it,' replied the secretary. Nothing got past her. She knew all the latest conspiracies and chatter.

'Well, what do you think about it?' asked the chief executive. Perhaps she was looking for reassurance from the person in the management offices who had been there the longest. She must have seen it all before: threatened closures, crisis after crisis. But the response from her secretary was far from comforting.

'I suppose these are uncertain times,' she replied.

The chief executive sat back in her chair. 'I guess so,' she muttered. What did it matter to Jan now? She was a year or two away from retirement, and if the chance came for an earlier redundancy, she would be crazy not to take it. She viewed the closure of the hospital with indifference. Yet the chief executive wanted Jan to tell her how the hospital had survived numerous previous threats of closure and each time had come back stronger.

'Shall we go through the complaints that came in yesterday?' asked Jan, taking the top off a ball point pen, ready to take notes.

The chief executive was in no rush. There would be no more complaints when the hospital closed.

'What do you really think, Jan? About the closure?' she asked, exposing a vulnerability in her position. 'What should we … I … do about it?'

Jan put the lid back on her pen and looked at the chief executive, who was now a different person to the one who had first sat behind the desk. Her grand plan for revolutionising the way the hospital ran was now in tatters around her. She saw a woman fighting for her job, fighting against the forces which were meant to be assisting her.

'It depends on whether you've got the stomach for the fight,' said Jan, candidly.

The chief executive did not respond, instead staring out of the window to the hills beyond. What was she fighting for? For the patients who lay in the beds? For the relatives who complained day in, day out about the standard of care bestowed on their loved ones? For the doctors who resented her? For the others in management who didn't listen?

Jan took up her pen again, poised to write, keen to get on with the morning's duties as quickly as possible. She had witnessed the unravelling of a previous chief executive in all its angst and barefaced shame. Strangely, she felt no compassion for either of them. They both had human sides and treated her well, but there was a coldness, an eagerness to accept the hierarchies of the hospital, a determination which she knew would take no prisoners should the need arise. If another chief executive fell, then so be it. It was a job that no one could do with any hope of achieving an outcome other than to keep the status quo. That was a job in itself. Medicine marched on with amazing breakthroughs and heart-warming stories, yet the view from the ground was diminishing budgets and rising expectations from the public.

Each chief executive had a shelf-life, and the time had come early for the current one. Whether through a series of uncontrollable circumstances or greed, time was called on each one.

73.

A FURTHER CURIOUS architectural feature of the hospital, aside from the extra-long corridor, now half-collapsed, was a drilled-out tunnel running beneath the main block and extending further under the car park, emerging via a staircase in the security office by the hospital gates. From this main passageway, rooms and cupboards had been fashioned, the majority of which were now storerooms for medical supplies or for noxious chemicals that needed to be hidden from view. A common rumour concerning the tunnel was that it had been constructed as a bunker for the use of local dignitaries in the event of war. When built, the town lay close to steel works and aircraft manufacturers, so the threat of attack from air raid was high. The security of being under a hospital was perhaps the reason for its location, since even an enemy wouldn't be evil enough to bomb a hospital. However, the allegation was not substantiated by fact, and the true reasons for the tunnel were not known, some considering it merely a folly of hospital architects who wished to incorporate as many unusual building designs as possible in a simpler time when things like that were possible and budgetary restrictions were less.

A subterranean band of workers, most clad in dirty brown coats and thick gloves because of the cold, damp nature of the working conditions, spent much of their time down there, checking orders and issuing supplies to the world above. If a ward required some boxes of face masks or disposable aprons, a receptionist or a student nurse would be sent down to the gloom with a shopping list to be checked off and dispatched with grudging disinterest. These were the unseen and unpraised, out of the limelight, yet vital in the vast healthcare machine.

Occasionally, management descended the steep staircase into the underground realm to check on the supply chain or to use it as a short cut (avoiding the rain) to the security office. More rarely still, the chief executive went down to conduct a walkabout; to show her face in all parts of her dominion. Since the problems of the hospital had escalated she had, however, taken daily perambulations along the length of the tunnel, perhaps as an escape from the stresses above. The workers in the tunnel paid little attention to her. It was questionable whether some of them knew who she was. It distracted them little from their duties, earphones in place, listening to the latest music trends, scurrying about like moles, their eyes well-adapted to the gloaming.

It was an ideal place to take a few minutes away from the chaos of the management offices; minutes that the chief executive needed in abundance. No one questioned her or bothered her with the minutiae of checks and balances or the latest staff shortages. She could be bunkered and anonymous. It was to her surprise, therefore, that on this occasion she came face to face with the figure of Elaine Stewart, emerging from a store cupboard, wearing a thick coat, a coarse grey bag slung over her shoulder.

The chief executive, instantly and subconsciously experiencing an explosion of anger generated by the trauma of the past few days, stopped dead in her tracks. Her head started to throb instantaneously, and she felt a tight constriction in her neck, accompanied by a rising feeling from her stomach, a form of nausea, deep-seated, in need of release. She pointed at the shoulder bag, which was bulging, a wedge of documents visible from the aperture, and, in a menacing tone, shouted, 'What have you got in there?'

Elaine Stewart flinched, as though under attack. She clutched the bag as a reflex action, the threat of the woman making her guard its contents.

'What?' Elaine asked, still squinting to identify her accuser. The neon lights illuminating the underground passage cast a shadow over the face of the chief executive making her features hard to determine. Taking a step closer, the chief executive came into full view.

'Chief exec!' said Elaine, surprised, yet standing her ground.

'What have you got in there?' repeated the chief executive, her tone no less accusatory.

'What are you talking about?' Elaine replied.

'In the bag.' The chief executive pointed vigorously, waving her finger, which trembled at its tip.

Elaine looked down at the bag, then clutched it closer to her.

'Don't talk to me like that,' she replied in a stern, confident voice.

The chief executive was enraged, pressing forward as if to seize the offending bag. At that moment, a man in a blue coat and woolly hat entered the passageway, momentarily diffusing the situation, snapping the chief executive out of her blinkered fury. She paused to compose herself, fighting her base instincts.

The man, clearly in no mood for conflict, darted into a side room, slamming the door, leaving the two women alone once again. The light above flickered and made a faint hissing sound.

Elaine continued to clutch the bag close to her body.

The chief executive, now deflated and ashamed of her outburst, sighed heavily. 'I'm sorry,' she muttered, putting a hand to her forehead and bowing her head a little. 'I just want to know why you're doing this,' she said, the calmness in her voice in sharp contrast to her words of a moment earlier.

Elaine Stewart made to say something but stopped. She took her hand off the bag, letting it fall down off her shoulder.

'We all work hard to make this a better place. The people down here and everyone above us don't deserve this.' The chief executive's words were strained. 'Why did you do this?' she asked again.

Elaine Stewart had no reply.

74.

THE DAY WAS bright and the air sharp with cold. Over the moors a dew had settled, displaying tiny shards of grey sparkle. Silhouettes of the trees contrasted starkly against the cold earth. The road was quiet, cars running slowly in reverence to the elements. Ice had been forecast.

The chief executive drove across this landscape from her home to the hospital. Thoughts of her encounter with Elaine Stewart were at the forefront of her mind. After they had met, the secretary (if that's what she should call her) had left immediately. The chief executive had spoken to the hospital's lawyers to determine what action should be taken against her. They were looking at her contract to determine whether a criminal case could be made against her but had advised the chief executive not to involve the police at this time. Combining the law and healthcare, two establishments deeply entrenched in complexity, would not lead to easy solutions. She had spoken to John Such, for whom Elaine worked. He had tried to ring his former assistant but had got no reply, perhaps not surprisingly. At least they had rooted out the source of the leak. Maybe the situation in the hospital would start to improve. Or maybe that was just wishful thinking.

Her encounter with Elaine had released some tension from the chief executive. The simple act of confronting the woman had been cathartic to some extent. From the expression on Elaine's face, the chief executive knew that she felt a sense of shame, like a child caught in the act of theft. That was something, at least. To have told her, albeit clumsily, the effect of her actions on the fabric of the hospital made the chief executive feel cleansed in a small way. As soon as she had spoken her words, she had known that Elaine didn't need to be told.

She arrived at the hospital just after eight o'clock. Her mood was better than on previous days. She said hello to various people on her way to the management offices, which made her feel better. Her tone of greeting, bordering on cheerful, surprised her. One of the porters, a jolly chap who seemed to spend more time talking than porting, struck up a conversation with her about the weather. She was happy to converse with him, something which she would have seen as an annoyance the previous day.

Walking on, she passed the scene of the collapsed corridor. There was already activity from the builders and workmen, who had thrown off their inertia of the past few days and were directing more heavy machinery into place. The large crane, recently extracted from the deep mud, was now on solid ground, ready for action. A heavy iron chain dangled limply from its jib while men connected its hook to the smaller chain wrapped around the trunk of the fallen tree. She stopped to take in the spectacle of industry. At last, the tree was to be removed.

She hurried on to her office. She had sent messages to her senior team to meet first thing. Jan would be making coffee at this moment and the others would be assembling, awaiting instruction. Indeed, they were waiting outside her door as she took off her coat and hung it by the main door.

'Bright and early!' she said in a friendly fashion.

John Such grinned, opening the door to the chief executive's office. They entered and took their seats. Eric looked nervous, uncertain what today's communication would bring.

'I'm sure John has told you about Elaine,' said the chief executive to Eric, trying to put him at ease. 'We need to put the whole sorry story behind us. The newspaper stories should stop now, and we can get on with it. We'll sue the paper. Take them to the cleaners!'

John Such raised an eyebrow. This was fighting talk.

'I'm sorry for employing her,' added John Such, 'I don't know how she got away with it. It looks like she worked for *The Herald* very briefly some years ago – although that wasn't mentioned on her CV – and then obviously was approached by them to go undercover.'

Eric sat in silence. The other two had hoped this would cheer him, but it had no such effect.

'Anyway, Eric,' continued the chief executive, 'how's pandemic planning?'

Eric sat up straight. 'All done,' he said.

'Good work. I knew you were the right person for the job. It appears that the Department of Health is stepping down the alert level, but it's good to have done this for future events. So, thanks very much.'

Eric nodded, acknowledging the compliment.

'Now we have to turn our attention to finances again. We've let it slip, for obvious reasons, but now it's vital we redouble our efforts.' She looked at the other two, who nodded as Jan Marling entered with coffee.

The chief executive continued. 'As we all know, there is a real possibility … a likelihood,' she corrected herself, 'that the two hospitals will merge and that one will close. I'll do all I can to save this hospital.'

Jan finished laying out the coffee cups, milk, and sugar before leaving with thanks from the managers. She admired the fighting talk from her boss, but knew, as she suspected the chief executive herself knew, that she would lose that battle.

75.

NOT TWO HOURS later, John Such was heading over to the headquarters of the local health authority. He cycled the mile or so, along back lanes, dipping down to the riverside before climbing up the gentle slope to the grand old house. For obvious reasons, he had not mentioned to the chief executive or Eric that he was meeting Jim Spier. The head of the local health authority was the enemy, the one who would close the hospital, and was not to be trusted. Whilst not entirely sure of the reason for their meeting, this was, undoubtedly, a traitorous journey – yet it was one John Such needed to make. His own opinion was that the chances of saving the hospital were next to none. The other establishment had so much else in its favour, not least the absence of huge debts and crumbling infrastructure. The recent attention from the press had put the final seal on its fate, as far as he was concerned. He needed to go into self-preservation mode. So, suspecting Jim Spier, with whom he had always got on, might be wanting to meet him to discuss future opportunities within the health authority, he made the journey, entering his office at the allotted time after changing into work attire.

'John, good to see you,' said Jim Spier as the younger man entered the room. 'Take a seat.'

John Such sat and looked around the room as the man behind the desk finished typing something on his computer. The artwork on the walls was pleasant; there were colourful images of flowers and birds in ornate frames. *This is a different class of office*, he thought.

'Sorry about that,' said Jim Spier, closing his laptop with a click and pushing it to one side. 'I'll come straight to the point. As you know, the hospitals will be merging, and we'll be closing down your site. I want you to become the deputy chief executive of the new merged hospital. You'll like working with Neil and the team. Good blokes!'

Jim Spier sat back, taking a drink from a large red mug of coffee.

'Well,' began John Such, assimilating the information. It seemed that the decision regarding the fate of the hospitals had already been made. Although not a surprising outcome, it clearly hadn't filtered down to the chief executive, who had been invigorated for a new fight. More games from the head of the local health authority; more pain for his current boss. It was a cruel sport. Why would he want to remain part of this organisation if the man pulling the strings acted in this way?

'I guess so,' he continued. 'Yes. I'll think about it.'

Jim Spier sat forward. 'I'd advise you to jump ship. There is no way your current job will be around in six months.'

'So, has that been formally decided?' asked John Such. 'I was under the impression that it was still up for discussion.'

Jim Spier sniggered, then sat back and put his hands behind his head, pulling his shoulders apart, stretching his upper back.

'John, come on. You know how it is.'

He did, that was true. The meeting concluded quickly. Once the head of the local health authority had made his point, he saw no further reason to continue the discussion. John Such left with much to think about. He got back on his bike after changing back into his cycling clothes, cycled down to the river, and stopped at a bench. Parking his bike up against a nearby tree trunk, he sat down with the riverbank in front of him. The river ran vigorously today, the sound of its flow soothing his mind, which was full of so many thoughts. He spotted a wagtail, bobbing in the shallows, its tail flicking nervously and its head dipping out of time. In a flash it flew off, a dart of black, white, and yellow. He unzipped his cycle jacket and removed his helmet, placing it on the bench beside him.

He was in no rush to return to the hospital. The game was up, and he couldn't face the charade which would permeate the atmosphere over the next few days or weeks. Who knew how long Jim Spier would keep the hospital staff sweating, just to play his ridiculous tricks on the chief executive? After just one meeting, he had little respect for the man, so was not enthused by the prospect of the job he had been offered, despite being flattered and excited to take over a larger challenge. He would always be looking over his shoulder. He might be the next target: fresh prey for Jim Spier. He had no idea what the chief executive had done to provoke his behaviour towards her. He suspected nothing other than being in her managerial position, and being someone to blame, someone to manipulate. He thought she was a decent person. He wouldn't go so far as calling her a friend, but, aside from her outburst when she had accused him of leaking information to the paper, he got on well with her and respected her management style. She was in the wrong place at the wrong time, but deserved a chance to save the hospital, to prove herself. That was not going to happen.

He closed his eyes, relaxing in the faint sun. He put off further the moment before his return to the management offices. A dog walker strolled by, breaking his reverie, his charge sniffing round John Such's feet and his bike before being called away. The dog barked loudly, then chased a squirrel which had dared to cross the path. The two animals disappeared into a hedge in the frenzy of the chase. The owner called the dog again, and after a moment it reappeared, wagging its tail, sniffing the trail once more. Man and beast walked off into the distance. *I should get a dog*, he thought, *or maybe go travelling*. Do something different to get away from the toxic atmosphere the hospital now wallowed in. He decided that he wouldn't accept the offer from the odious man. It was asking for trouble and was bound to end in further stress. It shouldn't have to be like this. He would escape.

He sat for a while longer in the cool morning air.

76.

Elaine Stewart was not seen again, neither in the hospital nor in the offices of *The Herald*. Despite this, stories of mismanagement of patients continued to appear in the paper. There was sense amongst the staff of the newspaper that the public were tiring of the constant denigration of the hospital, but Mo Kane persisted, heeding none of the warnings that it would backfire and thus reduce their circulation figures. He was still after the big scoop of further embezzlement. What no one in the grimy offices above the estate agent expected was the birth of a new rumour, generated from the heart of the local health authority – a rumour suggesting that the hospital would close and that all services would be relocated to the neighbouring institute seventeen miles away. Too late for that day's publication, it would appear the next morning, giving time for the hacks to flesh out the details, substantiated or not. Sources were to be found. Mo Kane had lost his insider, but there were so many other options for a journalist of his capability.

Reading that morning's paper, which contained nothing, therefore, of the health authority's latest plans of merger, Eric scrutinised the detail. He was not one usually prone to reading the newspaper, but he had picked up a copy from the canteen, which was being given away as part of a promotional deal. That the catering department had entered into a marketing arrangement with *The Herald* was surprising at the very least. It was akin to a rabbit offering to clean the farmer's gun.

The references to the hospital that day were centred around a story from six years earlier, at which time twin brothers had died within days of each other on the same ward and of the same disease. Obvious genetic predispositions to disease were ignored for the sake of sensationalism. The two had been local celebrities, being feted for their extreme strength, which had even propelled them to minor stardom in television shows after they had been spotted in a travelling show. They had been diagnosed with a form of gigantism, which accounted for their stature. The reasons why their lives ran in such precise parallel were not known. They had both died at the age of eighty-seven, with complications of cardiomegaly – a large heart in a large body. *If their hearts had been of normal size*, mused the article writer, *would they have lived for that long?* The co-incidence of their deaths was the meat of the story. Notwithstanding all that had gone before, the fact that they had both left this earth in the same way and in the same place was taken as evidence of wrongdoing.

Eric closed the paper and placed it aside for recycling later. The story defied logic, and it reminded him why he didn't care for reading the newspaper regularly. He was due to present his work on crescent moon disease later that day and so took out his laptop to review the files. The neatly arranged and labelled files on his hard drive, although a virtual presence, pleased him, their orderliness a comfort. He looked at the file icons within the computer window, aligned and succinctly labelled. The realisation that the documents were not needed, for the present time, did not concern him. Planning was enough for him. He checked the files once more but was disturbed by a knock on the door. He closed the lid of his laptop and got up to open the door.

John Such stood at the entrance, dressed in a tight cycling top, sweat on his brow.

'Can I come in?' he asked.

Eric nodded and stepped aside. John Such looked concerned. His failure to change into work attire indicated an urgency to his visit. He sat down. Eric remained standing, anticipating bad news.

John Such let out his exasperation with a sharp exhalation. 'What a mess!' he said, shaking his head.

Eric was unsure what to say but understood that he needed to listen.

'I've just been with Jim Spier, down at the HQ,' John Such said. 'It seems the decision to shut this place is definite. No reprieve, no chance to fight our corner.'

Eric furrowed the lines in his forehead a fraction, taking in his colleague's message.

'He's asked me to jump ship and join the other place.'

Eric sat down. 'Really?' he said.

A bead of sweat ran down the side of John Such's face. 'I'm not going to take it,' he said decisively.

'Oh,' said Eric non-committally.

John Such took a tissue from his pocket and wiped his forehead. He had needed to tell Eric this news as soon as possible. He viewed the fragility of Eric's persona as something he wanted to protect, as though he were his guardian, or perhaps a big brother, even though Eric was his senior by a few years. He looked out for him, checked he was coping with the latest stresses and strains, particularly in recent times when he had feared for his colleague – feared he would crumple under the heavy weight of the scandal he had inadvertently caused. To John Such's surprise, Eric had been oddly resistant to the crisis, adopting a stance of denial, burying his head in the pandemic project, refusing to let his mind think about the shame and disgrace which it might have created. Of course, Eric did not reciprocate or even acknowledge this compassion, yet John Such still felt a duty to confer it. They had started at the hospital at the same time and had been through the ups and downs of the management offices. They had shared much in as separated a way as possible.

After a while, Eric piped up, 'So, it's over then?'

John Such nodded. 'Yes,' he said.

77.

DECONSTRUCTION OF THE corridor continued at pace. The tree trunk which had wreaked such carnage had been chopped into discs and loaded on the back of a lorry, and a shredder had been brought in to make the remainder of the branches into sawdust. Piles of rubble were shrinking for the first time, a convoy of trucks distributing the erstwhile corridor to the corners of the county. Environmental control officers had, mercifully, now deemed the site to be asbestos-free, meaning that activity could be stepped up without the tedious safety procedures resented by the workmen.

The chief executive was unclear as to whether she should be making plans to replace the structure or just signing away the land to be developed for luxury homes: four bedrooms, three en suite, and a view of the valley. That was the way of the world. It had happened in other places. Decisions made hundreds of years earlier to site a hospital in the heart of the community – a future real estate gold mine – condemned its future. The land alone from the sale of a hospital could cover running costs of the new one for at least a year, it had been calculated. The health authority would claim that an out-of-town site was more convenient – better parking, more space for expansion – and perhaps this was right. The world had changed, priorities altered beyond description.

The uncertainty over the future of the hospital tied the chief executive's hands, yet she continued to plan for the future, albeit rather perfunctorily. She laid aside the finance question and turned her attention to the plans to restore the fabric of the broken hospital. Spending money was easier than saving it. Several local architects had been consulted to design an alternative corridor, but Jim Spier's decision by proxy at the recent board meeting put the schedule for building in limbo. One firm had already sent in preliminary designs. *Carbon neutral*, *locally sourced materials* and *sustainable* were terms used liberally in the description. It looked very nice and would be a striking build. Whether it fitted in with the drabness of the other buildings on the site was another thing. It was, after all, just a way of moving between buildings, a connecting route, so the grandiosity was perhaps not merited. It amused her to look at the pictures, with their stylised trees and pastel shading. Any excuse for escapism was not to be scoffed at. If she could just do this, perusing diagrams as though it were a mail-order catalogue, she would be content for a while. It was putting off the inevitable.

Her phone emitted a sound indicating an incoming message. It was the press officer of the hospital, asking for her attention on an urgent matter. *Everything is urgent to her*, thought the chief executive. She pushed aside the architectural documents and looked at her agenda for the day. Since she had no engagements for at least an hour, she decided to grant the press officer's wish. She walked to her door from where she could see the press officer's desk and, attracting her attention with a wave, beckoned her over. The press officer jumped up, gathered a few papers from her desk and strode over.

Once inside, the press officer could hardly contain herself.

'I've had *The Herald* on the phone, asking us to comment on the closure of the hospital,' she blurted out, falling over her words in the race to get them out.

She waited for a response from the chief executive, perhaps expecting a strong rebuttal; to be told that this was a fabricated, mischievous story. But the look on the chief executive's face suggested otherwise. Rather than an expression of shock at the outrage of such a suggestion, she appeared calm, thoughtful, almost resigned.

'Foxes, killing, closure,' said the chief executive after a moment.

The press officer slunk gloomily into a chair, confused by the obtuse nature of her leader's response. She knew, of course, to what she was referring. The three major stories in the press over the past few weeks. It had been an assault which had started with a ridiculous tale of little consequence, escalating into something unthinkable. Their utterance in the heart of management gave them credence.

'What shall I tell them?' asked the press officer, rocking on the edge of her chair in a childlike, agitated way.

The chief executive thought. 'Just say nothing for the moment.'

After the press officer had left, she closed her eyes and imagined a world far away from where she now sat. The trees were full of ripened fruit, the lawns were pristine, the views stretched far into the distance. However, her reverie was fleeting, disturbed by a knock on the door.

She sensed a commotion outside the door, raised voices and general tumult. Again, she heard knocking, louder this time, more urgent. She sat back and closed her eyes again, wishing it would all go away.

78.

NEXT MORNING, AS predicted, the papers ran with the story of the hospital closure. The source of the story mattered little now, the nails in the coffin having been firmly hammered down. What might have appeared most startling to those who, settling down over breakfast or morning coffee, read the front page of *The Herald* was the almost effortless switch from assault on the institution to outrage over its demise. Yesterday, the local community had needed protecting from the place, but today they needed to take up arms to preserve its existence. It was as if the newspaper had suddenly been placed under new management, its paymasters ordering a change of heart. Yet Mo Kane, editor-in-chief, remained in charge. His argument was that he could only report the news placed before him. Others thought that the closure of the hospital would deprive him of his juiciest material, and that its continued existence was thus paramount to him. Most understood, however, the fickleness of the ephemeral information machine and were aware that they had every right to vote with their wallets and not buy the paper.

Of course, Jim Spier read the paper, crumbling fresh pastries over the black and white text, slurping his double espresso. He noted with satisfaction that this signalled the end of the smear campaign against the health authority and thus the new merged hospital could start with a clean sheet. In addition, the conflicting messages from the newspaper over the past few weeks meant that the closure of the hospital would be more palatable in the community, which would struggle to get behind an institution which had, reportedly, brought such harm to its patients. For that he had to be thankful to Mo Kane and his band of troublemakers. In a strange way, he had beaten the awful man; a double bluff of sorts. That was one theory, at least. Who knew what the editor of *The Herald* had in mind for the next edition of his newspaper?

The story in the paper was naturally the talk of the hospital, in its coffee rooms and corridors. Its workers, although accustomed to increasingly outlandish revelations, were floored by the latest, most being unaware that such a thing was even thinkable. The hospital was viewed by many as an immutable presence in the community, a sacred cow, not to be meddled with. Shock gave way to disbelief, then outrage; all emotions covered in the course of a tea break. The chief executive had been briefed on the stories by the press officer as soon as she arrived in the management offices. She listened while the press officer read out the stories. She had not yet received official confirmation that this was the fate of the hospital, yet understood that the slowly turning cogs of the health authority were grinding irreversibly in only one direction. Her fate, and that of the hospital, had been sealed some time earlier. Her face remained implacable, her mind in slow motion, mulling over the lack of options available to her. She said little, other than to acknowledge what had been reported, the culmination of her life's work destroyed by a journalist she had never met. The press officer read the signals and asked nothing further of her.

After the briefing, she summoned Eric and John Such to talk about what to do next. Perhaps there was little to say, since there was no fight left in her. Her deputies sensed this from the moment they entered her room. The radiator in the office had broken overnight, so the room was bitterly cold, and condensation dripped from the windowpanes. The chief executive was dressed in her winter coat, her scarf around her neck. She sat behind her desk, elbows resting on its hard surface, a troubled expression on her face. It was like watching the condemned anticipating the moment when she would be hauled up into the courtroom to receive her sentence, although in this case it seemed unlikely that the sentence would be revealed by anyone other than the editor of the local newspaper. Being left in the dark about the health authority's position and having to read it in the newspapers was the final humiliation.

The three colleagues sat in an awkward silence for several moments. The cold gnawed at their extremities, the discomfort of an unseasonal cold snap brought inside the drab room. The chief executive struggled to find words and John Such, conscious of rumours concerning his duplicity, knew that anything he said to calm the waters might be taken in the wrong way. Eric kept quiet out of a sense of self-preservation, not wanting to be drawn into sentiments which would be detrimental to his psyche.

After a while, the chief executive turned from the taciturn to the aggressive, lambasting the newspapers, Elaine Stewart, the local health authority, the foxes and anything else which had rattled her thinking over the few short months of her tenure. Her tirade was out of place and unexpected to those listening who had assumed a dignified exit from her post. She stopped, apologised, and felt the weight of sadness and regret pulling her down. She had been wrong to blame others. It was her fault. She had entered a high-stakes game and had lost. There was little else to be said.

She asked John Such whether he had heard any more about the closure, knowing that he had consulted with Jim Spier in recent days. This was no time for deceit and underhand practice.

'I met with Jim Spier the other day,' he said quietly. 'It seems like he has decided.'

She nodded. 'Thanks for your openness,' she said.

'What will you do?' asked John Such.

'I don't know, yet. Maybe take time off to consider my options,' she replied, now thinking only of her own predicament.

'Eric – how about you? Do you know what's next for you?' asked the chief executive.

'Not sure,' he replied. 'As far as I know, I'm carrying on, but I haven't heard anything definite.'

They were like three comrades at the end of a war, their regiment disbanded, of no further use, each billeted to an unknown future. Yet their comradeship had never been sought out, nor cemented. They had been merely a team of convenience. No one in the group would mourn their parting.

The two men left the room, leaving the chief executive alone. She read again the article on which the press secretary had briefed her and then looked around her room, considering what she would need to take with her when she left the office for good.

79.

DURING THOSE TIMES of upheaval and change, the chief executive often wondered what she might have done differently in order to effect an alternative outcome. Her future prospects were indeed limited by her past life, all time being irreclaimable. The moments of her crisis were many and the pressing feeling on her chest grew stronger as days went by. A decision framed in the vast complexity of one situation may not be as profound in another, and yet we are only products of our circumstance, leaving nothing to chance, playing out some fateful narrative, in hindsight unchangeable. She should have found a rose garden to walk among the dead leaves and to hear the cry of the birds, she mused. Better still, settling her differences with the dictator's confidence, she would move on, not looking back, not thinking about the endless possibilities, which are, of course, the same. There is no place for the realm of speculation, which only leads to discontent. That was her biggest mistake.

Days spent at a desk, struggling with numbers plucked from an infinite pool of conceivable options or the consequences of a decision contingent on endless possibilities, versus days on the mountainside contemplating nothing, was, perhaps, the dilemma which she might have addressed on the first day of her work. But we are all enthused by the prospect of a struggle, one to overcome, to conquer, driving even the meek to thirst for the feeling of power. An old phrase suggests that only that which has been achieved by struggle is worth achieving. A war general will think victory much sweeter if it comes at a greater cost; surrender of an opposition is no conquest at all. Indeed, most of those about to be vanquished rage against destiny beyond the point at which defeat is inevitable. Human nature fights first, runs later. Yet, in which direction do you run? Towards the burning building, or away in order to gain enough distance from it so that it is no longer visible: a blinkered flight, a resignation for some, a bitter wrench for others. Packing up your stuff, muttering words about being hard done to, how badly treated you are, you reflect on nothing but the failure of it all, neglecting the truth that for every success there must be an equal amount of failure to balance the equilibrium.

The end had come for the chief executive. She had known for some time that the limitations on her tenure were mounting. What had started with a trickle had now become a torrent; her management skills were no longer able to overcome the impending threat. The absurdity of the newspaper stories played out the tragedy of her demise, a commentary of lies in the crumbling ship she had been employed to steer. She had been offered a role in the new hospital – effectively a demotion – but didn't have to consider the offer for too long.

It was her final day, and she took one last walk around the hospital. Work on the reconstruction of the corridor had ended. Piles of bricks lay abandoned, great craters filled with dirty rainwater lined the exposed foundations of the structure, neglected machinery exposed to the elements rusted slowly. The tents which had been constructed at pace were now shabby, coated with a film of mud, fraying at the seams and flapping in the wind. Walking through the darkened tented tunnels, the chief executive noticed the same patients being pushed in beds, the same relatives on visits to their loved ones, the same nurses – yet the gloom surrounding them meant that they were a changed group of people, carrying out their journey with some part of them removed. A light flickered above and was extinguished, adding further darkness to the surroundings.

She reached the end of the canvas walkway and stepped into the canteen. The mood was subdued, and the floor was patterned in muddy footprints. Mud was everywhere in the hospital, the temporary routes disseminating the ubiquitous sludge to all parts, like a carpet. It was as though the cleaners had given up the fight against dirt and come to accept it as part of the order of things; a new regime incorporating the overall feeling of resignation. An engineer had cordoned off the coffee machines, perhaps to service, perhaps to decommission them. Instant coffee in the form of reconstituted brown powder was offered as an alternative, which might have explained the quietness of the place. Small groups of people wrapped in dark coats were huddled around tables; muted conversations between the distracted and the downhearted could be heard. A group of nurses sat at a table in the corner, and next to them the windows were steamed up with the condensation of their breath. One of the nurses was telling a story to which the others were listening intently. The chief executive considered getting a drink but decided against it and moved on.

She walked past the entrance to Ward 19. A pair of doctors – an older man in shirtsleeves and a red tie, and a younger woman in dark clothes with a stethoscope slung round her neck – were in discussion. The older doctor's phone went off and he answered it, wandering off for privacy, leaving the junior colleague to wait for more instruction. The doors of the ward opened with a flourish and porters steered a bed with its supine occupant through the narrow gap. A nurse followed three paces behind, carrying a large blue box and a folder of papers. The woman in the bed was swaddled in layers of bedding, but her face peeked out and she looked directly at the chief executive. The two exchanged glances, the bed's journey having been paused when it became snagged on the door handle. The jolt this had caused surprised the nurse, who instinctively reassured the woman in the bed. 'It's OK, Muriel,' she said, placing a hand on a limb hidden deep beneath the bedding. In a moment, the bed moved on. A paramedic with a green backpack ushered people out of the way of the bed. The chief executive stepped aside, coming up against the wall. One of the porters asked the paramedic the location of the ambulance. 'The west car park,' he replied, pointing in the vague direction of the destination. The bed started again like a creaking juggernaut. The people outside the ward stood around in reverence. The older doctor finished his phone conversation and rejoined his colleague. Both entered the ward. The nurse now walked beside the bed, steadying its course. She looked back at the woman in the bed.

'Won't be long now, Muriel,' she said, 'the ambulance is waiting just outside to take you to the other hospital.' Muriel said nothing but looked ahead before glancing back at the chief executive once again. The bed moved on, picking up pace before turning the corner, out of sight.

The chief executive continued. She walked past theatres, X-ray departments and more wards, which were issuing a slow stream of beds, a flotilla of the ill at ease. An exodus to the other hospital had already begun; patients were being transferred for further care before the impending closure. Further on, the entrance to Minor Injuries had long since been blocked off, the facilities already transferred to a site on the edge of the industrial estate which was easier for ambulance access, or so the argument went. Workmen had been dismantling the unit for months, and it was now stripped of its resources, no longer recognisable as a medical unit. She stopped to peer in, beyond the blockade. No one was working that day, and the lights were off. Large cardboard boxes were piled up by the door, their utility and destination uncertain.

She sighed, still struggling to comprehend the destiny of the hospital when it was presented in such tangible terms. It was a dramatic decline. Six months of descent which would be complete in half that time. An emergency budget had been agreed for the final three months, whereas vast amounts of money were being pumped into the rival hospital to cope with the influx of new patients. The chief executive had agreed a redundancy package and was not required to oversee the last weeks. Of that she was glad, yet the snub was hard to take.

She turned round to continue her final round of the hospital buildings. She spotted John Such walking towards her. He stopped and addressed the chief executive with his usual happy disposition.

'Boss. How are you?' he asked. There was an irony in the use of the greeting.

'Yes, fine. One more round of the place before I'm off,' she said. It made her feel sad saying this, the words making her realise the finality of the situation.

'It's sad to see it like this,' replied John Such, nodding in the direction of the defunct Minor Injuries Unit.

The chief executive smiled. 'How are you John? What have you decided to do?'

She knew that he had been offered the deputy chief executive role in the merged hospital.

John Such hesitated, then shrugged. 'Yes, I've accepted the job. Starting next month.'

The chief executive forced a smile. 'Well done, John. I'm pleased for you. Really, I am.'

'Thanks,' he replied, 'and what are you going to do?'

The chief executive pondered for a moment to decide which version of the story to tell this time. Having been asked so many times, she had constructed multiple versions of the future which might meet the expectations of those asking.

'Taking a break,' she said, 'reassessing my situation. It'll be good to have a change.'

'That's good. You deserve it,' he said, appreciating the very moment he had said it that there was nothing redeeming about her situation as she neared the end of her time at the hospital.

The two parted, John Such walking away, hands in pockets, head bowed. The chief executive watched him go before she stepped outside the hospital building through the large electronic doors which led out into the green space outside the main entrance. Beyond the ploughed-up grass square, she spotted an ambulance in the half-empty car park. The woman she had seen leave the ward a few minutes ago was being loaded into it. The ambulance crew steered the bed onto the rear tail-lift, then elevated it into the air and from there into the back of the vehicle. The crew shared a few words, checked some paperwork with the accompanying nurse, then closed the doors of the ambulance with a distant thud before driving off.

Acknowledgements

Thanks to Karen Atkinson for editorial services and advice.

Thanks to Emily Fox for proofreading.

Typesetting by Book Polishers
Cover design by Creative Covers.

Printed in Great Britain
by Amazon

82298628R00162